A GUIDE TO
BERLIN

Also by Gail Jones

Sixty Lights
Dreams of Speaking
Sorry
Five Bells

A GUIDE TO
BERLIN

GAIL JONES

Harvill Secker
LONDON

1 3 5 7 9 10 8 6 4 2

Harvill Secker, an imprint of Vintage,
 20 Vauxhall Bridge Road,
London SW1V 2SA

Harvill Secker is part of the Penguin Random House
group of companies whose addresses can be found at
global.penguinrandomhouse.com.

 Penguin
Random House
UK

First published by Harvill Secker in 2016
First published in Australia by Vintage,
Penguin Random House Australia in 2015

www.vintage-books.co.uk

A CIP catalogue record for this book
is available from the British Library

ISBN 9781846559976

Printed and bound by Clays Ltd, St Ives plc

Penguin Random House is committed to a
sustainable future for our business, our readers
and our planet. This book is made from
Forest Stewardship Council® certified paper.

'(What I hate) Folding an umbrella, not finding
its secret button.'

Vladimir Nabokov, *Interview*, 1970

1

It was Marco Gianelli who spoke in the darkness.

When they were all standing together, shocked and numb, when they saw each other's faces remade as rogues, pinched, white, shrivelled inwards with guilt, dull with logistics and the banal business of dragging dead weight, he was the only one among them who was able to speak. He raised his arm in the snowy air and with this gesture assembled them. He asked them to pause.

There was a moment in which all they did was wait. Snowfall enshrouded them. A feeble wind spun the flakes. They heard traffic in the night, muffled and distant, they heard the heave of each other's raspy breath.

It was a formal speech, really, absurd in the circumstances.

Marco said that the death of any human was without metaphor or likeness. The death of any human was incomparable. It was not a writerly event. It was not contained within sentences. It was not to be described in the same way as the beauty of an icicle, or three wrinkles parallel on the forehead of a remembered governess, or the play of shadow and light on a swimming body, or the random harmony of trifles that was a parking meter, a fluffy cloud and a tiny pair of boots with felt spats.

2

Before the snows truly began, the city was a desolating ash-grey, and bitterly cold. Cass had never before seen such a grey city. It felt stiff and dead. There were the fleshless arms of cranes, slowly swinging, there was the rumble-slide of ubiquitous trains and trams, there were busy buses, skidding pedestrians, instructive red and green lights blinking their cartoon man, but still Berlin seemed to her collectively frozen. The white sky was menacing. The plates of ice on the Spree, uneven and jagged, resembled a spray of shattered glass after a wartime bombing. There must have been old people, she thought, gazing through the grime of an S-Bahn window, who looked down at the river and canals and recalled something blasted and asunder, piles of bricks, lives scattered, and a windowless episode in their childhoods. It would have been an easy connection, this shiny reminder of things broken, this pattern of severity and damage showing the forsakenness of the world. It was hard to imagine the icy water thawed and re-sealing, or the sky returning to a lively blue.

She had a sense of contraction, of huddling against the weather. Later, it figured in her mind as Stalinist classicism, the wind tunnel of the vast and inhuman Karl-Marx-Allee, and the shapes of people in padded jackets bending against the cruel air. A scene from Eisenstein, perhaps, with a gelid lens and the special effects of monumental vision, swollen by an aerial view and historical misery. Black outlines on white snow, impersonality, extinguishment. Exaggeration of this kind was irresistible.

In that early, fierce cold, Berliners coped better. They rode in sealed cars. They shut themselves in offices. Whole apartment blocks seemed to have not a single person about. In the city they dived into subways, seeking the shelter of corridors. There was an other-world of radiant bakery booths and the musty smells of takeaway food, of paper stands and convenience stores and stalls wholly of plastic and trinkets. Subterranean refuge was deeply appealing. There were tiny florists lined with clusters of unnaturally bright blooms – fuchsias, tulips, tropical orchids. Cass loved these above all: the tiny florists.

On the day of her very first meeting with the group, Cass bought ten tulips of startling orange, streaked with crimson. They appeared rare and magical. She bought them on impulse, attracted by their torrid colour. Near the exit to the U-Bahn stood rows of aluminium buckets stuffed to the brim with imported and hot-housed flowers. The Vietnam-ese florist, a sad-looking man with white hair, swept her choice from the bucket, shook it briefly, then laid the bunch on a metal table and swathed it in paper. His movements were swift and bored. Cass realised almost immediately that this was an untimely purchase. Now she would have to carry the tulips throughout the afternoon, guard them against bruising, hope the petals didn't break, or crush, or freeze.

She rose up from the U-Bahn with her tulips wrapped in a flimsy paper triangle and saw the blue U sign curved above her, hung like a secret code. She slid escalated into frosty air and the noise of the street, generously surrounded in her loneliness by so many sights almost meaningful. A small crowd stood ahead, waiting patiently at the bus stop. She would have liked to join their implicit community, and for a moment considered jumping onto the bus and going wherever it took her. But she consulted her map and headed north, walking as quickly as she could.

Goethestrasse was easy to find. This was an area in which all the streets were named for writers or philosophers, as if they added an intellectual authority or value to property. Leafless trees lined the street, which must be attractive in the spring. Cass located the building, an elegant *altbau* with an art deco vestibule and a hairdresser occupying part of the ground floor. She scanned the names on its brass plate, then buzzed 'Oblomov', as instructed. *Oblomov*: Russian. It was a palpable, egg-like, literary name.

The group's meetings, she'd been told, moved around the city, as if necessarily furtive or vaguely illicit. It appealed to her, this idea of unsettled conversation. She climbed the three flights of stairs, cumbersome and oversized in her winter coat, and when she arrived knocked on the door with a tentative tap, then a second time, to be heard.

Marco appeared before her, pulling the heavy door open.

'The Australian,' he announced in English. 'Our newest international. Here is Cass, from Sydney.' He leant from the doorway and ceremoniously kissed her on both cheeks.

There was Victor from New York. Marco and Gino from Rome, Yukio and Mitsuko from Tokyo.

'From Sydney,' Cass repeated, embarrassed for no reason.

'Four rhymers,' Victor quipped, 'and we two singular others.' He extended his hand, and, following his lead, each shook hers in turn. It was a conventional beginning, as if they were all acting a part. Only Yukio seemed reluctant.

'Sydney,' said Yukio, joining the echo-effect of their self-consciousness. He could not meet her gaze, but stared at the floor behind the curtain of his asymmetrical fringe. Cass was distracted by his clothes, a version of faux-distressed street fashion from the 1990s, all dangling chains, ornamental tears and discordant layers. He wore a peace-sign on leather string around his neck. Mitsuko was also idiosyncratically outfitted: gauzy blue stuff had been stitched in a frill to the bottom of her jumper, she had badges and jewelled spots casually disposed across her chest, and threads of yellow ribbon entwined wormlike in her chemically pink hair. Cass judged them to be in their late twenties, about her age.

She glanced at the others, cautiously appraising. Victor looked his part, a literature scholar in his sixties, professionally nondescript and self-effacing in beige. He had a walrus moustache and slightly florid skin. Gino was handsome, generically so and therefore unprepossessing, impassive in a black turtleneck. Possibly thirty. Marco appeared suave and a little aloof. He was dark, eastern-looking and self-assured. Cass shyly turned away. Though not usually her type, it was

Marco whom Cass thought distinctively attractive, and it had been at his invitation she had agreed to come.

The introduction acknowledged the prestige of their own cities, arrayed as exemplars. Victor, clearly the chatty one, was already inventing a joint future. They might be the beginning of a movement, a new form of literary devotion. He spoke as one who possessed a great fund of beneficence and fellow-feeling. There was a sense in which he simply assumed everyone was as visionary as he, and as bent on friendship and the artful sharing of literary adventures.

'Now we need a Londoner, a Parisian and a Muscovite!' Victor added. 'Beijing, New Delhi, Buenos Aires, Madrid.' He paused. 'Oslo, Lisbon, Reykjavik, Jakarta . . . Dublin, we need Dublin.'

The others smiled indulgently at his imperial announcement. They each held a glass of something dark, and Cass guessed the drinking had begun some time before she arrived. On the floor stood a chunky squarish bottle, already empty, and another two in waiting. Mitsuko, clearly pleased another woman had been included in their group, was offering a glass. It was Russian, Cass learnt afterwards. Some kind of brandy tinged ferociously with fermented black plums.

Victor rambled on. Engrossed in his own vision, he enjoyed both the listing of city names and the ambition of global connection. There was something emphatically enthusiastic, American perhaps, in the scope of his imagining. Cass thought of the way children arrange coloured pencils, angling and aligning their sharpened tips to produce a peacock fan.

'To world domination!' he raised his glass.

But no one really believed it. Victor was a fantasist, it was clear in the optimistic tone of his voice. Somehow each knew, even then, that their number would be no more than six. Theirs were a few circumstantial spokes, faint rays going nowhere. They could not last. They were adventitious. They were constructed essentially by happenstance and would be destroyed a few weeks later.

3

Only yesterday Cass had told Marco that she was not a 'joiner'.

On the bitter January morning, when ice on the pavements caused fractures and calamities to hundreds of toppling Berliners, so that fire-engines, as well as ambulances, were enlisted to pick up the injured, Cass photographed Vladimir Nabokov's house at Nestorstrasse 22. Shivering, cold, suffering pathetically in a minor key of frozen hands and feet, she aimed her phone through the watery light at the disappointing building across the street, and a man appeared, standing silently beside her. Taking her to be an American tourist, he introduced himself in English: Marco Gianelli. He lived almost opposite number 22, he said, and kept an occasional vigil on weekends. From his window, where he liked to read, he could spot like-minded souls.

'Souls?' she had asked him.

'"*Let us speak frankly. There is many a person whose soul has gone to sleep like a leg.*"' Marco smiled.

Cass recognised the quote. He saw the spark of recognition.

'You see? Like-minded. How many people do you know who might cherish and share those sentences?'

Before them stood the apartment block in which Nabokov had lived with his wife Vera from 1932 to 1937. Their son Dmitri, born in 1934, would have been an infant there. Now it bore a small commemorative brass plate – Cass hadn't noticed until Marco drew it to her attention – and at street level was a restaurant, sombrely closed and unlit, *Die kleine Weltlaterne*: 'the Little Lantern of the World'.

'Only true devotees,' he added, 'bother to take a photograph.'

For a few seconds all she could think of was her frozen feet. Then Cass was aware of Marco's visible breath, and hers, the way the rigour of the cold had brought their faces close, the sense of a deeper transaction and puzzling arousal. It was a pick-up line perhaps, but one superior and strategic: identifying a literary nerd, the assumption of shared experience, the seductive and insinuating facility of quotation.

Marco moved slowly and did not pressure or insist. He stood apart as she lingered, with nothing much to do or see, and when he proposed coffee in a warm place, Cass was grateful for the suggestion simply because it would release her briefly from the rude assault of the weather. A fire-engine sped by, to remind them of the danger of ice.

Later Cass would learn that Marco was considered the philosopher of the group. He seemed sensible, mature and level-headed. He knew the books but had committed only a few lines to memory. He knew Nabokov's life, but mostly in a general outline. He was interested in the writing, he told them, *primarily the writing*, not in what he later called 'our collective mania'.

In the unspoken consent of small groups, they saw him as

their leader, even though Victor had the more obvious claim. Victor deferred – they all did – to Marco's old-fashioned and serious manner. Marco talked quietly, with eloquence; he drank in moderation; he seemed the neutral, calm figure in their eccentric crew. He displayed a Roman sophistication they had seen in movies, a way of tilting his head back after the first listless drag of a cigarette, a habit of leaning towards women as he listened to them, implying automatic intimacy, a tendency to flick open the *Corriere della Sera* when he was bored with conversation. He wore citrus aftershave and expensive clothes. He liked to smooth his springy black curls with a gesture of his palm. Only Marco spoke English, German and Russian with equal fluency; this confirmed his access to extra levels of significance. It was as if he possessed a layered understanding of their lives in words, and as if only he, having contrived it, knew the true meaning of their intersection.

They walked together up Nestorstrasse, turned right, walked a little further, then entered a tucked-away bar. It was one of the few places nearby, Marco claimed, that served halfway decent espresso. Like Italians everywhere, he felt responsible for the quality of local coffee and obliged to apologise for the disgraceful variations that existed beyond his country.

Cass unwound her scarf and removed her gloves and coat in the shadowy bar. The heating was infernal and the air was foul. It was a grim interior.

'I know,' said Marco, catching her expression. 'But the coffee is drinkable. Trust me.'

There were three stags' heads, glumly staring, hung high along the wall. In an old mirror with faceted edges and a

11

smattering of gold letters, she saw them both reflected as Marco helped her remove her coat. She retreated from the poor translation that was her German version. Around them beer posters announced inebriated excellence with rampant bears, winking lions and the stern command of Gothic type.

The grizzled bar owner hailed Marco – '*Eh, paesano!*' – and they exchanged a few jolly words of Italian together.

It was hideous, really, the clammy air, the taxidermical decorations, the unripe banana stench of stale beer. The windows were wet with condensation and semi-opaque. There was an unhygienic, blurry light. Her own reflection had disheartened her, so pallid and barely there.

Marco seemed at home and stood by quietly, waiting to pull out her chair. He ordered the coffees, making a joke, which was met with a gruff laugh from the patron, now invisibly busy behind his crowded counter. Then Marco leant across the table as if confiding.

He had studied literature at university, he said, but was now working as a real estate agent, catering mostly to wealthy Italians who wished to buy a pied-à-terre in Berlin. Short term, he insisted; writing was his true vocation. His aim was to save enough to retire at forty-five to write his family history. He was thirty-nine, he had three sisters and an elderly mother with arthritis.

It was a life summary of poignant or wary concision. No wife was mentioned, no adoring girlfriend.

Cass, habitually reserved, was taken aback by Marco's disclosures. Was she expected to reciprocate? Should she confect a mini-biography? She was not sure why he'd told her of his literary ambitions and family. She responded simply. This was her first trip to Berlin, she had once studied in art school, then at university, and now worked part-time in a small bookshop in an inner suburb of Sydney. She too hoped one day to become a writer, but considered it unlikely.

'Everyone wants to write,' she said softly. 'It's a universal affliction.'

She felt suddenly exposed, having proclaimed incompetence. When her cappuccino was placed before her she recklessly filled it with sugar.

'Nabokov,' Marco returned to their shared subject, 'lived in ten different apartment houses here in Berlin, often renting just a room, sometimes only for a month or two. The Nestorstrasse place was unusual because it was more truly a home. Five years, a long time. He knew few Germans and lived almost entirely within the Russian émigré community.'

Cass nodded, wishing for something spongy and buttery to soak in her gritty coffee. She was overcome by discomfort, as if her attraction to Marco seemed suddenly to place her at a disadvantage.

'But you knew that, of course.'

He was testing her, she was certain. He was intrigued by her nationality and for some reason especially pleased that she was not English or American. Australians were inessential; that might be the key. Perhaps he imagined her in some bucolic or colonial mode, unformed and derivative. Or romping with childish fauna: koalas, kangaroos. Perhaps he thought her gullible and susceptible to old-world persuasions.

She looked at his beautiful hands, fiddling with unconscious fussiness at a sachet of sugar.

'As a child,' he went on, 'I was fascinated by Australia. Two of my father's older brothers emigrated there in the seventies, just after I was born. I never met them, but my mother has a cache of their letters which I used to read and reread. They are vivid letters, full of improbable information and naïve boasting.'

Marco paused, halted before whatever came next in his story. Cass was too polite to ask what his father did, and too reticent to offer more details of her own. He drank his espresso in a single gulp and looked away. Some memory had captured him, some private recollection had pulled him inwards.

And it was then, resting on the brink of disclosing conversation, that Marco changed the subject and told her of his group. He listed the names and offered a little information on each. He had known Gino for years in Rome – before he trained in real estate he'd been a literature postgraduate at La Sapienza with Gino. Though neither stayed there very long, they'd formed an enduring friendship. He'd met Victor only recently, helping him find an apartment. He was a college professor on a six-month sabbatical. A lovely man, Marco added. Very high-spirited, very funny. Yukio and Mitsuko, both writers, had stopped beneath his window, just as she had, to photograph the Nestorstrasse apartment. Yukio was a blogger in Japan of some considerable fame; Mitsuko was an essayist and English–Japanese translator.

They all met as a group each week, sometimes twice in a week, inspired and compelled by a shared interest in the work of Vladimir Nabokov. They tended to make speeches, Marco said, often effusive and cluttered with personal symbols. It was a new kind of community, not academic, not social, but some new species linking words and bodies with an occult sense of the written world. Like the parasite, he said wryly, that Nabokov claimed spelt out the word 'deified' in the jelly substance of its cells.

'Victor hopes to confirm this,' Marco added, 'and presents us with images of organisms that seem to display cursive writing. Mitochondria. Golgi bodies. He hands around photocopies of images taken through microscopes.'

Cass laughed. She couldn't help herself.

'Yes,' said Marco, 'I know it sounds a little crazy. But what a beautiful idea, don't you think? It's in *Ada*, the tiny being with "deified" written inside its body.'

'Everywhere,' Cass said, 'there are signs and symbols.'

'So you must join us.'

'I'm not a joiner. Really, I'm not.'

Marco was earnest in pressing his case.

'Consider how empty most social encounters really are; how nothing is revealed, or known, nothing is risked or truly given. The inner self is disqualified in the rough currencies of social commerce. Who cares about complication? Who cares about Nabokov?'

'Who indeed?'

She saw now that she had slightly offended him. Marco looked down at his hands.

'Forgive me, I'm lecturing. I must sound like an old fogey. All we want is that our self in words be more precise, and mean more. Matter more, you might say. Make true connections.'

Cass thought, Yes, he does sound like an old fogey. But she was also touched by the plea, and by the evident sincerity. Outside, a second fire-engine sped through the ash-grey streets, alarmingly scarlet and incongruously silent. Cass and Marco both noticed it, but neither commented. It fled past, a pale fire, into the frosty distance.

In the end he persuaded her. It may have been the sense of rare meeting or incipient sexual attraction. It may have been his charming appeal to an inner self, so primly defended. Nothing much at this time merited her full attention. The city was mysteriously closed in hibernation, and somehow inaccessible. Her vantage was one of ignorance, and her intuition was that whatever was concealed would take time to unconceal. She had come to Berlin to write, an ambition as vague as it was hopeful, verified only by her saying so. There was no evidence of her writing, for she had not yet begun. Her torpor would eventually – *necessarily* – lift. But she was a kind of tourist, after all, and bent on swift amusements. The weather oppressed her. She sensed herself frozen inside. She was like one of the ubiquitous cranes located high on building sites in Mitte, a stiff shape merely, stuck mechanical in mid-air.

Cass wondered what happened at the meetings, sometimes held in coffee shops, sometimes in empty apartments to which Marco had access. She was without friends in this city, aimless and contingent: why not follow the possibility of a literary fellowship? Marco said that the meetings so far had been rather anarchic; they were all a little odd, he declared honestly, and none of them were really 'joiners'. At the next they would begin a 'speak-memory' game, in which each would introduce themselves with a densely remembered story or detail. They had made a kind of pact, a narrative pact, to speak openly and freely. There was no compulsion, Marco insisted. No pressure or obligation. But each would try to speak with candour in whatever manner or genre they chose. Victor had offered to go first.

Outside the bar, on the footpath, they murmured shy farewells. Marco scribbled an address on a piece of paper.

'Oblomov,' he said.

Cass had no idea what he was referring to.

'Five pm, tomorrow. Please join us. Please.'

He seemed reluctant to leave. They stood motionless for a few expanding seconds. Cass half expected another fire-engine to appear and zoom past, since the world was like that now: Berlin was already declaring itself in replications and convergences. Blue U and green S signs seemed everywhere suspended, faces were not entirely distinctive, the same yellow bus roared everywhere between orange LED-lit signs. Colour drew her attention; any interruption to the overall grey caught her gaze. She had noticed too the surreal apparition of fibre-glass bears – life-sized and brightly decorated, standing in erect human postures – a ubiquitous public art of comic-book taste.

Prone to awkwardness in these situations, Cass spun on her heel with what might have seemed a decisive impertinence. She pushed away from Marco into the freezing air, feeling the turbulence, and the faint thrill, of scarcely admissible feelings.

4

The central heating was on and the apartment was cosy.

Cass placed her paper sheath of tulips near the doorway so she would not forget them. She loosened her scarf and removed her gloves and coat. This was the repetition that a European winter imposed, this on-again, off-again, this robing and disrobing.

Mitsuko, acting like a hostess, handed Cass the mysterious drink and led her with a delicate touch at the elbow into the sparsely furnished room. What struck Cass most were the empty walls and the pale squares and rectangles where once had rested paintings. Oblomov's disappeared images were now secretive shapes. There was a black leather lounge and two matching leather armchairs, but no coffee table, so that the drinks were served on the floor. There were two vintage standing lamps, of enamelled green metal, Venn-diagrammatically arranged to pour rings of light where a coffee table might have been. Cass recalled the squat she lived in when she had first fled home – sitting on the floor around candles in bottles and dope in plastic bags, and the queasy joy of having only a few books and a duffel bag of scant possessions. She had followed a boyfriend to London and her parents and brothers had been scandalised.

Victor's geographical announcements, manic and apparently lighthearted, had been a sign of his nervousness. His voice was curiously thin, high and insistent. He had rattled on – listing cities, engaging in fanciful speculations. Now he sat himself down and prepared to speak in a more tranquil tone. Mitsuko and Cass sat with Victor on the lounge, Marco and Gino each had an armchair, and Yukio sat between them on the floor, his legs crossed like a buddha. It was not an arrangement Cass, in her forward imagining, had at all anticipated, sitting opposite Marco, faced with his inquisitive scrutiny.

'We are grateful,' said Marco, 'that Victor has agreed to be the first in our speak-memory disclosures. This cannot be easy.'

He nodded to Victor. 'So, shall we begin?'

It was the simplest of commencements, no pomposity, no introduction.

Victor cleared his throat, a little too loudly, like a worried actor, warming up. Then he began. 'So, here goes, kiddos.

'I was born in New Jersey in 1952. Momma said I came out yawning, and liked to tell the story: "You came out yawning, little one, you came out yawning!" Like I was over it already and bored with the world. But she was wrong. I was never bored. I always wanted more and more world.

'She was forty-two then, an old mother in those days, and I was to be their only child. My parents loved me in an impassioned way that I found embarrassing: Momma would fuss over the smallest things – she was always tweaking my clothes, pulling at my sleeves, adjusting the cute bowties they inflicted on boys at that time. She was obsessed with cleanliness, spitting on her hanky and wiping away invisible smuts or blemishes; holding my chin with her thumb and index finger, tilting my face upwards, wiping and rubbing so that I imagined my face shone like a lamp. Her eyes would fill with tears at the slightest provocation: when I handed her a drawing, or recited some fragment in Yiddish, inept and stammering, or showed her a school certificate, given simply for attendance. I had a sense of power over her and my father, who was silent to the point of anonymity, a shade of a man who had left his full self behind him in Poland.

'My mother stayed at home and took in ironing for better-off households, so that our front room was always filled with piles of clean washing, as if there was a huge population hidden away in our house, forever casting off their clothes. I loved pushing my face into the piles, like a housewife in a TV commercial. It was like a secret vice, I guess, because it seemed so womanly and so wrong.

'My father worked in an umbrella factory – on Ferry Street, I think it was – doing who knows what, he never really told me. I was always asking him, "*Tateh*, what is it you actually do?" He would wave me away, so that I was left in the dark, contemplating the mysteries of making an umbrella. At school I told the kids that my papa was a cop; it sounded much nobler, somehow, and much more plausible.

'But Papa gave me my first real sense of the mystery of *things*, specific things, how something ordinary might carry extraordinary detail. Once, when he'd become tired of the ignorance of my questions, he drew an umbrella and named all the parts. There was the ferrule at the top, there was the open cap, the top notch, the ribs all joining at the rosette in the centre, there was the runner, the stretcher, the top and bottom springs. There was the shaft, the crook handle, and at the end of the crook handle there was the nose cap. Above was the canopy, that lovely shape, the dome some call the parasol. I remember him saying this in Yiddish, *"Some call this the parasol."* He sat back in his chair, surveying his named umbrella, and this was the closest to contentment, even happiness, I'd ever seen him. He was transfixed by his own drawing, and by the modest vocabulary of his labour.

'When the factory closed down in the early sixties, and he was dying of some unknown illness that made him even less substantial and more withdrawn, Papa one day, out of the blue, entered a kind of confused monologue, mixing Yiddish and English, about the bits and pieces of umbrellas. I understood then that he probably made the springs by hand. He'd been a watchmaker before the war, and it made sense to me then, that he might find a more simple expression of the skill his eyesight no longer enabled. He had a contempt for newer umbrellas with metal shafts and mass-produced springs, and owned a stick umbrella from the olden days, beautifully fashioned, a pointy miracle, which stood propped like a kind of furniture by our front door. I never saw him use it. I don't know where it came from. I know only that the old umbrella was his single treasure. When I popped it open after his death, the canopy was torn in two places. He must have known this, but kept it still.

'Other boys had basketball pennants in their rooms, and baseball cards and posters, especially after the Mets started in sixty-two. Other boys had small metal toys, cast-iron cars and tanks, and plastic figurines of cowboys and Indians. I had just a few books and my dead father's useless umbrella.

'My parents, Solomon and Hanka, later Solly and Anna, were Polish survivors of the Holocaust. I know very little of their story and they evaded my few questions. But at some level, too, I was guiltily incurious. I was a pretty dumb kid when it came to family, I can tell you.

'I know they were from Warsaw and had been in the ghetto. And I know they were both in Auschwitz, because I saw the numbers tattooed on their forearms. I have no idea of their actual experiences, or how they were taken, or when, or how each of them managed to survive. Even now, mostly when I'm watching movies or documentaries on TV, I feel a kind of despair that arises from knowing so little. I look for their faces in photographs and grainy footage. I think for a second: *Hey, that's my father!* But it never is. *Hey, that's my mother!* But no, not once.

'So every torment is possibly theirs, and nothing wholly is; I insert them into any memoir, anxiously imagining, then have to remove them again. Their lives in Europe are remote and obscure and their times in the camp are appallingly *generalised*. It pains me now to know so little. And it astonishes me how well we all avoided the topic.

'What I know of their story only starts after they were released. This much I know. They were two years, three maybe, in a displaced persons camp run by the Soviets, and this was where they met. Momma once told me they refused to be repatriated back to Poland because they'd heard there had been executions of those on the Left, and of participants in the uprising. Some had survived the camps, only to be killed when they arrived home. So they held out, waiting and waiting, hoping to get a passage to Palestine. When this didn't happen, they settled for America. On the boat they already heard about Newark, New Jersey.

'Newark, New Jersey, they heard, was a paradise for Jews.

'I think it was very hard when they first arrived. My mother spoke a little English, she had been well educated, and came from a middle-class family. My father spoke not a word and was reluctant to learn. A welfare agency set them up in two rooms with a few possessions, and not long afterwards Papa started at the umbrella factory. When I came along, they must have been mighty surprised – there were times when they looked at me as if I'd arrived from Mars.'

Here Victor halted. The group remained silent, wondering if his story was over. Mitsuko was examining her fingers. The men were all looking down. Cass was conscious of Victor sitting beside her – she'd entered the dreaminess of his story, she'd let it dissolve her Berlin surroundings into his New Jersey past – but now she was aware of him physically, the way he hunched over in his telling, the way he fiddled with his watchband, all the small giveaway signs that spoke of the effort of revelation. Marco looked up and caught her glance, but then looked away almost immediately and did not speak. Someone would soon pour another glass, say something trivial, and make time move again, back to the present, in this room, in Oblomov's room, on Goethestrasse, in freezing Berlin. Just as the strain of this quiet indecision took hold, Victor recommenced.

'I was a clever student, impeccably behaved, and I managed in grade school to blend in and seem like one of the others. But high school was a nightmare. I was fourteen when my father died and I felt ashamed of my stricken mother, and our lack of family, and our obvious poverty. No amount of lying disguised it. No amount of academic success. Everyone I knew had aunts and uncles, grand-parents and cousins, and we had no one. The rabbi visited once or twice, when I quit Hebrew classes and refused to take my bar mitzvah, but otherwise I can't remember a single caller to our apartment, apart from clients dropping off and picking up their ironing. Momma had no friends to speak of and said Americans had no souls.

'After Papa's death, she underwent a bewildering change; only in adulthood I realised it was a kind of breakdown. She lost it, completely lost it. She began casually to insult people on the sidewalks and in supermarkets. They understood nothing, she said. That was her line. *They understood nothing.* They played golf and had swimming parties, the women baked each other cakes and took their children to Dairy Queen and pizza bars, and all this seemed to her frivolous and a spiritual dereliction. She especially resented the wealthy Jews who lived on Keer Avenue, with their free-standing houses and their Cadillacs and their thin strips of emerald lawn. She resented their American speech and their extended families.

'I remember once we were walking together and she stopped before the window of a hairdressing parlour – this was in the days when women sat for hours under those metal hoods that looked like the heads of aliens – and she just started berating them, gesticulating and shouting loud insults in Yiddish. I could see the women, all in white capes, all in a row beneath the metal heads, turn towards her in unison. All together, like automatons. They looked stunned at first, at this crazy foreign lady shouting at them from the pavement, but then one began to giggle and the others followed suit. It shocked her, their jollity. It made her shout even louder. I'm guessing she never went to a hairdresser once in her life. She had grey hair, even when I was born, always bound in a loose bun; something from the old world, maybe, something from before the war.

'I wanted to flee, but had to stand there, watching Momma go crazy.

'By the mid-sixties white people had largely abandoned our neighbourhood. The third ward, that's what they called it. We lived in the third ward. Unemployment was widespread and people were unhappy. We were the only white family left in our block, and Momma gradually turned her scorn to the blacks. I never understood it. She shouted at them to get a job and clean up their children. Told them they had no souls, and they told her: "Fuck off, ole white lady, who you think you fuckin' are, speak to us like that?"

'There were race riots in sixty-seven – maybe you heard of them? The National Guard was sent in. Open gun battles in the street, dozens of buildings set on fire, twenty-six dead; hundreds, I dunno, maybe thousands, wounded. I remember the smoke and the scream of fire-engines and the sound of gunshot pinging outside our window, and I remember thinking: I *really* gotta get outa here.

'Afterwards it seemed the streets were never cleaned up. Everything smashed up and broken. Whole buildings in ruins. They despised us, the third ward. I got nervy and weird. I used to chant "umbrella, umbrella" to help me fall asleep.

'A scaredy-cat kid, that's what I was: "umbrella, umbrella".'

Victor managed a tight sardonic smile.

'Momma died later that same year, suddenly keeled over on the stairs. I was relieved, and I was destroyed . . . I had a chance, and I got away.'

The body somehow knows when it is proper to punctuate.

Victor leant into the crossed pools of light and poured himself another drink. He leant back, tilted his head and gulped it down. The room was silent, subdued. This was the hush of respectful listening. As if given permission, Gino took up the bottle, gestured an offering, and the others presented their glasses to be refilled. No one spoke. Victor had allowed himself to swerve away from his mother's death. He had held his story steady.

'Long story short: I was completely fucked up and went AWOL for a year, living rough in Brooklyn. But I was a good kid, with good manners, people saw that immediately. Too old-school to be a bum. Too young to be completely hopeless. A woman found me reading a book under a bridge and we struck up a conversation. She took me off the street, just like that; she took me off the street and decided to look after me. Leah Rabinovich. That was her name. Fed me baked ziti and German beer and supported my last year in high school, and after that my time in college – don't ask me how. She was Russian, or at least she'd been born in Russia and she had an apartment in Brighton Beach, stuffed to the ceiling with books.

'She rescued me, Leah Rabinovich, she was the one who saved me. Leah Rabinovich. A widow, no kids, it was just fate that we met. Russian fate, you know?

'One day we were talking and I asked her about her childhood. She said a little, not much. I gathered she had left Russia when she was ten, in 1920. Then Leah went to her bookshelves and drew out the autobiography. I'd heard of *Lolita*, of course – everyone had – but I'd never read any Nabokov, and it was a charmed encounter. It was like entering the luminous room of an imagined Europe, seeing a prewar world intact, particularised, densely notated, that my parents, or my grandparents, or my aunts and uncles, might have known. And even though I knew this to be someone else's world entirely, and nothing whatever to do with Poland, it served a deeply reassuring purpose. It was like something lost returning – all those detailed descriptions, all the colours and faces. Quirky visions, fancy words. Old things, long vanished.

'You all remember it: the little boy Vladimir is scrambling on rocks by the seaside, muttering a chant in English – "childhood, childhood". He is thinking of Robin Hood and Red Riding Hood, and the hoods of fairytale hunchback characters, he is peering at the tepid seawater glistening in the dimples of the rocks, he is watching his younger brother and their governess, in the far hazy distance, strolling hand in hand along a curved beach.

'This was so familiar to me, this sense of solitude and observation, this longing for a pure and concentrated reality. The way stray words knit with specific moments.

The intuition that this, more than anything, is our truest experience.

'Outside it was all motherfucker and goddamn and don't give a shit – excuse my French; it was Lyndon B. Johnson and the Vietnam War and Martin Luther King blown away; it was the Apollo program, Jimi Hendrix, sitcoms on TV. The world was crashing in. But I was a boy caught in the bubble of an enormous grief, equipped only for the past.

'And for this resurrection in formal prose, Russian-style. And for encountering a Europe my family might years ago have known. And for the novelty, above all, of unconventional seeing.'

Victor paused again, as if noticing that he had entered a literary-critical speech.

'I was a dumb fuck, I know it, but I was a dumb fuck with books. Excuse the French.'

He took a swig of his drink.

'I kid you not, kiddos,' he said, opening up a nervous smile. 'It was just like that. Like I could see a way forward. Like certain things made sense all of a sudden.

'The umbrella and my wish to bury my face in fresh clothes. Momma shouting at that row of women in the hairdressers. My papa in his own world, his own third ward, occasionally visible.'

Victor held out his glass, Gino filled it. 'Drink up!' he instructed.

They knew then that Victor had finished his speak-memory. For a few seconds they just sat, looking blankly at each other. Then Marco leant forward and shook Victor's hand, as if congratulating a man who had just won a trophy. Gino mimed a toast. Mitsuko skipped up, like a child suddenly released from a tiresome duty, and almost ran to her backpack nestled by the door with the coats.

'Snack time!'

She extracted a green plastic box, which she snapped open with a flourish. In it lay rows of sweetened rice balls, sprinkled with sesame seeds and coconut. With a pair of chopsticks, she tweezered the rice balls onto paper plates and handed them around. They sat still in their small circle, the six of them, and in silence ate their modest snack together. It was almost infantile, the way they licked their fingers, the messy challenge of Mitsuko's rice balls.

Victor drank and drank again. He was a short man and more than usually susceptible to drink. They all watched as energetically he drank himself towards oblivion. Before long, Gino stepped onto the balcony for a smoke; they could see his shape outside in the cold night, behind the sweating glass, and the orange spotlight of his cigarette lifting and falling. Yukio and Mitsuko, their shoulders touching, began a low conversation in confidential Japanese. Marco was jotting something in a sky-blue notebook. Victor noticed Cass slightly apart, observing him.

'The non-rhymers,' he said. 'We have to stick together. Right?'

It was an attempt at a joke, but he sounded tired. Already his speech included a weary slur. But there was a mellow expansiveness, too, and a sudden affection. Victor was neither abashed nor emboldened by his disclosed story; instead, with generosity, he asked Cass about herself, how she was spending her time, newly arrived in Berlin. After a few blundering responses – having little to report – Cass was relieved when conversation moved to the topic of Nabokov's short stories. They exchanged favourite titles and made a plan to visit the aquarium mentioned in one of the tales. Then came a moment in which Victor seemed to slump and melt away. Now, his story done, his strenuous memories rehearsed, he looked like a man ready for the luxurious and necessary forgetting of sleep.

Cass felt the beginnings of a fondness for Victor; she would see later how swiftly their attachment arose. This had been the special effect of Victor's speak-memory. How could one not care for this gentle man who had wanted someone else's past and whispered 'umbrella' to the violent night to help him sleep? It was a feeling borne of respect for the story he had offered them. It occurred to Cass that he might have a history of confessions to a psychiatrist and that his storytelling was not an entirely new thing. Wasn't this commonplace, almost a cliché, for New Yorkers of his age and class? The bespectacled shrink, the overpriced quack? But quickly she dismissed her thought as stingy and suspicious. There was no sense of habit or repetition in what Victor had told them, nor of fabrication, nor hidden agenda. He had entrusted his sorrow. He had spoken of shame and grief. And it suited her to believe that this was a first disclosure. The slow drift of her thoughts wanted Victor protected.

Heading to the U-Bahn, returning, Cass held her tulips to her chest. Her shield of organic life against the callous weather. They were damaged, she could feel it. Something loose, a few petals, moved in the triangle of paper. Animated by the evening, by literary oddity and the glimpsed inner life of Victor Edelman, she quickened her step, then almost slipped, and was required by good sense to slow down.

The streets were black and shiny with ice. Gravel had been cast on the pavements, but walking was still a difficult and treacherous enterprise. Cass followed the trails of dark gravel and now walked with care. She hardly noticed where she was going, carried on pale streaming lights, stiff and tranced with the cold, alcohol-affected. But somehow, by random instinct or luck, she managed automatically to retrace her steps. The streets bore an unreal gloss and unfamiliar names, but still she managed.

Then there were wheels, and noise, and something brash bearing down on her. A double-decker bus thundered close, its interior a jaundiced yellow, its patrons held high above, framed as silhouettes. She jolted away. In retreat, the bus resolved to a lucid vision. She might so easily have fallen beneath it, this seeming premonition.

Cass reached the steps to the U-Bahn, trembling with delayed alarm. She sensed wordless, deep in her nerves, how near to her end she had been. How near to absolute nothing. She grabbed at the railing like a falling woman. Her gloved hands were hard and clawed, her steps were uncertain.

5

When Cass opened her eyes, the first thing she saw was the tulips. It was true: they were the light of another, warmer world, their candle heads streaked with red, still bright and aflame. She was reminded of the Nabokovian regard for the weird vibrancy of things, the writer's capacity for relish and glorification. Tulips might be joyful or troubling objects; they might carry any meaning. Now they bowed limply in an almost human posture. More petals had detached. There was no vase in the cupboards, so the tulips stood in a milk carton, propped against overbalancing. It was an ugly vessel, but nevertheless served.

Fond of symbolic markers of time, Cass had arrived in Berlin on the first day of January. She expected New Year splendour, but walked into a mess. Her unremarkable street, spiked with leafless trees, was strewn with blackened debris and the curly innards of dead fireworks. Beer bottles and scrunched paper lay on the pavements and in the gutter. Everything was closed up, locked down, and vaguely shoddy. One or two weaving cyclists braved the ice on the streets, precariously atilt, but Berliners of all ages must have been sleeping it off, after so wild a party.

Her block, number 50, faced a cemetery. It looked plain and forlorn. At least it would be quiet, she thought. At least she might work here. Write here. Find a foreign sense of purpose. In a building further down the street, an apartment on the second floor had burnt out. Above each window was a residue of black smoke, rising up in a blurred paisley. The caretaker, Karl, who handed over the keys – looking blurred too, but from vodka, judging by the sour smell, and bent with the evidently sore joints of his seventy-plus years – announced in English that she had missed all the New Year's fun, that the fireworks were *fantastische* and the fire-engine had stayed for two hours. He'd glazed a little, trying to find the vocabulary for pyrotechnical dazzlements, then slipped without noticing into rambling German. All she heard among the clotted consonants was *feuerwerk, blitz*.

Karl's bloodshot eyes were unfocused and weepy. He turned away and led Cass slowly, almost creaking, up three flights of stairs. She felt sorry for this man, too apparently tired to be dealing with strangers, too ruddy with drink and seasonably undone. Her single suitcase seemed impossibly heavy, but she watched his labouring back and couldn't ask for help.

When Karl stood aside, puffing with his own exertion and leaning on the door frame, Cass saw that the studio was small, unadorned, painted in dove-grey, a pokey rectangle but for its balcony that jutted out into the wider world. A white door, which stood ajar, led to a tiny shower room.

There was a miniature fridge, rumbling, and on the kitchen bench a set of knives plunged into a wooden stand. Two coffee cups were visible, and an electric jug. Against the wall was a bed, a little larger than a single, but not quite double, with two pillows and a new-looking doona folded neatly at its end. Two chairs, chrome and formica, seventies vintage, stood at a matching table so narrow it might have been fashioned for a child.

She liked the place immediately. This was the promise of an austere, uncomplicated existence. This was the empty single room in which she might recover her own presence.

From the balcony Cass saw the cemetery, walled and peaceful, and beside it a small park. She was high enough to peer over extensive graves; they were set in a neat geometry, their headstones marked with bare vines and spots of brown moss. She would discover later that a few pedestrians used the cemetery as a shortcut, but they only took the central path, never deviating among the plots, so it retained an untouched air of self-containment and enclosure. In the distance the lacey ring-shape of a gasometer seemed almost to float. As industrial relics go, it was charming, even ethereal. So here, up high, there was a kind of German romanticism: sky, distance, relic, *memento mori*. It was an unanticipated pleasure that the studio faced a space, and not a building, that it had a view not to other windows and balconies and furtively glimpsed lives, but to weather and perspective and poetic conceit.

Cass offered Karl money but he refused with an indignant huff. He looked disappointed – she had somehow insulted him. She watched as he withdrew gingerly down the stairs. He did not look back as she called out a second thanks, but lifted one arm in acknowledgement, then clutched again at the bannister, gripping hard, like a man who has foreseen his own death at the bottom of the stairwell.

Cass closed the door behind him and stood for a moment, once again simply looking outside. Cemetery, gasometer, louring sky. Bed, fridge, a narrow table with two chairs. She dragged her heavy suitcase to the centre of the room. On the sink behind her was an upturned glass. She ran the tap for water and drank too quickly.

On that first day, newly arrived, she saw briefly beyond her own exhaustion. But with the door closed, a warped temporal order overtook her – the airline spin around the globe, the desultory hours in bright airports, the grumpy queues, the uniformed staff, the lunacy of long-haul travel. The spiritless after-effects crumpled her where she stood. She took off her shoes, stretched on the bed, and immediately fell asleep.

Now Cass looked back on her arrival and considered how swiftly she had entered their circle, the five international others. How helpful Karl had become, how unlikely a support. She had spent the first week in Berlin aimless and uncertain. She'd bought a bulky down coat so that she might survive the cold. She'd tasked herself with exploring the city, and made excursions here and there, visiting places that might suggest centrality or importance. But her movements were aimless, half-hearted and largely without motivation. The cold seemed to her extraordinary: surely an extreme. The vistas, for the most part, were grievously bleak. The entire centre of the city appeared to be a building site, spoilt brutally and with the air of an abandoned film set. It had been a mistake, Cass told herself, to arrive at the beginning of winter. There were omens even then of sorrowful times to come, there were obvious symbols of disrepair and ruination. At home it was summer, thirty degrees in Sydney. Here she shivered in Europe's ostentatious reversal.

At the end of her first week in Berlin she had stood before the Nestorstrasse apartment, taking a photograph with her phone, and meeting Marco Gianelli. He was charismatic, she realised, in an anachronistic way – this was what had attracted her. She saw in his neat clothes and tactful manner something she'd rarely met in the men she had known at university, with their practised uncouthness, their masculine argumentation, the way they assumed ownership of the women they lassoed into their grasp. She had endured them, her series of clever boyfriends, who expected her to pick up their towels and edit their poor prose. They had all exemplified the modish paranoias of their age. They were conceited over-achievers and smugly privileged. It had been a relief to fly away, saying the word 'Berlin' and implying, even to her brothers, that she might never return.

All Europe was fundamentally exotic to Cass. Berlin was exotic. Marco was exotic. There was the moment on the street in which he drew her attention to the Nabokov plaque. There, he said, there is the textual evidence you need. He stood back, he was patient, he was uncondescending. He did not have a thesis to write, not anymore. She held up her phone and snapped the plaque and wondered why, of all the possible sights, she might want this dull place stored in her repertoire of images.

It had been January 6th, the day of their first meeting. The temperature, glistening in illuminated lime numbers hung high above a chemist, read –4°. As she walked away from the dingy bar with the excellent Italian coffee, she saw Christmas trees, one after another, discarded on the pavement verge. They lay on their bellies, a sorry sight, their cone shapes squashed.

One bore a handwritten sign Cass translated to herself: 'Now, I am useless.'

She could not remember noticing discarded trees on Nestorstrasse. It troubled her that Christmas decorations, both frivolous or sacred, still appeared here and there throughout the city. There were festive snowmen still on Ku'damm, metal snowflakes and Bethlehem stars remained strung high over Alexanderplatz, and some shops persisted with dimly luminous displays, askew trees with empty boxes, looped tinsel, dangling baubles. It was difficult to resist the conclusion that she was surrounded by untimely signs, that ordinary numbers, January the 6th, –4, were the registers of a fake or redundant knowledge.

In a text message, Marco asked her to meet him at the Pergamon Museum. His message read, 'Care for a stroll around Babylon? Entrance, 2 pm?'

The simplicity of the invitation made it easy to accept. Cass had yet to visit one of the city's prestigious museums. It would be warm, she imagined, toasty warm, and museums had a solemnity that would make her meeting with Marco seem somehow neutral and educative. She was at once enticed and hesitant. She had imagined time alone, *longed*, truly longed, for contemplative time alone, and already she was succumbing to romantic possibility and the magnetism of her own attractions. But she also despised the false coyness women were expected to display, the sensible containment of feelings and opinions, the demand of high-level tolerance to the inconsistencies of men. She thought how as a child she had striven to be like her three brothers, how tough she had become, how rudely boyish. She wrestled, gave Chinese burns, refused to wear dresses; she swore, she mucked about, she was not sweet or dependable. Her mother had wrung her hands in despair. Now, in a new city, she might recover independent feelings.

It was still sub-zero, she guessed, without the *Apotheke* sign to confirm it. Cass located the bridge across the Spree. Plates of grimy ice lay on the water as if thrown like garbage into a chasm. She fancied she heard them scrape in a high pitch, rubbed together by undercurrent. As she crossed to Museum Island, Cass saw that it was another building site, a solid chaos of intentions and structures unfinished. Vast puddles of slush lay on broken concrete. Machines and implements were scattered in disarray. Like so much in the centre, it was under construction or reconstruction. Scaffolding, cranes, the temporary business of architects and workmen, the portable toilets, the short-term fencing, the crash-barriers and the skips. Rubble, more rubble. There was a history of Berlin to be written on the topic of rubble. Wreckage, waste, the sense of corruption or crime scene. A long blue water pipe, held high on a frame, encircled the whole. It was the way of the world, perhaps, that the dignity and sobriety of old public buildings, their temple facades, would be assaulted and covered over by indiscriminate modernity; that new buildings, more severely efficient, would eventually replace them.

Cass saw a few others struggling with frozen expressions and tightly compressed lips. Everyone wore black padded jackets in a kind of mournful uniformity, and battled the same bladed wind that swept across the open spaces, their fists jammed into pockets, their heads resolutely down. In the courtyard in front of the museum, a mass of gloomy punters surged in a dense queue, moving forward by small increments to the warm haven of the entrance hall. She saw their breath in the air, their virtuous and orderly loitering. When Marco hailed her, holding up tickets, she was overcome with relief. He lifted his arm as if involuntarily, as if pulled by hidden strings, and then he strode to her side. Here he paused, fondly waiting. Cass was aware she must look a fright, and hated herself for caring. Her nose and eyes were streaming. Her face had set in a stiff mask. But Marco said only that he was very pleased she had come, lightly kissed the air at her cheeks, then guided her, without touching, up a rattling ramp and towards the makeshift doors.

Inside, past the gift shop, everyone was crowded at the cloakroom, discarding coats and encumbrances and collecting headsets. All was loud and clamorous. The barbarian horde of a large group of schoolchildren had taken control, and shouted to each other as they stowed their backpacks and clothing. A maddened schoolteacher, with octopus eyes and a stiff straining neck, shouted back, so that the room jangled to the ceiling with conflicting and contiguous voices. Cass ought to have been critical but felt secretly charmed. They were so rebellious, these kids; they all flirted and gossiped and would not be wholly controlled. Each and every one seemed to possess a mobile phone, and this too connected them, the incessant, busy fidget of new-zapped messages, the will only to connect. Into the museum of dead worlds they carried electronic charge. One boy, thinking himself unseen, stole a kiss in a sideways peck from a bashful classmate. Others everywhere collided.

This time he touched her. Marco reached for Cass's shoulder and gently pulled her towards him.

'Come,' he said, leading her away.

They stepped together into huge rooms of ancient loot. Porticos, walls, statues and friezes, the altar of Pergamon, the Market Gate of Miletus. Labouring Turks, enslaved to nineteenth-century technologies, had somehow packaged entire monuments for shipment to Berlin. Gigantic dimensions shrunk everything human. Cass was suitably astonished, but also unmoved. Before them stood the Ishtar Gate, the model of archaeological feats and megalomaniacal drive.

'Built by Nebuchadnezzar,' Marco was saying, '575 BC.'

Cass looked dumbly at the massive gates, speculating on what she should feel, and why it was that here, surrounded by reverential murmurs and breathing melancholic museum air, that she felt almost nothing. She scanned the prestigious surfaces and experienced only detachment. Expatriated signs and symbols to be gawked at, all immemorial. Was this History, then, this sense of stony alienation?

Marco pointed informatively to the lions and aurochs, striding in regular sequence across lapis tiles. He was speaking in low, impassive tones of gods and goddesses. There was the drone of authoritative commentary in his voice; Cass wondered at how remarkably well informed he was, how he might almost have been a paid guide, or studiously out to impress her.

But still she felt nothing. Her clarity of vision was prompted by his presence, not by any special reverence for objects two thousand years old. A broken umbrella in an oily puddle might have affected her more. What was missing in her, that she had the urge to retreat?

Marco noticed at some point that Cass was no longer listening. They moved to smaller rooms, with smaller, more acceptable marvels. They stood at a basalt water basin, carved – so the sign said – from a single piece of stone, and decorated with images of men who had both legs and the bodies of fish. 704 BC.

'Early surrealism,' she said wryly.

But now it was Marco who was inexplicably absent. Without any warning he gasped, as if in deep surprise, and collapsed beside her. He had suddenly buckled, his knees giving way, and fallen to the floor. He lay still for just a second, prone, strangely resting, then began to shudder and seethe, his body battered inside by waves of convulsion. Cass saw him arch as if pulled and cracked on a wheel, his head thrown back. Popping eyes, a gaping mouth, and what might have been a grunt emitted there; Marco clenched with the junk electricity of his body. In an instinct to protect them both, Cass wanted to look away. Still he seethed, with visible and invisible currents. She saw now the whites of his eyes, the sweat on his brow, how he twitched even across his face and to the very ends of his fingertips. Others had noticed too – she heard voices swimming around her, pitched in high tones of concern and exclamation.

A large man in a uniform arrived from nowhere. He was at once upon them, active and intervening. He pressed down on Marco's shoulders to try to hold him still. When she looked into the man's face Cass saw Karl, and in the welter of the event thought she must be mistaken, or confused with the surprise of Marco's condition. Only later Karl explained that he had a few hours' work at the museum on Fridays and Sundays, that it was a routine, easy job, another kind of caretaking, in which only mischief or accident provided excitement and conversation.

Karl's large hands held on, and at last Marco became still. There was ebbing retraction, his brain settling down. Cass saw that she too was on the floor, and that a small crowd had gathered, human voltage drawing them in, and the delicious scandal of a poor man rattled and undone. She held her hands to his face. His eyes returned. There was no focus, no recognition, and Marco appeared utterly baffled. Tears rested in his eye sockets, squeezed out in the moment of return.

There were more uniforms, now, as other men moved the crowd away. With unusual courtesy, two museum guards pulled Marco upwards, and half-carried, half-dragged him to a room hidden behind the exhibits. They sat him down and offered to bring him a cup of tea. Marco was unresponsive and seemed incapable of speech. Cass accepted for him, as if she were his girlfriend, or wife, suddenly assuming the mantle of his protector in this public setting. She could hear the men discuss whether or not a doctor should be called, her schoolgirl German heightened and alerted by what she had witnessed.

'Aqua,' Marco said softly.

He was distraught as he said it. He could not bring himself to look at her.

Karl extracted a silver flask from a pocket inside his jacket and handed it to Marco. It was vodka, he said afterwards.

An official-looking woman with a mirthless smile appeared before them to offer a blanket. Marco took it meekly, like a child, and as if given permission, dropped his head to his chest and almost instantly fell asleep. Cass sat beside him, waiting. All around them the air seemed to whorl and hum. Left alone now, with sleeping Marco, Cass was aware of the sound of museum visitors beyond the thin partition, of their parallel world and quiet, peaceful strolling. They were visiting legendary kingdoms, gazing to take in details, commenting respectfully on ancient ambitions and the vigour of fantasy religions. It was a comfort, this low murmur, this ambient seep, as though everyone had consented by polite contract to whisper in the same tonal range. A guide returned with a cup of tea. Cass gratefully accepted it.

She might have dozed. Time fell away. When Marco stirred, Cass found that her arm was stiff, and that an entire hour had passed.

He had been humiliated, she saw. He did not want to speak of it. They parted outside the museum, shivering, in the early dark.

'I was intending to suggest dinner,' Marco said apologetically, 'but another time, perhaps? This condition always leaves me violently tired.'

She was struck by his phrase, 'violently tired'. He made a sign to go, clearly wishing to be alone. He'd been overtaken by a cloudy strangeness that made small talk difficult. Cass headed back across the footbridge, back into the fierce, icy wind, and towards the S-Bahn station that rumbled high up in the distance.

There must be an etiquette to such events, but she had not known how to perform it. There must be a discipline, a medical discipline at least, that might comfort and settle those whose brains had misfired and brought them tumbling down. She'd hung around, ineptly, then she had left. She'd really done nothing at all. Nothing at all. Marco seemed to assume that Cass had been repulsed, but the force of his distress and disturbance had intensified her interest. As he walked away she had the impulse to call him back, but let it fade.

On the train Cass saw how faces looked eroded by the cold. In the dim light everyone appeared both indistinct and familiar. The woman sitting next to her was speaking loud Russian into a mobile phone and all she said sounded angry, like an accusation, or a curse. There was a jointly blond pair who might have been any modern couple, dressed in brand names and alike, both swiping their text messages. Sitting opposite, a young man, gaunt and unearthly, had his eyes closed like one who has fallen asleep sitting up. Cass stared at him for a whole minute before noticing the tiny buds of earphones and the thin cords dangling into his buttoned-up jacket. He was otherwise transported, she thought, lost to the world. He was supernaturally removed, travelling essentially on sound.

6

They were meeting a second time at Oblomov's apartment on Goethestrasse. Though she had neither seen nor spoken to him since the episode at the Pergamon Museum, Marco was there again at the door, acting with composure. He looked healthy and handsome. There was no bruise or mark, no evidence of the fall. Nothing betrayed what had passed between them. The episode in the Pergamon might never have happened. He admitted Cass with a slight nod, and she saw once again that the others were assembled, and had already begun drinking.

'Am I late?' she ventured.

'No, not at all.'

Still, she felt the pang of what a child might experience in a playground, the simple exclusion of secrets and others turning away, or of being in a game in which she was spectator and must stand alone as others played. She felt their gaze as she unzipped her overcoat and discarded her gloves and scarf.

'Today is my turn,' said Mitsuko. She kissed Cass thrice.

It sounded like a boast. Mitsuko wore a black velvet

cape, festooned with mauve flowers, fake pansies, made of felt. She had smaller felt pansies arranged in her hair. Cass admired the hippie audacity of her style; she might have been a famed retro singer coming home from a gig. It was Yukio, this time, who handed her a drink, and discreetly kissed her once on the cheek before slipping away. Victor gestured a greeting from the floor, where he was arranging piles of paper. Gino stepped in from the balcony, leaving his smoker's privacy to offer a casual mini-salute.

Cass was pleased to return. She had thought of them all, how unlikely a coalition they were, how misfitted and intimately haphazard. It had pleased her to be considered part of their group. She was not a 'joiner', she told herself again. Yet she had treasured Victor's story and the trust of its disclosure; and she had carried with it an impression of the others' kindness towards him.

They sat as before. The drink, as before, was unidentifiable and strong.

'Okay,' said Mitsuko. 'I don't have a crazy mother or an umbrella father,' and here she glanced at Victor, believing she was offering an empathetic introduction. He nodded graciously, slightly embarrassed, but understood and acknowledged the kind intention.

'My parents are ordinary, sweet and ordinary. I grew up in Hagi, Yamaguchi Prefecture. It's on the west coast of Honshu, not far from Nagato, if you've heard of that, with its famous hot springs. Hagi is a little town, a port town, with a ruined castle at the foot of Mount Shizuki. So I am not a Tokyo girl, I am really a Hagi girl.'

Mitsuko looked across to Yukio, who smiled his encouragement. It was a sensitive exchange. They confirmed each other in the manner of couples newly in love, setting up a code of shared stories and a cautious protocol with others.

'Hagi is a town renowned for its pottery, and my father is a potter. In the 1590s a Japanese warlord from Hagi invaded Korea and abducted its potters, so the tradition begins then – every Hagi schoolchild knows this story. My father is the last in thirteen generations of potters, and very proud of his work. I'm sure it is a sadness to him that he didn't have a son, and that I had no interest at all in becoming a potter, but he is a philosophical man, and to this day he is still happily potting, back there in Hagi, fulfilling the dream of his ancestors to outlive their own time. Behind our house is a large kiln hundreds of years old, built into a hillside. There are many kilns like this, and ours is one of many ancient potteries.

'As a child I believed that history was a kind of smell, the scent of baking clay – musty and biscuity. Or of the sunshine drying seawater on human skin. I had no specific image of the past, because the pots of the eighteenth century look like the pots of the twenty-first century, but I somehow knew that this was it, that something as immaterial as a smell might carry time itself, that the dusty past was inside us, that the earth was inside us.

'A child from Hagi cannot resist an obsession with time.

'I love the wet clay that smatters my father's workroom, and the fine dry suspensions hanging in the air. I love the mess of his labour, and all the little instruments and wooden tools, unchanged for centuries, that a potter uses every day. I love to watch him at the wheel, turning it with his foot, as

47

his father and grandfather and great-grandfather have done before him. There is the slick and the shine, and the flecks of clay spinning away. It's mesmerising, watching a rotating pot, seeing the hands cradle it and shape it, hearing the low sound of the turning wheel. This is my earliest memory. The pot turning on the wheel. And my father's long hands creating a shape.

'Hagi pots are very prized and collected all around the world. There are delicate cups, with a translucent white glaze and there are heavy, lumpish teacups of rough, gritty clay. These have a creamy thick glaze, slightly pink, that has been likened in haiku to a woman's blushing skin. My father makes the second kind, but secretly I prefer the others, and my vision is always of powdered green tea spinning and spiralling in one of the fine cups. Because the clay is slightly porous, tea stains and recolours the pots as they are used, entering into the crazes and crackles, making the white slowly turn pink.

'I like this idea – that an object sucks in the memory of its use. I often wonder if this happens with other objects, too, at some level of perception we don't see or haven't yet learnt to recognise. Is this possible, do you think?'

It was a rhetorical question: Mitsuko had her own answer. She turned to Cass briefly as if to say, *Yes, it is possible; I know it is possible.*

'I believe I would have been happy to stay all my life in Hagi, with my beloved parents. But at the age of sixteen I went to live with my aunt Keiko in Tokyo. I was a very clever student, and my mother, who is also clever and wanted success for her daughter, decided I should finish my high school in Tokyo, and try for a good university, Waseda or

Keio, Japan Women's University or the University of Tokyo. I was a dutiful daughter and in those days, not so long ago, I already knew I wanted to be an English translator. English was always my interest – I love the English language. I was excited about going to Tokyo, and I wanted to meet the new world with diligence and a good heart. People forget how high-minded a sixteen-year-old can be.

'From the beginning, Aunt Keiko was a disciplinarian. She felt responsible for my success and imposed strict bedtimes and study times, strict mealtimes and little leisure. I went along with it for a while, then inevitably rebelled. I began to take bus rides away from my usual route between school and home, and always explained my late return as enrolment in a new after-school study class. In this way I began to know the city, and to find in anonymous wandering a wonderful freedom. In Harajuku district – perhaps you have heard of it? – I discovered music subcultures and street fashion and the world of Lolita Girls. It was a revelation, seeing young people dressed in cult outfits and fetish clothes. You have seen photos, maybe? Before I had heard of Nabokov, I had become a Lolita Girl. There's *kawaii*, the cute version – all cupcake dresses, lace and frills and pastel colours – the girls wear bonnets, corsets, ribbons, blonde wigs and petticoats, many petticoats. Often they carry parasols. This fashion is for girls who grew up with Minnie Mouse and Hello Kitty and want to look like dolls, even as adults. They wear special contact lenses to make their eyes look rounder. They pose a lot, attend make-up parties and gather in chattering pink groups.

'I was a goth Lolita – I wore only black outfits. I didn't carry fluffy toys like the *kawaii* girls did, and I didn't join clubs or giggle or make peace signs in front of cameras. I considered myself an intellectual and wanted a darker style. Aunt Keiko was dismayed, but nothing she said or did dissuaded me. I remember the first time I appeared in my costume, she staggered back as if I had pushed her. She was very conservative, more a typical Japanese lady in her early forties, single, but with a good income, I think. She didn't understand me, or why I might change from a bookish, timid niece to this Manga-style creature.

'When I finished high school I was admitted to university to study English. It helped that I was clever – my academic success protected me. I discovered later that Aunt Keiko never told my parents. She never once mentioned my transformation. She was deeply ashamed of what I had become.

'I'm not really sure what happened to me. I was not unhappy, just seeking something different. It was months before I told my aunt I had left university. I had found work as a "rental sister". Do you know *hikikomori*? These are young people, mostly male, who have withdrawn from the world and live entirely in their bedrooms at home. They lock themselves away, they don't get jobs, they don't want to be outside in the real world, or meeting with others. This is a very big problem in Japan. People say it is a kind of Japanese sickness. *Hikikomori*. Yukio will tell you more about this.'

Mitsuko again wanted his smile before she continued. Yukio flashed her a sign of approval. The others knew immediately that she was speaking of how they had met.

'I was employed by an agency. *Hikikomori* agency. Parents paid the agency to find ways to get their sons back into the world. For many we were what you call in English "the last resort": the parents had tried pets, Shinto priests, bribes, threats.

'I was a very good rental sister – I had a high success rate. The fact that I dressed as a goth Lolita helped, I think. I often began by slipping a photograph of myself beneath the doors to the *hikikomori* bedrooms, then notes, then gradually I began to speak softly at the door, so softly I could hear the young man drawing closer on the other side. Sometimes it took weeks before the *hikikomori* spoke in return, or sent a little piece of paper back under the door. I was patient and persistent. I was careful and smart. The guys knew I wasn't just some cute good girl who would normalise or disrespect them.

'I moved into a tiny rented room in Aoyama district, and Aunt Keiko finally had to tell my parents what had happened. They arrived one day to find me sleeping – the rental sister job was mostly nocturnal, as *hikikomori* are – and I made them tea and sat them down and explained what I was doing. I was not wearing my costume or my black make-up, so I didn't scare them away. I explained I was taking time away from my studies, supporting myself as a "counsellor" to disturbed youth, and that I would be staying in Tokyo. My mother wept then kissed me and my father said calmly and softly that I must find my own path. There was no big fuss and no persuading. I write to my parents – the old-fashioned way, with pen and paper – every week. We are still very close. They have met Yukio and like him. They are my perfect, ordinary parents.

'With my salary I began amassing a collection of books. Other young women bought clothes or went away on group trips. I wanted to keep up my English studies, and

I suppose I always knew that I would return to university. At a second-hand bookstore in Jinbōchō I discovered the works of Vladimir Nabokov. Of course, it was the title *Lolita* that at first attracted me. It was hard to believe that something I thought Japanese had derived from a Russian man living in America. I felt stupid not knowing. But I remember that I wasn't really interested in the Lolita girl Dolores Haze, and Humbert's obsessions, to be honest, weren't a surprise to me. We have *salarymen* in Tokyo a lot like Humbert Humbert, the "panting maniac". It was the writing and the image patterns, it was the unusual vocabulary, it was the peculiar, vivid way he knew about secret inner lives.

'When I first began, I could not read Nabokov without a Japanese translation and a dictionary: he is a difficult writer, even for English speakers, I think? But the work was also a wonderful challenge. I felt that as a goth Lolita I should know this book, and slowly developed my skills and moved on to the others. I love the stories most of all. They are all so sad and beautiful. Characters sob a lot. Characters are often Russian men and insecure and have very troubled *souls*.

'After I rescued Yukio – you have guessed he was a *hikikomori?* – my life completely changed. He had money he made through selling stories online – he will tell you about this – and we began to live and travel together. I ceased being a goth Lolita; somehow it didn't seem necessary anymore. Somehow I lost interest. First we went to Hagi, so Yukio could meet my family and see our pottery. We went together to the old kilns, which pock the hillsides like caves, and to the pottery museum and the ruins of the old castle. And then we stood by the ocean, and tasted the tang of salt in the air. I told Yukio my theories about the curious scent that is history, and the way objects carry time, and my belief that powdered green tea spiralling in a pale Hagi cup is for me the supreme image of all possible images. I had never told anyone these things before. Yukio listened, and understood.

'And then – this is a true story – one day we were standing facing the sea together and a butterfly appeared. It must have been windswept across the waves. It came speeding towards us, a patch of bright orange, and flew past; and just as quickly, it was gone, it disappeared from the field of our vision. It was a sign, we both agreed. It was a moment we have talked of often, when we both turned and peered into the distance, with the wind and the waves crashing behind us, looking to check that what we saw was a real thing, a true orange butterfly, and not a figment or an illusion that we had conjured together. High brown fritillary – *Fabriciana adippe* – I think that's what it was.'

'The butterfly?' asked Victor.

'Yes, the butterfly. High brown fritillary. But this one was orange.'

'You can google it,' added Yukio.

They were quiet now. There was a gleam, a polish, that surrounded them all, Cass thought. Light from the crossed lamps collected them in a primitive and artful arrangement. The storyteller against death. The retrieval of a few lucky images from the semi-darkness of the past. There was no irony here, no superior *whatever* to the presence of others. She thought at this unlikely moment of Karl's massive hands gently but firmly on Marco's shoulders, the blue veins prominent and bulging, the sausage fingers pressing down, the fan of each hand seeming to command the jerking body beneath it to halt and recover.

Mitsuko looked pleased with herself. She was absent-mindedly fiddling with the imitation pansies in her pink hair, relaxed and newly social now that her telling was done. She plucked one, reshaped the petals in finicky pulling actions, then placed it back in its jumble. They were all watching as she performed what might have been, in its elegant simplicity, a Zen ceremony dedicated to the worship of cherry blossoms. The hovering silence that followed was like that of a sleeping household, all at rest, all self-enclosed, all comfortably dreaming their own dreams.

7

After Mitsuko's speech, they decided they were irrevocably committed, and that each remaining story should swiftly follow. It was Marco who suggested it, speaking as if a social experiment was taking place. Each would consent, following Victor and Mitsuko's example, to revelation. Earlier, rather than later, so that none would suffer a relative advantage or disadvantage of knowing. It was an acceleration, he said, of the usual processes of friendship; it was a narrative artifice to which they might all pledge their mysteries.

Gino snorted. 'Pledge our mysteries? Jesus, this sounds like the church.'

Marco was unperturbed. 'Why does "mysteries" make you anxious? Why not pretend for the duration that we are all mysterious to each other?'

'I like scepticism,' he responded, 'though I am flagrantly superstitious.'

They were staring at each other in a fraternal challenge. Victor was delighting in their argument and hoping for more; Mitsuko and Yukio were both uncomfortably silent.

'Fine. Let us hear of your scepticism and superstition.'

'No mysteries.'

'No mysteries. Not a single one. We shall abolish all mysteries.'

Now they were smiling at each other. Something in their shared past had resurfaced to trouble and interrupt the present. Marco was calm and obstinate; Gino was worried, perhaps, about what he might be called upon to reveal.

'Say no more than you wish.'

'*Certo, Marco; certo, professore!*'

Gino shrank back into himself, implicitly conceding. The idea of their contest was intriguing to the others. Cass thought of Mitsuko's tale – she had never heard of Hagi, or Lolita girls, or *hikikomori* – there was so much to discover behind each face in the room. But already she too was apprehensive, worried in advance at what she might be able to say, or not say. This was a pact of strangers and carried the danger of capricious misunderstanding. Perhaps, being the newest recruit and a kind of visitor, they might not expect her to offer up a story.

'*Alles gut,*' said Victor. 'Save me from being the only two-bit putz who spilt his guts at chez Oblomov . . .' This was for Gino's benefit.

So it was resolved to continue in the spirit of sympathetic listening, and to enjoy the drinking, and the conversation, and the temporary community. Cass expected Marco to renew his dinner invitation, but after Mitsuko's talk they all dispersed into the dark, and she watched as he turned and walked away in the opposite direction, just as he had done after they left the Pergamon Museum. It occurred to her that having witnessed his shame, further intimacy might no longer be possible. This evening Marco had been distant and formal, not unfriendly, but simply removed. There was a moment in which they had accidentally touched, each studiously winding their scarves in the vestibule, and she saw a brief flush overtake him, and the shade of an idea, perhaps an invitation, begin to form, before he turned away and shrugged silently into his overcoat.

Yukio's speak-memory, entwined with Mitsuko's, took place the next night. It was perhaps inevitable that they should wish to be paired. Yukio frowned in concentration. They saw a seriousness in him now, less visible in the couple, as though Mitsuko absorbed an aspect of his character he might only express when he spoke as one.

'My English is not so good as Mitsuko. But I will try.

'When I think about this story, my story, and Mitsuko's Hagi story, I think we are made for each other and we needed to meet. But now, my story.'

Yukio sat on the floor, cross-legged. He closed his eyes for a second, and then he began.

'In 1995 there was a gas attack in the Tokyo subway, somewhere near Kasumigaseki station. Sarin gas is very deadly – one tiny drop can kill a man. Psychos left sarin in plastic bags in the subway, and broke the bags open using the ends of umbrellas.'

Yukio glanced at Victor. 'Ferrule,' he said carefully, making sure to pronounce the 'l' as best he could.

'Ferrule of the umbrella. It sounds a crazy idea, but that's how they did it. With umbrellas to break open the plastic bags. Many people died, I don't know how many. And very many were sick, and are still sick today. Some are blind, forever. Some cannot move. I watched Kasumigaseki station on Japan TV. The same pictures on TV, again and again. There was Takaheshi, the stationmaster, lying on the ground dead, with a spoon in his mouth. This is a horrible image. Dead with a spoon in his mouth. They said his name, Takaheshi, Takaheshi, and I had never seen a real dead man, with a real name, on television before. A Japanese man.

'And many others coughing and crying, and one man . . .' – here he consulted Mitsuko for vocabulary – '. . . *foaming* in the mouth. Lying on the ground. No breathing at all. I was very, very scared. I was ten years old then and everyone at school talked all day about the sarin gas attack. There were many very bad stories. We lived in Waseda, a long way from the station. But it was my city, it was my subway.

'I had very bad dreams. I was afraid of the subway. I was afraid of men with umbrellas. In Japan we have typhoons and earthquakes and nuclear and tsunami, but then, just a boy, I was afraid of the city. Sometimes in my dream I was a long way in the north, Sapporo, in the snow, in the mountains of Hokkaido, and there was a typhoon in my dream, spinning and spinning, like cartoon or like manga. But this was not as scary as the sarin attack in the subway.

'I have an older brother, Ichiro, five years older than me. He was excited by the attack. He teased me because he knew that I was afraid. I hated my brother. He is now a salaryman for a big company – Nikon, you have heard of it – and we don't talk to each other. My father is also a salaryman for Nikon, and early I knew that I was not like them. My father is a hard man and very strict. He was hard on Ichiro too, but Ichiro had girlfriends – very handsome, my brother Ichiro – and magazines about women. He was popular, he was confident, he was very good at IT. I was just the kid brother who was afraid of Tokyo.

'My mother was loving and very worried. She cared for me. But she could see I was going a little crazy. She cooked my favourite pork gyoza, she bought me computer games and manga, but it didn't help.

'I think now it was maybe my mother's idea: I was sent to live with her parents in Nagoya, in Aichi Prefecture. My grandparents cared for me too. I liked Nagoya. I wanted to stay there forever, with my Oba and Oji. One day my grandfather taught me to play chess. We sat by the window of his apartment, where the sunlight fell on the chessboard, for many hours. Many times my grandfather let me win. But later I was winning all by myself. I liked the small pieces and thinking about the chess moves. I liked the shape of the board and how it started in full rows and slowly became scattered and then at last became empty. I liked how the small pieces made shadows across the squares of the board, it was a beautiful thing. A simple thing. Most of all I liked the puzzles inside my head, those squares of black and white, and the pieces moving this way, that way, and other pieces disappearing. The pawns, the queen, the knight, the bishop. All the little shadows and small disappearances.

'Mitsuko says this feeling is *mono no aware*.'

'Sensitivity to things,' said Mitsuko, 'the pathos of things. Melancholy, shadows, tiny objects vanishing . . .'

'When I was fifteen I was sent back to Tokyo. My grandfather became ill and it was too hard for them to keep me. Back in Waseda, I went to school for one more year, then I refused to return. It was easier to stay in my room. I had a fixed world there. I had my own world there. My double-click world. There was a lot to see inside my laptop. I studied and I taught myself. I studied very hard. Everyone thinks *otaku* . . .'

'Obsessives,' Mitsuko chipped in.

'Everyone thinks we just play video games and read manga and waste our life, but double-click was my real education. I was disciplined and serious.

'First I changed my time. I woke up at night-time and went to sleep in daytime. This way I knew there would be hours when everyone was sleeping, and I could make my own room-world in silence. My mother left food outside my door, and I would collect it when I knew everyone was asleep. Sometimes I even went outside, to 7-Eleven, in the middle of the night. I took my father's money from his wallet and bought snack foods, batteries, sweets, magazines. I didn't stay out long. The darkness was scary. On the internet I read that Yakuza were hunting young *otaku* men to kill them for their body organs. Maybe true, maybe not. There are many scary stories on the internet. There had been murders of young men like me in *kapsaru hoterus* . . .'

'Capsule hotels,' Mitsuko said, 'where you sleep in a stacked room, the size of a coffin.'

'They died, or woke up with a hole and no kidney. So it was better, much safer, in my room at home.

'At first my father would bang on the door and shout. He said there were hospitals for people like me. He said he would not have a *hikikomori* for a son. He cursed and he threatened. Ichiro, who no longer lived at home, would sometimes visit to bang on my door for maybe hours. Then he would tire and leave. I had fixed good locks. I knew my father was ashamed and would not tell others what had happened to his second son. I knew he would rather have me hide away than shame him in public. Sometimes my mother passed letters under the door saying she still loved me and begging me to come out. Once, when I went to the bathroom, my father seized me and I hit him. I was ashamed I hit my father, but I still stayed in my room.

'In my room with my double-click, I had my own education. I watched one English film a day, so I learnt English language. Not so good as Mitsuko, of course. I bought *Star Wars* and watched those movies many times, copying the speech. My favourite film is *Blade Runner*.'

Here Yukio closed his eyes and recited with dramatic gravity, as if offering a sonnet: '"I've . . . seen things you people wouldn't believe . . . Attack ships on fire off the shoulder of Orion, I watched c-beams glitter in the dark near the Tannhäuser Gate. All those . . . moments . . . will be lost in time, like tears . . . in . . . the rain. Time . . . to die . . ."

'There is a whole world of *otaku* still talking about *Blade Runner*, forever, like outer space. I studied other things, too: medicine – you will be surprised how much medicine was on the internet, even then – I studied chess moves, geology. I learnt about constellations of the stars. I kept little notebooks of symbols and ideas. I wrote stories about life on other planets.

'After four years in my room things became sad. I was skinny and sick. For some reason my parents started again to try to get me back into the world. They battled with me, I stayed still, protecting myself. But in my double-click world I had begun to feel lonely. I think I knew I could not live in my bedroom forever.

'When Mitsuko arrived, I was angry my parents had told my life to a girl, and I was sure I would not open my door to her. She came almost every night for weeks. I could hear her behind the door, reading aloud to herself in English, sometimes talking to me in Japanese. I learnt she was practising her language, but she was also waiting for me to come out. After the first week she pushed a photograph of herself under the door and I was very surprised. Her voice was sweet and low, but her photograph looked nothing like the girls I had known. She was in her goth Lolita costume and dressed in black. She had black make-up and red lipstick and long wild hair. She was the same age as me and I was impressed that she was already so confident as herself. She was out in the world, and dressed like that.

'I began to wait for Mitsuko's visits at night. My parents gave her keys and she let herself into our apartment about two am. Sometimes she stayed for just an hour, sometimes two, even three. Once I think she fell asleep behind the door, because I did not hear her say goodbye, and in the morning I was woken by my mother's voice, exclaiming.

'After a few weeks I began to talk a little to Mitsuko. I was curious about her. I think I was already in love, but I didn't know it yet. I began to wait for her voice and long for her visits. And I began to ask her questions about herself – this was the first time for many years I was curious about another person. She told me all about Hagi and her parents, she described her room in Aoyama and her strict Aunt Keiko. She told me her strange ideas about time: we all live in different times, and only sometimes these match. This is called friendship, or love, this matching time. We talked about forever, what that might be.

'*Infinity* – that was one English word Mitsuko taught me.

'When I asked Mitsuko about her English language, she said she was translating a difficult story, she had discovered a Russian writer who knew special things about the world and memory and how words fit in. I had never heard of Nabokov. One night Mitsuko put under the door three pages of her translation of the story "First Love". In this story – you know it – a boy is in a train, travelling to the seaside where he meets a little girl called Colette. They are on holiday. She is English, he is Russian. She has a dog called Floss. When they are looking at a starfish together, she kisses him on the cheek. Only this. It sounds like nothing, but it is a whole world. I didn't know anyone had written a story in this way, noticing everything, taking a child's mind seriously.

'When I read the first pages of the story, I remembered my train trip to Nagoya. I was on the *shinkansen*, the fast train, not like the train in the story, but I understood how the boy watched the world rush away, how he saw the telegraph wires go up and down, how the white daytime moon follows the train, how he hears new sounds and notices a voice, or a cough, or words from other passengers, floating to him in the new world of the train.

'Mitsuko explained the story to me. I remember that after she left me with a copy of her translation, I read it again and again. It was different to anything I had read before. I think the story reminded me of how to see. Myself and others, my grandparents in Nagoya. The world outside where people meet, and talk, and change each other. I had a very safe room-world – everything around me was set up in tidy piles, everything had a place, everything was dead, and easy. My TV, my computer, my comic books. But this story reminded me of the chess games I played with my grandfather. Small shapes in the sunlight. His wrinkled left hand, with spots and long fingers, reaching slowly for a piece and bumping one of my pieces out of the way. I wanted that world to come back. I wanted little shadow things. Another person's hands, and something playing between us.

'Mitsuko took her time. She waited. I waited. The first time I left the room with her, we went for a walk together while my family slept. She was not wearing her costume, so I saw her as she was. It was very strange for me to be near a girl. I was nervous and shy. I saw small things, and looked away when her face was close. We didn't say very much. I remember I asked her what "meerschaum" was; it was in the short story. She spoke very softly as she explained. It was like she had made a new thing in the world.

'Everything shone under the streetlights, everything was close. Afterwards she said goodbye in front of my building. I wanted to kiss her, but she turned and walked away into the darkness. The next night she didn't come, and I was in a panic of waiting. I thought I would die. Really, I thought I would die. But on the second night she came again, at two am, and something in me had changed. Like the little Russian boy looking down at the starfish. I opened my door and saw her round face there, smiling, and looking back at me.'

Yukio paused. Mitsuko was staring into her lap. It perhaps occurred to each listener that one meets couples all the time but is never told the story of their love, is never given access to the blazing first moments in which a connection is made. It was a startling, rare thing, to be told of falling in love, accentuated on this occasion by Yukio's sincerity, by his wish to capture the essence of his transition from *hikikomori* to lover. Victor seemed especially moved. He was dabbing at his eyes beneath his spectacles, possibly disguising a tear. Gino and Marco were looking intently into Yukio's face, as if expecting or silently willing more words. Cass saw that Yukio would say no more, and that the proper conclusion to his narrative was Mitsuko's round face at his door.

A love story, a first love story. After Mitsuko's disclosure it was somehow fitting that Yukio tell the other side of the encounter, that he match her gentle words with his own declaration. No one spoke. Mitsuko and Yukio seemed both to be blushing with pleasure. Unable to endure the quiet pause any longer, Victor let out a single, ecstatic burst of applause.

8

So again they were gathering their coats to depart. And again feeling or instinct flickered unacknowledged between them. Yukio and Mitsuko left swiftly, their twin shapes bounding, released and joyful, down the long zigzag stairway. They were heading to a nightclub in Neukölln, they said, to hear a famous Japanese DJ play remixes of David Bowie. Super-cool! It would be super-cool! repeated Yukio. Victor was tired: no remixing DJs for him. No Ground Control to Major Tom. He offered bear hugs as he left. Whacked, he said.

Gino shuffled and lingered. 'I suggest that we three have dinner together.'

Marco hesitated, perhaps feeling a little caught out, or wishing he had bounded away with the Japanese lovers. His face concealed whatever he might truly be thinking. 'Of course,' he said softly. It was only then he looked directly at Cass. 'I promise I won't disgrace myself again.'

Gino discreetly declined to follow up. 'So, it's settled. I took the liberty of booking nearby.'

Outside, he linked arms with Cass, determined to

support her across the uneven flagstones. It was an assertion gallant and kind, and declaring his own physical superiority. Slightly taller than Marco, there was also a rigour to his body, a hint in the veined neck and broad chest that he was of the new class of man who reshaped in gyms. Millions out there, thought Cass, millions fashioning their bodies. She was a walker, miraculously alive just as she was, without lifting and pumping. Slim, slight even, and secretly disdainful of energetic movements going nowhere.

Together they walked through the freezing streets of Charlottenburg, this evening festive and bright, but also slowed, somehow, flowing in distended duration. Lights in beaded strings looped around the restaurants, warm interiors were ablaze in tones of amber, and a soft radiance arose behind moist glass windows and doors. A man stepped from an apartment, pulling a triangle of yellow light; the door closed again and the triangle contracted and disappeared. They each saw it, the tricksy and liquid aspects of the evening and the forms of illumination that shifted shapes. There were few people on the street – too cold still – but within each restaurant were dispersed cosy couples and groups, leaning together in apparently fixed tableaux. At one window two children, a boy and a girl of about five, pressed their noses to the pane of glass, looking outwards. The palms of their hands were splayed likewise, held up in four pale stars. Marco stopped, stooped to their level, and pressed his face towards theirs. The children sprang back, excited. Their hands left ghostly impressions on the glass, white traceries of palm prints, which faded as they noticed them.

'*Scimmie*,' he said. 'Monkeys.'

They walked on in silence. After Yukio's story, casual chatter was no option, the world needed no commentary that evening; it was self-sufficient. When they arrived at the restaurant, hyperbolically Italian (chianti bottles hanging from the ceiling, the Italian flag decoratively draped above the bar, *trattoria*-style fake wood panelling coating the walls), they had each to make the effort to move from reverie to conversation, to break the hypnotic sense they had of someone else's words still acting within and upon them.

The Italian restaurant was, unpatriotically, depopulated and quiet. Gino and Cass ordered pasta, Marco ordered veal, and they all spoke in euphemisms about Victor, Mitsuko and Yukio. It was in part the anxiety of knowing they would soon join the speakers, and needed to find, each one of them, a credible self to display. Gino said everyone should have a sabbatical as a *hikikomori*, remain inaccessible for a time, and then be greeted extravagantly by love. Everyone, he continued, might move between radical isolation and ardent connection. Think of an astronaut returning; think of the shift from zero-gravity aloneness to jubilant over-attention.

When an aged waiter with speckled hands interrupted to pour their wine, Gino took the opportunity to touch Cass's lower back. Sitting in the middle, she understood that she was a token between Marco and Gino, that they were obscurely competing for her attention. She ignored the subtexts and the hints, she tried to remain self-possessed. Yet there was undeniable desire and the stirring of delectable sensations. She told herself later that ignoring Gino was an act of forbearance, but in truth she had been pleased at his explorative touch. She hoped Marco would move closer, or brush lightly at her thigh.

Gino spoke with a lack of focus of his few months in the city. He was writing freelance pieces on the topic of 'haunted cities' and composing a book, he said firmly, about his personal Berlin. This was, he announced, an unconcluded city, all open systems, broken circles, damaged stars, ravaged 'scapes, so that the polluted past wafted like toxins into the atmosphere of the present. He was pleased with his own metaphor; Marco saw it too. Cass thought the allusion melodramatic and unhistorical – and too easy, somehow – history as poison wind. Gino's tone was sure. She was reminded of academics who spoke of their own projects with a certain highbrow disdain, wishing both to promote and stylishly bluster, but also convinced that no one else would really understand.

Encouraged by their lack of objection, taking silence as assent, Gino went on to speak of the features of Berlin that he intended to write about: the ghost stations of the underground, the various unreconstructed ruins, the site of the former Gestapo and SS headquarters, now known as the Topography of Terror. Museums were one thing, he went on, but it was Nazism and Nazi kitsch that had a universal appeal, indivisible from Hollywood movies and one's own haughty self-righteousness. Everyone is better than a Nazi; everyone takes assurance, pleasure even, at knowing how barbaric others have been. There was a consolation, an immoral consolation, he granted, in looking back at the history of this tragic place.

Gino was warming to his subject now, wanting to offer morbid insight and cryptic knowledge. He was claiming his

69

own sense of affliction as a mark of good taste. Cass caught Marco's gaze and wondered if he too, at this moment, was feeling repelled.

The waiter returned. He unobtrusively took their plates, piling them together, and whisking away the empty bread-basket, which he placed balancing atop the whole. They ordered coffees. Cass was thinking of how she and Marco had let Gino take over, presenting his version of Berlin as if it spoke for them all, not objecting, not arguing. His adjective stayed with her: unconcluded. Every city, she reflected, is surely unconcluded.

Marco took the waiter's actions as an opportunity to break Gino's spell. He mentioned that they must all soon move from Oblomov's apartment, that he had sold it that very morning to an investor from Milan.

'Don't worry, I promise I won't talk about real estate in Berlin.'

'He won't say,' added Gino, 'that he is selling the city. That he is one of the agents of foreign hype – a foreign agent, no?'

Marco did not respond.

Only when the conversation became Nabokovian did they all begin to relax. Following the prompt of Yukio's story, Cass said he had reminded her of the moment she discovered the word 'lemniscate' in Nabokov's work, and had needed to consult the dictionary. What a distinctive thrill it was, to have a familiar shape named.

'Lemniscate? I don't remember it.'

'Me neither,' said Gino.

'It's the shape of infinity. It's the figure of eight lying on its belly.'

And so their conversation swung to those connoisseur pleasures that new words brought with them. Marco loved 'conchometrist', one who measures the curves of seashells; he thought it might have come from *Pale Fire*. Gino liked 'kibitzer', the non-participant in a game, the one who stands at the side, observing, giving advice. They all loved 'fritillary', as Mitsuko clearly did.

'And I too', said Cass, 'didn't know what a *meerschaum* was.'

They were good-humoured now. They spun out words as if drunk on them. When it came to a summary, Cass opted for the simple 'drisk', as one of her favourites: it was a type of rain, drizzly and misty, a very *European* rain, which the author considered exclusively Russian.

'We don't have "drisk" in Australia,' she said. 'No way. There is no Russian rain falling in Australia.'

It occurred to Cass then that she had drunk too much.

Gino liked 'ensellure' – it was that concave in the lower back, in the lumbar region. He had discovered it in *Lolita* and thought it opened an entire, personalised erotics. He stared at Cass as he said this, willing her to agree. There was a pause in which he might have gone on to describe his own arousal.

Marco ignored him. He placed his index finger at the centre of his forehead: 'ophryon', it was called. The middle transversal supra-orbital position. Third eyes. Headaches. Inspiration. Epilepsy.

Gino quoted Nabokov to the effect that writerly inspiration begins with a prefatory glow, not unlike a benign version of the aura that epileptics sense just before an attack. He looked knowingly at Marco, challenging a confirmation or refutation. Cass saw then that he knew of Marco's condition, and wanted to provoke him. Had Marco told Gino of the incident in the Pergamon Museum? Now, she thought, he would say something of their time there, reverse its power to silence them, thank her for staying, perhaps, or offer an affectionate squeeze of the elbow as he told Gino a deftly comic account of falling in front of the water basin of fish-men, dating from 704 BC. But again he did not.

'Shall we get the bill?' Marco asked.

Seeking the toilet before they left, Cass blundered by mistake into the kitchen. She had expected to see an ample Italian woman with huge forearms and a food-stained apron hefting a saucepan or stirring a gigantic pot. Instead, she saw two reedy men who may have been Sri Lankan. They stared at the intruder with no visible interest at all, completely indifferent; then turned back to producing authentic Italian cuisine.

Gino and Marco walked her as far as the subway. There were others also leaving restaurants and entering the night. Everyone was bulky in hats and coats, extra-large with the winter. Even in the buses that thundered by, people were bigger, slower, clumped and indistinct at the smeary windows, like a specially captured tribe. But there was a lustre to the air, and a quality of bright delineation. Cass felt strangely immortal. Now, right now, she cherished the city she was in, saw how Berlin supplied and allowed her this tipsy elation, this clever conversation, this sense of participating in a new internationalism and a time beyond her own.

As Gino and Marco retreated, she heard their voices,

almost indistinguishable, begin a new conversation. They may have been speaking about her. Italian vowels rose and fell in departing music. Cass felt suddenly self-conscious and drunk. She felt like the kibitzer, just as she had when she'd arrived for Yukio's talk. She realised she had wanted one of them to invite her to his bed. It was an abrupt, self-interested, elementary knowledge. She stood silent for a while, watching the two men disappear, then descended to her train.

9

Gino's speak-memory was to be the last in the Oblomov apartment. Cass arrived early and found Marco alone. He opened the door and could not disguise his expression of surprise at her untimely arrival. He ushered her in, and stood back as she performed the ritual once again, placing her bag on the floor, unwinding her scarf, unzipping and removing her coat, adjusting by degrees to yellow warmth after the black cold outside.

Marco kissed each cheek.

'So cold!'

'Yes, it's freezing out there now.'

They needed this formal exchange, this impersonality. Behind Marco's head the shapes of the disappeared paintings appeared more symbolic than before: what had once hung in the vestibule? What had visitors seen as they entered? Perhaps there had been a gilt-framed mirror in which they saw merely themselves, arrived. Perhaps Herr Oblomov had peered at himself there and wondered if he was about to die soon, abrupt and irrelevant, of heart attack or stroke, leaving his classy apartment to the care of apathetic strangers.

More in awkwardness than passion, Marco leant forward again. His hand reached for the back of Cass's head, he touched lightly, and he kissed her mouth. Both felt an immense and instant relief. She could feel it in the variation of his touch and in her own relaxation. She hoped he wouldn't apologise, and he did not. When he drew back he smiled and looked directly at her.

'Restoration.'

It was an enigmatic word, and Cass did not ask what he meant. She saw a burden lift from him. She composed herself by brushing back her hair with her hand.

'I've wanted to kiss you since Nestorstrasse, since we first met.'

It was astonishing, how feelings work; she had often thought this. It was a simple enough reflection: that without witness two people might become personal and simplify. Might move closer. *Ramify.* Astonishing too how a new kiss still carried uncomplicated exhilaration.

But there was no time to think on this, or to consider if she was immature, or needy, or a sucker for seduction. These were cynical times. The door buzzer had sounded; someone downstairs wanted admission. They were both startled to hear it and for a moment stared at the handpiece on the wall, and the closed door, as if together they might ignore it and hide.

It was Victor. His joyful American voice crackled though the wires: 'Major Tom to Ground Control! Super-cool!'

They stood apart as they heard him clomp up the stairs.

'I thought I'd come early!'

Victor greeted Marco warmly and then turned to Cass.

'I have a daughter, Rachael. You remind me of her.' He hugged with a vigorous, clumsy embrace.

'Rachael,' he added proudly, 'is a pediatrician. In Jersey. Very successful.'

'Nothing at all like me, then.'

But Victor wouldn't hear of it. He spoke of how close they were, he and Rachael, he boasted of her beauty and wished she would marry and settle down. Rachael had been upset after his divorce, years ago, but now she understood, he added.

Victor wore a shapka this time; it was of artificial fur, a tourist item, and the dangling earflaps looked childish and comical. Goofy. Snoopy.

'Alexanderplatz. The poor schmuck selling them looked so miserable I had to oblige. *Fish fur*, Momma would call this.'

He held the hat out for inspection. It had a red star in the centre, where the ophryon might have been. In tourist areas, even in unpromising midwinter, Cass had seen vendors with their trolleys of fake Soviet-era memorabilia. They were gritty-looking men, tough, all down on their luck. They had the faces of Stakhanovites, carved by ice and hard as coal. Just that day she had seen a group of Spanish students larking about, trying on the shapkas and flinging one between them. It sailed in the air, barely flapping, like an incompetent bird.

Victor was discarding his coat onto the floor.

Marco and Cass maintained their distance. Victor took his seat and was already uncorking a bottle.

'Come, let's talk.'

His research was going nowhere, precisely nowhere, he said cheerfully. He had wanted to work on Russian émigré writers in Berlin, but found it had all been done before; there was nothing left to uncover. He would return to textual analysis and give up the dream of literary history.

'It was always a pretext,' he conceded. 'I just wanted an excuse to come. The elevated railways remind me of Chicago. The old women in the subways sometimes look like my momma. The sausages are fantastic. The lakes are mysterious. I can't quite bring myself to go to Poland, so this is the next best thing. Is that nuts, do you think?'

'No, it's not nuts. We go where we are able. We find our way slowly.' Cass was aware she sounded like a counsellor, full of easy platitudes, but Victor seemed pleased with her answer.

'That's just what Rachael said.'

'There is a street in Rome, my home city, I cannot even walk past,' Marco added.

Neither asked him why. The door buzzed again. It was Mitsuko and Yukio.

'We thought we'd come early,' they shouted through the intercom.

So in the end the five who were early waited for Gino. After the appointed hour passed, they discussed the possibility he had decided he could not go ahead with the speak-memory, and had disappeared somewhere, perhaps even returned home. But thirty minutes later Gino arrived. He was well dressed and assured and seemed entirely unaware of his tardiness or of the critical speculation.

They sat, once again, in exactly the same places. Their assembly was already composed of ritual behaviours and intricate assumptions. Oblomov's imageless room hung quietly around them.

Gino took a large swig of his drink.

'I cannot tell my story,' he began, 'without first telling you that my family is obsessed with the idea of coincidence. For us, signs and symbols converge, duplicate and interweave. There is no moment or event that is not referring to another moment or event. This is not just delusion, or some family madness. My family make up a design, as we would say in Italian.

'I was born in Bologna on the 12th of December 1980, which is also the date that my father, Aldo Scattini, then aged thirty-seven, died from injuries received at the central train station in August that year. So from the beginning I was destined to carry his memory, and my mother was bent on a lifetime of sad comparisons. Curiously, I was named not for my unfortunate father, as if this honorific would too closely link us, but in memory of my mother's father, Gino Lorusso, who was also killed in the central train station, though many years before, during the wartime bombings of Bologna, in 1943.

'I have four older sisters, Lucia, Maria, Claudia and Antonella. I was the longed-for son, and since my birth coincided with my father's death, I became the "little man" of the household. My childhood is saturated with the singsong of my quartet of sisters: "*Ah, uomo piccolo; ah, que bello . . .*" and their repetitious faces bending above me.

'For my mother, my existence was more emotionally complicated. She doted on me, but she was a widow with five children and believed herself abandoned and fated to struggle. She carried about her a gloomy doom-laden atmosphere, her own weather, as it were, which was never sunny. She died five years ago, and when my sisters and I peered into the coffin, we saw that she wore the same expression, as if cemented, she'd carried throughout her unhappy life. It was one of grim disappointment, puckered in a sullen pout. Her bosom was immense; oddly, it was only seeing her lying down, in the coffin, that I saw how stout she was, how unusually top-heavy.

'Seeing her at rest helped us all. Antonella said the satin in the coffin was the wrong colour – she had asked for pink and it was standard white – this too somehow helped; I remember we spent ages discussing banal funerary details. My mother's face nested in a frilled, babyish bonnet of the wrong-coloured satin, she held a frail, breakable rosary between her chubby fingers.

'I mourned my mother. But I was also relieved that her lifelong unhappiness was at an end.

'Like Yukio, my childhood was marred by imagining disaster. My father, Aldo Scattini, had been seriously injured in the bombing of the Bologna Centrale train station on the morning of the second of August 1980. His name is not on the memorial plaque at the station: it lists 85 people, most of whom died on that day. He lingered too long to be an official casualty, or perhaps he was simply forgotten or overlooked. My mother resented his exclusion, as if having his name printed officially might have made a difference to her grief.

'Perhaps it would have, who is to say? Perhaps she might have borne the loss better. Or perhaps it would have become a trivial detail, like the colour of satin in a coffin or the shocking contrast between a big bosom and the light trail of an arranged rosary.

'At the train station today you will see the clock stopped at 10.25 am, the time of the explosion. I used to think this a glib and insulting thing, and believed for years it should have been consigned to the garbage. But now it seems to me profound, this broken, stopped clock. Now I know a little more about stops and starts; I know that there are time signatures to certain events, and that the world of objects stands there, mutely unchanging, to remind us that we are careless and inconsiderate of our own given time.

'As a boy I read obsessively on the Bologna bombings. I knew that Bologna was then a Left-wing city – *Bologna Rosso* – and that Right-wing fascists had planted the bomb. It was compelling information. As a vulgar teenager it pleased me to think of my father as a victim of fascists, but this is no solace, of course, and a moral distraction. His death was meaningless, entirely meaningless, and there is no profit in thinking it was for a cause, or carried historical purpose.

'My father, Aldo Scattini – I still love saying his name – exists in a nebulous, slightly brown photograph, taken at the time of his wedding. He wears a moustache like a cowboy and appears stiff and unsmiling, a young man evidently having second thoughts. My mother is slim and almost elegant – hardly recognisable – at his side. She holds a spray of gardenias and clematis that spills over her fruitful belly. I recovered other photographs of my father after my mother's death, but this was the one that I knew him by, since it stood in the centre of our sitting-room mantelpiece throughout my entire life. This is the photograph, the cowboy, that I held in my mind as a child, that still returns to me in dreams, or when I think of or imagine him . . .'

Gino paused in his story and looked around him.

'I've never told anyone else of these things. It must be this drink' – here, Gino held his glass up, as if to a toast –

'this tricky Russian drink is making me chatty.' He smiled a wan smile.

He was silent for a minute or so and might have been reconsidering his participation in the speak-memory. The room seemed to close around them with the claustrophobia of withheld speech. As they began restlessly to shift, Gino recommenced.

'It was a hot August day, the day of the explosion. In Bologna we have very hot, humid summers – many locals go on holiday, to the seaside, or up to the mountains. But the central train station is always busy, and on this August day the second-class waiting room, where the bomb exploded, was crammed full to bursting because it had air-conditioning. Anyone with children, any exhausted tourist, was seeking shelter in the relative cool of the second-class waiting room. My father was not, as it happens, but he was still crushed under the rubble as the whole side wing of the station exploded.

'He was carried to hospital in a bus, number thirty-seven. It was passing by and became an ambulance. Only my mother and Lucia saw him in hospital; all the long months that followed my sisters were kept away. When I was old enough Lucia told me that he'd been brought in with his chest collapsed and bleeding from the ears and eyes. This gory detail haunted me all my childhood. I hated Lucia for telling me. For seeing him like that. It was a boast, needing to tell me.

'There is a terracotta sculpture in Bologna Cathedral, *Compianto sul Cristo morto*, a lamentation of the death of Christ, and all the mourners standing above the holy body have their mouths open in horror. This is how I thought

81

of my own father – that all around him, all who saw him, would have had their mouths open in horror. So my father also reminds me of these figures of clay, standing in a dim candlelit corner of the Bologna Cathedral. You can see them for yourself; they are bathed in the tawny light of little chapels and crypts, they stand timelessly for the silent shock of a young man tortured.

'I was never a believer, but I always admired these analogues, the way art gave us a true expression of what left our mouths hanging open. I found the priests of my childhood dull and incompetent, they reeked somehow of personal failure and wasted ambition, but I loved the velvety air of the cathedral and the way footfall echoed, the sense that voices always floated upwards towards the apse, and were caught there, very high, circulating like stray birds. There is an amplification of muffled and whispered words – perhaps you've experienced this, perhaps you know it too. If a metal candle stand is knocked over in an old church, there is a shattering clang, louder that you can imagine, so that even as a priest rushes to upright the blasphemous object, everyone is reminded of these special qualities of the air, the way this is an enclosure, and one that both registers and exaggerates.

'Accidents of all kinds do this too, I think – show the invisible energies around us, and the waves of a higher-order empiricism . . .

'I moved to Rome as a young man to study art history, still a plausible career in Italy. But I was already lost to literature – never a very plausible career anywhere, really, and changed courses early. My father had been an accountant, but with his own literary aspirations. He had left behind a small library that showed his classical tastes, and was devoted entirely to works in French and Italian. He clearly adored Dante, and the only thing he owned of value, and which I have inherited, is an old edition of *Paradiso,* dating from 1748. He seems never to have owned *Purgatorio* or *Inferno,* or at least they were nowhere to be found in his collection. There are also scraps of his poetry, clumsy and sentimental, full of shining moons and the pearly moon-face of some lost love and though amateur and incompetent their existence moves me enormously. It may have been an element of my mother's sadness that she'd kept these poems, because not one line of verse seemed addressed to her. They're written in an immature hand, but I look at them and think: this is my father's handwriting. This is my father's true sign.

'On that hot August day in Bologna Centrale, Aldo Scattini may have been solving a knotty accounting problem, but I like to imagine that he was composing a poem. It suits me to imagine that in the agony and mayhem of the explosion, he was halfway through a lyrical composition, and that a word or two stayed undamaged when his body was broken. On bus thirty-seven, his eyes and ears streaming, perhaps he stayed sane repeating the fragment of a line, a word or two, or a memorable phrase, possibly on the conventional topic of moonlight. I know nothing of course; this is all wild surmise, and a symptom of my rather anxious and futile need to connect. But it is a necessary imagining. My spiritual practice, you might say. Each year on my birthday and his death-day we lit candles in the cathedral for my father, and I was obliged to look into the red eyes of my weeping mother and sisters and realise that my own undistinguished life was no compensation.

'And only recently did I consider my namesake, Gino, who died in the bombing of the Bologna Centrale train station during the Second World War. He was a member of the resistance, my mother once said. He was a true hero. She said this often: "He was a true hero," and I was never entirely sure if she was encouraging or criticising me.'

Gino patted the outside of his jacket to locate his packet of cigarettes. He found it, tapped one out, then absentmind-edly turned a cigarette unlit in his fingers as he continued to speak, his voice lowered.

'I truly love Rome. It was a relief, to be honest, to leave the world of women in Bologna and enter the noise and masculine commotion of a new city. All those motorbikes! I bought a battered red scooter. From the moment I arrived, I sensed the possibility of a bigger life, one less hemmed in by my family and our mournful repetitions. At Sapienza University I wrote on Calvino and Nabokov. Each, as you know, is a superstitious writer, attracted to coincidence and the fearsome pleasure of patterns. In this study I felt a modicum of control and understanding. I felt I could approach my assassinated father by a symbolic route. I felt too the solace I experienced seeing the *Compianto sul Cristo morto*, the sense that art might convert something destroyed – exploded – into something else entirely, ennobled and justified, solid, approachable.'

Gino paused again. 'Marco knows that I failed to complete my doctorate.'

'As I did,' said Marco. 'We are legion, we failures. Next time, my friend, we will both fail better.' It was a warm-hearted response, an affirmation.

'But it was important to study in this way. Now I am

84

travelling for a year and find myself here, visiting Marco, initially, but compelled to stay for a reason I cannot fully comprehend. I call it research, but I'm not entirely sure. I'm not entirely sure what story I am writing.'

Gino's speech drifted away. It was an unconcluded story, sounding as if he had become bored, or simply decided not to go on. In the silence that followed Cass was thinking of the cowboy father, and the red-eyed sisters, and Gino's mother with the huge bosom and perpetual sadness. Cass had been struck by his eloquence, and by the unusual formality of his telling.

Gino cleared his throat.

'I need a cigarette.'

He rose abruptly, upsetting his half-empty glass. Mitsuko drew an indigo scarf from somewhere in her voluminous jacket and mopped the spill. It was a peculiar moment – in which each of them saw the puddle of Gino's drink glistening like a miniature lake on the parquetry, in which Mitsuko's hand swept, wiping the liquid away, and then a gesture, no-nonsense, as she flapped the scarf as if to dry it.

'Butterfly effect,' she said.

None could resist a symbol.

And so Gino turned away abruptly, and stepped out onto the balcony. This was his place, this little platform, jutting into the sky above the street. It was clear he wanted no comment on what he had disclosed, and no chorus of solicitude, encouragement or approval. The others fell into hushed and inconsequential conversation.

Yukio told them that his blog on Berlin was doing very well: Japanese were interested in the artistic reclamation of a city so ruined by war. He was taking photographs of ugliness, he said, with no apparent irony. Brutalist architecture, rubble piled around building sites. The arrangement of cranes in Mitte. The graffiti in Kreuzberg and along the S-Bahn lines. 'Super-cool,' he added.

Mitsuko said she had begun a new translation. A young British writer, only twenty-six, described London in the same way, like a second Berlin.

'Everywhere is Berlin,' she announced in a merry tone.

And then, as if in afterthought, Marco mentioned that he had read that there were fifteen thousand unexploded bombs buried somewhere beneath the city. Could this be true? His sentence stopped the casual wander of their conversation. Cass had nothing to add. Victor looked alarmed. The five fell silent, each contemplating a newly exploded Berlin.

10

Marco and Cass parted but agreed to meet at the end of the week, after the next speak-memory. Marco's embarrassment had entirely dissipated. He smiled as Cass left with Yukio and Mitsuko. When she turned to look back, he stood at the top of the stairs, benevolently watching as they descended in single file.

'Gino is my brother,' Yukio said. 'More than Ichiro.'

'Yes.' Cass felt she understood.

Gino and Yukio had scarcely exchanged a glance after the talk, but the group had sensed the charge in the air, the bolt of immediate fellow-feeling. They saw how carefully the two men avoided each other. The bruise of their own families, the terrible histories of railway stations. Both had admitted to their own unmanning.

At the entrance to Oblomov's building a fat legless man, almost spherical, sat in a wheelchair smoking a cigar. Ash dusted his belly. He had the gravity of a statue. They pushed through his turbid air, excusing themselves, and crossed the street at a diagonal, heading together for the crowded bus stop on Kantstrasse. Yukio refused to travel in the underground.

'I wonder,' Mitsuko said, 'if the man in the wheelchair knew Mr Oblomov.'

Oblomov, the missing Russian art collector. The émigré ghost in whose evacuated space they told their stories. Cass imagined a network of individual connections, friendships, unguessed links, like forms of hidden inheritance, which might lead back to Vladimir Nabokov himself. Oblomov's father might have known him as a boy, or seen his hatted head pass by, or sold him a Russian newspaper on the street. He might have been a student, or a neighbour, or a near-relation. It was the word 'brother' that had triggered this connective imagining, so that Cass was seized with a wish to net the world into a system of real affiliations. Vulnerable, lonely figures, a man smoking in a wheelchair, might be the survivors of a linking chain of historical compatriots.

When they arrived at the bus stop, Yukio said he wanted some time alone. He may have been allowing the women a chance to speak together, or he may have been disturbed by the story of the deaths in the Bologna Centrale Station. Mitsuko and Cass left him there, waiting in a crowd of padded bodies, and headed together towards the S-Bahn. It was Mitsuko's idea. She said she adored trains but travelling with Yukio rarely had the chance to try one. The elevated S-Bahn appealed to her: she could look down on Berlin, she said, she could see it from above, sweeping backwards into the night.

Charlottenburg Station was of seventies red brick and blankly functional. But there, up high, was the bright grass-green S button, and a busy crowd streamed in and out of its gaping, bunker-like entrance, gradually engulfed by fluorescence or darkness. Cass handed Mitsuko one of her tickets.

It was early, possibly seven, but the night freeze had set in. On the platform they saw breath in the air and the bodily huddle against the cold. Mitsuko's pink hair was a startling flare of colour in the waiting crowd.

'Noodles and coffee,' she said, rubbing her hands. 'Yukio will join us later.'

She studied the rail map for their route – to Alexanderplatz, then a change to U8 for Kottbusser Tor.

It was an enthusiasm they shared: the circuit delight of a train map, its multi-coloured intersections, its neat calculus of routes and connections and oblong-symbol changeovers. Cass secretly loved the image of ring lines with their lace-patterned interiors; and the threads unravelling outwards, and the names of far-flung stations. London was like this, too; she carried the London Underground map in her head, and enjoyed the predictable sequence of names and the tranquillising effect of their reiteration. As a child Cass had assumed that everyone was under the spell of such ideal forms; only in adolescence did she discover the disappointing truth.

The train appeared almost immediately, exhaling and slowing before them. The automatic doors *shoosed* open. Mitsuko leapt up and in, but the seats were all taken. They stood together by the doors and their faces, close as lovers, were bleached and somewhat drawn in the thin, spilling light. Yet in the anticipated freedom of a train ride Mitsuko was cheery.

'Alexanderplatz,' she whispered, nodding upwards to the map arched on the ceiling above them.

The train was approaching the next station, just at the beginning of the long platform, when it juddered to a halt. Mitsuko grabbed Cass's forearm and smiled a timid smile.

The other passengers were curiously quiet and subdued, studiously formal and not looking at each other, but there was some sort of commotion developing outside. Just visible, a policeman appeared from nowhere. A woman in a uniform waved a red flag. They heard a whistle and saw an official-looking man running up the platform, along the clear strip, too dangerously close to the canyon of the tracks. It was only then, after the speeding man, that an announcement was made and a low collective murmur sprang up among the passengers.

Mitsuko had not listened, and Cass could not understand the loudspeaker German that had reverberated through the carriage.

'Excuse me?' she said. 'Do you speak English?'

The young man beside her turned. 'Ambulance mission,' he responded in a bored tone. 'This means a suicide. We will all have to wait now. They won't open the doors and we will just have to wait.'

Mitsuko's bleached face contracted; she seemed to go limp. Cass put her arm across her thin shoulders and squeezed.

All around them passengers became busy with handheld devices. They were unconcerned, or self-protecting, enjoined and apart in the senseless distraction of screens. Ten minutes passed. Twenty. So many screens, privately shining. Mitsuko was sending an extended text message to Yukio; Cass stood by, silently unoccupied. She had become aware of the thick human smell in the carriage, of the stifling air, of the isolation of each individual, of the swollen sense that they were all contained, a massed human cargo, against the sight and inconvenience of a single death.

Outside, police had begun evacuating the station. Their silver labels, *POLIZEI,* sparkled on their backs, under the lights. Then, without further announcement, the carriage doors opened and all were funnelled in solemn order towards the exits. Cass and Mitsuko did not look back. They rode the escalators down to street level and set off to walk to the next station. Shaken by what they knew but had not witnessed, they walked solitary, rather than together, in a tight withdrawal and in silence. At Zoo station they recommenced their journey. Almost at once, Mitsuko began to weep. Berlin did indeed slide past, but she saw only the streaming world of her tears, her pink head hung low. In her soundless weeping she looked like the single mourner.

It flew behind them, the tracked spaces of Berlin at night. Cass saw, below, the streaks of red and white light that marked the passage of cars; she saw streets stretching away, she felt how the train curved around the dark-as-death shape of the Tiergarten, and crossed over the black and ice-shining Spree. She saw the central station, the Hauptbanhof, and the Charité Hospital, she saw the university and Museum Island. There were lit windows, regular squares and livid patches of abyssal dark. There were countless hidden lives, countless hopeful or hopeless souls. And at last she saw, swallowing their train, the gargantuan mouth of Alexanderplatz.

Cass guided Mitsuko. She found the U8 line. One of the new trains, daffodil-yellow and decorated with a Brandenburger Tor design, drew sleek alongside them. It was this local emblem, repeated as a motif, that she dumbly stared through, suddenly tired. At Kottbusser Tor station she took Mitsuko's arm and led her slowly to the exit under the vast steel archway, so high it might have been holding up the night. Addicts with their dogs, and shady dealers dressed in black, hung abject and half-present in the exit shadows. A dreadlocked man wearing a Dead Weather hoodie stepped forward to offer a grubby folder of cannabis. His unhappy face, in the deep-purple cave of his hood, mumbled afford-able euros. Cass was tempted, but held back, not sure what Mitsuko would think. He slunk backwards, his sly insist-ence fading, and she saw a scrawny brown dog yanked and dragged away.

It seemed to Cass that although they had travelled and arrived together there was a new distance between them. In her apartment Mitsuko prepared a simple meal of noodles with fried mushrooms. Neither had much appetite. Conver-sation was patchy. When Yukio appeared, Mitsuko rushed to be held and laid her pink head on his waiting shoulder. He whispered, low and comforting, in a sibilant Japanese. Cass wondered how she had described what happened on the train. She watched them embrace and enter the safe absorption of each other, aware of her own frozen feelings and uncertainty of response. The invisible dead: what might it mean in this city? How, in the context of its history, ought she respond to one unknown body, crushed and smeared beneath the irresistible wagon of a train? It was exhaust-ing to weigh and properly consider the matter. Her mind became empty, her instinct defensive. She wanted neither to think nor to feel.

Yukio had bought cannabis from the men near the station. He held up a plastic bag in his long slim fingers and waved it, offering. Cass was relieved. She wanted not this austere clarity and her philosophical bent, but to be blunted and deranged. She watched as Yukio rolled a joint with tidy and finicky skill, licking the paper with a swift, spontaneous flick of his tongue, extracting one or two stray threads, patting the tube into place. Then he rolled another, placing the first, like a regular smoker, behind his ear. Before long the air of the sitting room was smoky and permeated; they were each puffing away, flushed and urgent, as though desperate to be calm. Cass noted how much she liked the tiny crackle sound of dope igniting, that barely audible combustion, that pure time of the inhale. And so they settled, and began to relax, and might have slipped into each other's arms, so dreamy they soon seemed, so close up and so far.

In the end, they sat talking late into the night, finding their way slowly back towards each other. Yukio spoke a little more of his time as a *hikikomori*, describing himself as an astronaut, high in his ever-night capsule. Cass was reminded of Gino, how he too had spoken in the restaurant of spaceships and isolation. Something men shared, perhaps, a boyish aspiration or affection. Mitsuko confessed to a nostalgia for that nocturnal time, when they met while everyone was asleep and the darkness was wholly theirs. Cass had nothing to contribute to this easy romanticism, she was tired, she was stoned, she was suppressing yawn after yawn. When she could continue no longer, she asked the lovers if she might stay and sleep on their couch.

It was pure elation when Yukio switched off the light – the great relief when the body knows it can succumb to heavy sleep. How grateful she was. She removed her boots and arranged a cushion under her head. The effect of her long day and its jarring sequence of feelings was that she could not have contemplated returning alone to the train station, facing the cold once again, travelling back through the mean streets or the rushing tubes of the late-night city.

A thin band of light issued from beneath the closed door. Cass lay on her back, very still. In the dark she heard the lovers continue to talk in sweet, rippling tones. Their Japanese washed around her, tidal and sedative in its effect. It was an ocean of whispers she wanted to sink into.

It may have been a few minutes, or even less – her doped brain disassociated and imprecise – but she stayed awake and afloat for a short, drowsy while. She was thinking not of the anonymous body beneath the train, dragged in agony to kingdom come, though she maintained a vague and impersonal sorrow in response. There was a ruined family out there somewhere, a destroyed mother, or sibling. This was the necessary abstraction of invisible death. This was her rigid control and her refusal to be affected. Instead, she was recalling the man smoking in the wheelchair outside Oblomov's building: his tough, balled form, his messy spray of ash, his obstinate and casually lifeless persistence.

11

In the dark morning a branching frost lay at the windowpane. It glittered, an unearthly plant, in the rays of the standing lamp near the couch. Wrapped in a blanket Cass rose, stiff from uncomfortable sleep, and tapped on the glass to see if the frost would shatter. It remained intact. Its crystal form was a wonder, like so much here in deep winter. It looked such a brittle deposit, but held on, gently ablaze and unsynthetic, scattered like filigree on the surface of the glass.

She tried to recall her dreams, but nothing coherent remained. They had all been there – Marco and Gino, Yukio and Mitsuko, Victor and herself – but nothing bound them in a story, there was no sense truly to be made. They were merely coincidental, figures becoming wisps of human meaning, then threading away, like blown smoke. Wind; she remembered there had been wind in her dream, and that she had felt cold. But this may have been her awkward rest on the couch, the body half-sensing.

An hour later it was still dark, and Mitsuko and Yukio had not woken. Their apartment was immensely quiet and still. Cass took paper and pen from her bag and scribbled a short note. In the stuffy room she loitered, quiet as a thief. When she had located her coat and scarf, she drew them on, thinking how abnormally loud the rustle of clothing could sound. She left carefully, gliding on tiptoe, pulling the door shut behind her.

Now Berlin was all trains. She saw how fundamentally the city had mapped itself in rail, how the layers it held, the archives, the spaces of its forgettings and transports and covered-over deaths, were reflected horizontally in striations of overgrounds and undergrounds. It was mid-January, freezing, she was a foreigner to the city, and it may have been presumption or madness to imagine it thus: that these configurations of tracks and stations were the structure of its hieroglyph. She rode the U-Bahn heading south towards the ring line. Again, the Brandenberg Gate formed a veil on the windows of the train. The design monument of choice: the firm Doric columns, the prancing horses of Victoria's quadriga, the city represented, reduced, to a neat white stamp.

It was not any dark morning in any northern European city, but precisely *Berlin*. In the rushing underground Cass consulted her map, and counted the lines and the stops. The U-Bahn had ten lines and about 170 stations. The S-Bahn had fifteen lines and 166 stations exactly. They radiated in a wild way not visible on the official plan, which made the routes uniform and intelligible, just as the London map did. Around the city were the cast-iron, wrought-iron, steel and iron stations, the arcade genre of modernity, the horizontal claim, just as skyscrapers were its assertive vertical. The stations of East and West, not of any cross. The speeding into tunnels, the hollow roar of concavities.

Cass glanced up to see a man looking directly at her. He had seen her pore over the train map; he had witnessed her ridiculous counting. Catching her gaze, he turned away in a kind of knight's move, pulling down his cap like a secret agent. He wore a torn jacket over workman's clothes, spattered with old paint. He was rushing to work as she was rushing home; they were both captive in the train, they were both in the belly of the beast.

Almost immediately Cass thought herself histrionic: she became wry and self-critical. It was her Australian-ness, she thought. One must not be earnestly conceptual; one must not think too hard on the allusive, or the enticingly symbolic. One must not mention the war. She both embraced and resisted this business of national definitions; and when she refused them, other people could be relied on to ask, and to insist.

The doors parted, *shoosh*, and the man in the cap left the train in a sliding rook's move. Cass stayed put. She was pulled away from daft conjecture to await the S-Bahn ahead. She had somehow added the horizontality of a chessboard to her figurative imaginings. It was Nabokov who likened the bishop's move to a torchlight, scanning in the dark, swinging into angles, and now she thought of herself as a lighthouse, fixed and bright, searching for some legible shape to light on. A voice announced Hermannstrasse as the next stop, and she rose, readying herself, keeping the train map fixed in her head, then moved diagonally.

On the S-Bahn platform Cass saw daytime. Not sunlight, but sunrise, somewhere behind the fog. The milky trace of a lost sun hung over sleepy buildings. Above ground, heading west, she looked down at the gaping emptiness of Templehof, a pool of pure mist, and the dereliction, on the left side, of wastelands of rubble and rubbish. Graffiti in tag-lines and throw-ups covered flat surfaces near the railway. She rested her head against the glass and let the world drift and roll away. At each station a blast of icy air entered the open doors, and when she stepped out onto the platform at Innsbrucker Platz the shock of the cold almost drove her back into the cabin. But she needed a shower, and a coffee. She walked up Hauptstrasse, still hazy with her own confusing visions, and then on to her apartment.

Cass had just opened the door to the building when Karl appeared, real and shabby before her, unselfconsciously scratching at his balls.

'Fräulein Turner, good to see you. Coffee maybe, before the day?'

He was standing at the door of his ground-floor rooms, and it occurred to Cass that he was aware she'd not made it home during the night, and had been worried, or simply vigilant, or neo-Stasi, on her account.

'I stayed with friends,' she explained. 'Japanese friends.'

It sounded fictitious. Why in any case did she feel the need to account for herself? Why did she feel protective of her own privacy when he had not actually asked a question? She looked into his face and it was then, seeing the tacit plea there, that Cass realised that Karl wanted simply to talk. He tilted in a Chaplinesque bow and gestured to his doorway. She consented to join him.

The room looked like something from the Eastern side, she guessed, circa 1965 – the furniture was of angular blond wood with feature handles in fake brass, an elliptical plastic clock hung high on an orange wall, a table of cheap kitsch – shepherds and milkmaids, terrier dogs with bowties, a set of glasses with 'Dresden' scrawled in a Gothic script – stood arranged together on a kind of altar against the wall. On a side table sat a glass ashtray, stuffed with bent butts.

Karl swept his arm low like a courtier. 'Welcome!' he said proudly.

'Schön! Beautiful!'

She half-expected to see a lithograph of Stalin or Honecker hanging on the wall. He had a pot of coffee already made, and Cass waited politely as he bustled in the kitchen, heating milk, wiping clean a second cup with what looked like a dirty rag. Karl was talking in rapid German and she asked him to speak more slowly.

'So, then I moved to the West side,' he said; and Cass realised she had missed the main features of his biography.

She sat with his bitter coffee warming her hands. He was telling her his story, spilling out his own speak-memory, unprompted and relaxed. Her German was simple and it was an effort to keep up. She was piecing together his narrative largely from randomly heard nouns and verbs. What Cass established was that Karl had been a widower for many years, and that his wife Clara had died of cancer when his two children were young. He had raised them himself – this announced with pride – but both carried a life-long sadness at their mother's passing. Both had never really recovered from the loss. As well, he said, his son Franz had *epilepsie* – Cass didn't need a translation – and this was why he knew what to do last week at the Pergamon Museum. This was why, he said seriously, he didn't panic, as the others did. He wondered how her boyfriend was, he said in a rhetorical aside; and whether, like his son, he was ashamed of his condition. *Beschämt*, ashamed; how did she know that word?

'It's under control now, medication is better these days,' Karl went on, 'but he is a broken man; he lives with gangsters in Moabit, and only visits his papa occasionally.'

'And your daughter?'

'She is gone,' he said simply. 'My daughter Katharina is gone.'

There was self-control in the statement, and resignation. Cass knew not to inquire further. Karl leapt up and returned with a tin of butter biscuits, which he offered with a thrust. It was impossible to refuse. Cass sat before him crunching on a biscuit as he continued to talk. Now and then he included sentences or words of English, mightily pleased with himself, but his monologue was largely in German and now slowed and pared for her audience. He looked reformed, somehow: he was less puffy and sweaty; his moustache had been trimmed. He was self-assured, or his story-telling had made him so.

As she left Karl seemed happy and unburdened; he seized her hand like an old friend. He'd asked her nothing about herself, Cass realised, but this had been a relief. She had not wanted to explain anything, or account for her 'boyfriend', or to tell entertaining tales about a quasi-mythical Australia. That would surely come later.

In her room, blue and violet, as if in deep water, Cass undressed and walked into the steaming shower. She stood there for a long time, soaking her hair, inhabiting the soothing sensation of time suspended. She wondered what had possessed her, to count the train stations of Berlin. It had been like a temporary obsession, to break the code of the city, to imagine that somewhere in this pattern lay essence or historical secrets. Still, the pattern remained. She had an eidetic faculty that made it easy to remember maps and suchlike; it was a party trick, mostly useless and sometimes startling; an inner, exceptional compass others seemed not to possess. But it occurred to her now that it was also rather close to delusion, that she might be overcome and infatuated by her own visions of organisation. As a child she had dizzied herself noticing arbitrary diagrams and maps, storing them for a further, lonely consideration.

Nabokov was hyperthymesiac; he carried too many past memories. He forgot too little. The past was ever-present. It was a dreadful risk to mental health, to forget too little. It was an affliction, not a boon, to recall involuntarily and excessively and without the requisite dose of irony. She told herself these things, as if a teacher lived in her head and must instruct and reprimand. She told herself she must resist her fascination with forms and her somewhat fanatical tendency to referential mania. She felt foolish. Trains. Trains indeed.

As Cass was dressing she noticed a change in the light. The blue violet of shadows had lightened and there was a radiance splintering across the wall. When she turned she saw it: the first snowfall since she had arrived. Doubtless, there had been snow in December – it was an unusually harsh winter, everyone said so – but since she arrived in January she had seen only ice and endless grey. Now the windows were trembling and alive with slow-falling flakes. She pulled on her jeans, socks and sweater and rushed to witness it. The sky was white-spangled all over in a pointillist stipple. She felt her heart beat faster. She remembered reading somewhere that if one watches falling snow long enough, it seems as if one's building is floating upwards. This was true. Verifiable. Already she was ascending, already her elation was a levitation.

Cass flung open the glass doors and stood on the balcony. The cold stung immediately. But she leant out, her wet head gathering the adhesive flakes, her face dumbly upturned, her mouth wide open. She forgave Berlin its cruel winter for this first moment of snow. Below, it dappled the street and the cars and the people walking past. She saw how it accumulated over every broad and elaborate surface, how umbrellas had popped open to catch it on vinyl circles of black. Bare branches against white were gradually disappearing; the sounds of the traffic became sifted, muffled and restrained. And her own body, it seemed, also lost definition. She might have been dissolving into airy whiteness. She might have been experiencing transfiguration.

When she closed the doors Cass was so cold that she knew she had turned blue. Her head ached as she wrapped it in a towel and then began vigorously to rub it dry. But the rapture remained. After so many grey days, there was now this ordinary excitement, and the world becoming beautiful. She would wait until her hair dried before she ventured outside. But this was enough, for now, this thrill of a crystalline sky.

12

When Marco arrived in the evening Cass had not long returned from a second walk in the snowfall. Her first, in the morning, had been in a spirit of discovery. She had walked through the cemetery, now looking like a period-drama film set, then up streets already draped in creamy shapes. There was a delicious glassy crunch beneath her boots. There was a lustre upon windowsills and building façades. She saw the plump layering that took the edges off things, and gave a rounded, more organic look to the city. It was possible – she knew it – that this novelty would not last, that she would tire of sumptuous white as she had tired of fascist grey (finding it soaking inside her, altering her moods), but outside and within it she could not really believe this was so. A thin wind picked up, and began to spiral the white flakes in unwinding circles. Cass was reminded of the coiled colours lodged magically in her brothers' glass marbles. She felt an instantaneous, novel delight.

It was her first experience of enwrapment in the soft surround of snow. When she could bear the cold no longer she slipped into overheated shops, lingering in her damp coat, discreetly stamping her feet. But before long she was out again, trudging with pleasure.

Her second walk had been to buy milk and cakes. Marco had rung asking if he could come by after work, and instead of postponing his visit, which felt too soon and importunate, she had instantly agreed. The afternoon was dark, the snowfall had become dense, more impressive, almost entirely filling the sky. The world bore a mirrory-blue shine she'd never seen before. The muffle-effect, too, was more pronounced and almost eerie. She had hurried back, freezing, her shopping tucked under her arm, aware suddenly of a kind of hazy, incipient fear.

Marco arrived early. No one in this city, apparently, arrived at the appointed hour. Cass was anticipating coffee; then perhaps a meal in the Greek café down the street; and she was imagining Marco's face resting against hers. But the buzzer rang before she had warmed herself back into emotional equilibrium and recovered the poise that she knew she must practise.

'Ciao,' he said softly. 'Snow at last, yes? Hexagrams!'

He shook his cap free of hexagrams. Flecks lay on his shoulders and on the back of his coat. He discarded it apologetically, faintly showering the floor, and hung it with his speckled scarf on the hook nearby.

He pecked at both cheeks in a wholly formal way.

'I hope you don't mind.'

'No, not at all.'

Cass felt herself blush. She did not know what he referred to. The visit itself? His presumption in meeting three days before they'd planned? Some yet unannounced mistake, or liberty? He had said nothing in particular but she was discomforted in his presence. This was a condition of genuine attraction. She knew how vulnerable she was, how sexual yearning had lodged in her.

'I wasn't sure,' he began, 'if we should meet, just the two of us, before our speak-memories, or after. We don't yet know each other's stories, but this is the usual case, is it not? This is the usual way a man and woman meet? And I realised that if we met on the Saturday, as we had planned, you'd have heard my story, but I would not know yours.'

It was sophistry, or delicacy, or his fear that she might have an advantage.

Cass looked up into his face and drew him down for a kiss. This time, robustly, it was her initiative. This time she claimed him as her lover. She did not waver or hesitate. She closed her eyes and felt that his cheeks were still cold from the outside. She slid her hands beneath his sweater and found that the warmth of his body carried a distinctively erotic shock. How important it was to her: that first slide of a curious hand. In so many films a man enters a room and begins pressing a woman against the wall, or flinging her into a bedroom with lusty energy and a rough tearing-off of clothes: all exertion and demand, all muscular haste, and agitation, and masculine power. But she saw them quiet together in the corner, standing near the doorway. Each was stilled and mysteriously centred by the other, each was waiting.

Marco unzipped Cass's jeans with his left hand. When he explored her with his fingers he looked into her face, uncertain, asking a question; and she held his wrist there firmly, answering a silent 'yes'.

They undressed quickly in the cold room and slipped under the covers. Cass enjoyed her own nakedness. She wrapped herself around Marco. Curled herself into him. Felt how easy it all was.

The light was still on – neither had thought to extinguish it – so when they paused in the gasp and shudder of their meeting there was the surprise of seeing each other so close and so clearly. Her chin gently touched his. Her open palm cupped his cheek. There were so many inklings and intuitive gestures that composed their encounter, so many flipped switches of common circuitry, already brilliantly in place.

'Hello,' she said.

Marco laughed, his face astonishingly near. With a pang of tenderness she noticed for the first time that his teeth were a little crooked.

Later, when he napped a little, his dark head deep in the pillow, she looked at his naked shoulders and his curved back, and stored the details for future recollection. She was thinking too of the word 'hexagram'; she was constructing a new pattern of reference.

It was not romance, she told herself, nothing so conventional. But the advent of the snow, and his warm human arrival, and such an unforeseen abundance of mutual pleasure. She moved her bare legs under the covers, adjusting to his napping shape, sliding her thigh between his. She tugged the doona higher. Then slowly she collected him again in her arms, nudging him gently awake with her pelvis. There was the tranquil seesaw of each body, and the temporary design of two that they made. There was the post-coital heat and comforting accord. She felt absurdly happy.

They decided to stay in. Cass found a wedge of cheese, which they ate with a packet of crackers and a cheap bottle of shiraz. She poured the wine and they clinked glasses, unsure what to toast, since both were still in a state of expansive disinhibition, fuzzy and lethargic with their own immediate physical relief. Marco had hummed in the shower; now he grinned and chattered. When the wine was finished, they ate the fresh schnecken rolls Cass had bought, and drank new-brewed coffee at her tiny table. It was a time of raw appetite; both ate with vigour.

'So,' said Marco, 'what do you think of our group? Are we not remarkable?'

'Complicated,' she responded. 'We're a complicated group.'

As all groups are, she might have continued. But there was something else, some way in which, entering their pact, learning the details of each life, they were binding themselves irreversibly to each other. The aloof and with-holding habits of social meeting had already been replaced by something less predictable and more precious that made their storytelling possible. Only in fiction had Cass encountered the lengthy declaration of life stories; only in specialist study had she ever gleaned the delight of order and correspondence and the way the act of telling itself was a kind of technical comfort. This was a new under-standing. She saw she was habituated to secretive privacy and the hiding of her feelings.

'I need to tell you something.' Marco looked suddenly weary. 'Gino is using.'

'Using?'

'Ice, methamphetamine. He used to use heroin. He had a problem in the past and started again after his speak-memory,

107

though he'd been clean for months. There's a deep misery inside him. Speaking didn't seem to alleviate it.'

Cass felt at a loss. She'd not realised. Or noticed.

'Only since the speak-memory. But you should know, and be careful. There's a volatility there. He can be aggressive. Unreasonable.'

Here Marco looked away, as if he had said too much, or too little. Cass waited for precise details, but none were forthcoming. She felt overcome with confusion and a sense of alarm.

They were silent for a moment, then Marco began irrelevantly to chat. 'Before he married her,' Marco said, moving from the topic of Gino, 'Nabokov gave Vera a list of the twenty-eight women he had slept with, not including Svetlana, the woman who was then his fiancée.'

'What a bastard, what a boaster.'

'He was being honest. And it was his way of committing only to her.'

Marco was looking directly now, as if in challenge.

'Rubbish. He was placing her in his list. She was another treasure flying by that he wished to catch and pin.'

Marco looked taken aback. Cass would not meet his eye. What was he trying to tell her? Why would he refer to another couple, at this moment, when she thought only of the sufficiency of one? Was it an act of comparison? He may have been trying to entertain and inform, as he had in the Pergamon Museum, asserting his knowledge, readjusting the uncertain balance between them. Or he may have just added her to his list, finding in Nabokov a self-aggrandising analogy. She hardly knew him, she thought. This might be an end, not a beginning.

'You may be right.'

Marco was trying to conciliate, trying to regain her trust.

'I do not admire the man,' he went on. 'Except as a father. He seems to have been an excellent father. What I admire is the work.'

It sounded weak, and a familiar literary-critical distinction. The work is admirable, the writer flawed, narcissistic, more or less reprehensible.

After that it took some time before their conversation again steadied. Both had become more guarded and circumspect. Cass saw now that her room was ugly. What she had at first taken as austerity, a kind of artful restraint, looked bare and deprived. A new bunch of tulips, powder-pink this time and still holding their prayerful shapes, was its only patch of colour and beautification.

She speculated on what Marco's Nestorstrasse apartment looked like, and what she might learn visiting it.

'I should go,' he said abruptly, and was already rising from the table and heading to gather his coat and scarf. When he finished buttoning he stood still for her brief inspection.

Like a dutiful wife she extended her hand and adjusted his scarf.

'So.'

'Yes, so. Thank you. Thank you for everything.'

He offered a weak smile, kissed her briskly on both cheeks, and then was gone. It was just nine o'clock. In her room, suddenly so confined and so plain, with only a few books and her papers and the tulips to console her, Cass felt abandoned. She wondered about Gino. She wondered what history existed between Marco and Gino. Then, bored by her own ignorance, disappointed at their parting, she wondered half-heartedly how she would spend the rest of the evening.

Of Marco's presence there was only a vague scent of citrus in the room. She imagined invisible particles, twisting in ampersand with every slight movement of her body. *And, and, and.* This was the shape of her desire and its relentless wish for connection. She would never be satisfied. For all her practice with her own feelings, her restraint, her repression, her acting unafraid, there was still this glorious upset of the enlivening charge of one other.

13

The next address was a stately old apartment in Wilmers-dorf. Marco seemed only to deal in up-market properties, or perhaps he chose only those that matched the lost time of their retrospecting speak-memories. A new apartment would not do. They all wanted the old, incrusted place, somewhere which, even empty, would seem to carry embedded secrets and a hidden history. Creaking stairs, figures in the carpet, the allure of relic architecture and gentrified remains: this was the antiquarian aesthetic they all silently coveted.

Cass would walk, it was not far, though she needed new boots – hers were leaking in the snow. There was black slush in the gutters and on the roads and pavements, but new snowfall swathed and recoated the sullied world. She had retained her initial exorbitant thrill. Each time she found herself in snow she felt again the charm of the first moment she had rushed to her window. Each time she faced the fierce arctic air, she was relieved when it sprang alive with a bulge and billow of soft flakes.

The street was a sombre one, toned by the denudation of winter. The lighting was poor and the pavements empty.

Nevertheless, a kind of porch light had been left on to show the way, so that a pallid shine lay at the entrance, and the names on the buzzers were faintly illuminated. The name this time was Kępiński. Cass considered it: Polish? Kępiński. Just as she was about to press the button beside the name, she dropped her umbrella. As she turned to retrieve it, she noticed a brassy glow beneath the coating of thin ice. It was a row of three 'stumble stones', commemorative paving stones wrought of shiny metal. She bent down to examine them and discovered that three members of the Levi family had lived here, Moses, Esther and Judith Levi, and that all had been murdered at Auschwitz, in 1942.

Cass stared at the names, so carefully inscribed. She stayed crouched for a moment, contemplating the three small squares, the shape of narrative residue. She had seen these brass stones before and knew what they were, but had never inclined to look, nor paused to contemplate. Her crouched posture seemed appropriate. She considered it respectful. Such an unobtrusive commemoration. Yet she could not imagine Moses, or Esther, or Judith Levi, and knew that her mind was closed to the frightening scale of historical violence. Their miniature tombstones lay slanted to the west, in pitchy blackness, and appeared like mislaid pieces rather than deliberate inclusions. What she saw was the shape of tessellation, the artful arrangement of the stones, calculated and logically interacting, the tight fit of the pavement stretching away down the street. The information that lay there was so easily disregarded and overlooked. And it was horrible to consider stepping, unbearably heavy upon the names.

Cass rang 'Kępiński'. Marco's voice said, 'Welcome,

come on up,' and the door growled as it opened. There was no hint of how they would be together, or what manner he or she should adopt.

This apartment building contained an old-fashioned lift, a tarnished metal cage with clanging doors. Less architecture than contraption, it rattled and shook as it ascended, as if complaining of its endless entrapment in the journey up and down. Marco was waiting at the open door.

'Welcome,' he repeated.

They were all there, once again. Cass had arrived on time, but still managed to be the last. The surprise was that the apartment was furnished. It was a let, Marco explained, and would be rented fully furnished. Was she interested? he asked, half-facetiously. She could not read his mood. He seemed fidgety and distracted, but also fixed on her face. He wanted her attention, but seemed mostly silent. She realised at once that Marco was fearful of his own speak-memory, just as she was of hers, and that the strain in his behaviour was the effort of holding himself together. Subtly she took his hand and patted it, as one might an old man in a nursing home. He pulled his hand away.

Kępiński's sitting room was lavishly appointed. There were thick brocaded curtains, of emerald-green damask, frilly standing lamps, not entirely perpendicular, and commodious settees and armchairs, all corpulence and plush. There were touches of gold around mirrors and on the frames of mediocre paintings, and in the light over all. At the centre of the room hung a giant chandelier, which on closer inspection was missing more than a few of its crystals. And at the periphery was an old oak writing desk, clearly never intended for use, upon which stood a tulip-shaped reading lamp, fashioned in a tone of pink not unlike that of the blooms in Cass's studio. No bookcases anywhere, no books were visible. Victor was sprawled in a decadent pose on a chaise longue. He waved his glass.

'The manner to which I am accustomed,' he called to her. 'The manor to which I am born!'

Yukio stepped forward to embrace her; Gino ground his cigarette and was stepping inside from the balcony.

'Kępiński is probably a long-lost cousin!' Victor continued.

Cass looked over to Gino and saw what she now realised were signs of chemical fervour. Gino was all mind-zap and twitch and stimulated emotions. He had begun talking rapidly to Mitsuko, who was pretending to listen.

Marco stood apart, pouring himself a drink. Now they were all assembled, there was a theatrical air to their meeting. Mitsuko wore a triangular garment of magenta wool, Yukio a suit of royal-blue velvet. But it was less costuming than this new Kępiński location, and the sense of embellishment and faded glory it superficially implied. Marco stiffened formally and began his speech.

'Let me begin by saying that I find myself feeling nervous. When we each agreed to participate in the speak-memory exercise, I did not really imagine what it might yield. I expected something, I suppose, less confiding and more random. I expected a backward glance, token and brief, offered up in this improvised community we have created.

'Now that it's my turn, I'm aware what effort this might have taken, and what unusual courage. So I thank you all.

'I was born on April the 23rd 1974. April the 23rd, as you know, is Nabokov's birthday, and Shakespeare's birthday, a petty fact Nabokov delighted in, as if it meant a literary transmigration or intermingling of souls. It means nothing to me, confers no warm glow of association, but I'm reminded how coincidence matters to us all, so claim this one only as a banal beginning.

'When I began reading the master, I recorded his precise images, believing these refined my own existence in the world. My words and the writer's lay side by side. I look at my notebooks now and think: this is what reading is, no? A silent propinquity made of words. And this is what attention is, seeing and notating with care.'

He was beginning to calm. '*Eh, professore!*' Gino called out, offering encouragement.

Victor raised his glass. 'To silent propinquities!'

Mitsuko and Yukiko had bought with them a connoisseur's vodka.

It seemed to Cass they had developed a rare kind of happiness. They all ignored the refrigerated night, hanging, slightly quivering, behind the window, they all abandoned inhibition, to some extent at least, they sat in a circle of six, the communicating points of a brief star. Mitsuko was carefully refilling the glasses. In the bottle rested a single yellow-faded blade of grass, which it was claimed added the flavour of the windswept plains of Georgia to the vodka.

'Like Gino, I grew up without a father. Mine was an enduring grief; he disappeared when I was eight and never returned.'

Marco stopped. He swallowed hard. They saw a constriction in his throat, the tension of holding back emotion.

'Let me begin again.'

They were all settled now, and embarrassed by Marco's embarrassment. In kindness, each looked away from his face. Marco began for the second time, now more collected.

'I grew up in the *rione* of Trastevere – do you know Rome? It is a suburb, you would say, in the historical centre, on the west bank of the Tiber. Nowadays this is a prosperous area of cafés and tourists, but when I was little it was rather neglected and poor. My mother still lives on Via della Luce, with one of my three younger sisters, Francesca. My other sisters, Fiorina and Rosa, have both moved away, into marriages, and I am now the proud uncle of two bouncing little boys.

'We were close as children, linked by our formidable mother and absent father, but also by word games, fantasy and the world that siblings sometimes share. We trusted each other. We confided. We were utterly devoted. We spent hours happily playing in each other's company. We also published our own little handmade magazine, populated by preposterous characters we had invented, and full of faraway journeys and ridiculous events. My contribution was Montefiore, a clownish man, adorable and stupid, who had the ability to transform at will into a horse. He was in love with Bella, Francesca's invention, known as the most beautiful woman in Rome, despite her great height and toothy smile. You must imagine drawings in coloured pencil, and stories that went on and on, tall tales that we elaborated with rococo ornamentation. Nothing was too outlandish, nor too dubious. Rosa's character was a Neapolitan fishmonger who had migrated to Mars, from which he made comparative commentary on our small Roman world; Fiorina developed a domain of talking insects, led by a stag beetle. These fictions, altogether, grew hugely silly. Even today we sometimes refer to them as a kind of code, a family secret unknown to anyone else.

'What my mother called my affliction also united us. Although the oldest, and the only son, a privileged place in the Italian family, I suffered from epilepsy. It made me vulnerable, how shall I say, in almost feminine ways.'

Marco paused: Mitsuko was whispering in Yukio's ear, translating 'epilepsy' into Japanese.

'I think I was seven when I had my first *grand mal* seizure, and in my childish mind I thought for years that my father had left because of it. I felt responsible, somehow. The doctor who sat me down to explain my condition likened the brain in my skull to a defective light bulb, flashing. I understood that he referred to electrical discharge, but this terrified me because I knew electricity could be fatal. I was appalled that spontaneous electrical activity might happen inside my head and my body, with violence and without warning. The doctor, a turtle-faced man with waxy skin, did nothing to allay my fears. When I convulsed on the floor my sisters would rush to aid me; I would wake with a headache and sore tongue to their faces bending above. They would hold me, one or other; I slumped into their laps, as if in the form of a pietà.

'When I think back to my childhood this is a persistent memory: the ambivalent and tormented feelings of that pose. My sisters' embraces were loving – they sought to reassure me – but they never quite relieved my sense of self-disgust.

'Epilepsy is still a concern, though until last week it had been seven years since I'd had a seizure.'

Marco addressed this remark to Cass.

'Seven clear years. I thought it was finally over. All these neurons firing and sparking out of control.'

Marco held out his glass. Mitsuko refilled it.

'Excellent vodka, thank you.

'So I have this image of myself jerking and quaking, a puny creature, a pint-sized freak. My sisters tried to save me from social disgrace. Francesca, one year younger than me, once punched a boy on the nose when he mocked my convulsions. She said she was proud when he snuffled into his bloody handkerchief, and cried.

'My epilepsy no doubt added to my mother's trials. She grew impatient and at times irrational and shrill. She never once explained why our father had left. For the first months she maintained the fiction that he'd gone to visit his family in Napoli, but gradually she tired of so dull a story, until eventually, one day, she simply shouted that he was not coming back, then burst into tears. We were shocked by her honesty – we'd preferred the lies. And we were shocked to see our normally stoical mother with her face buried in her apron and her body hunched in distress, sobbing like someone savagely beaten. She told us nothing more. Our hopes dwindled and Papa became a mythic figure.

'A little later my character Montefiore set out on a quest to find him. There was a sighting in New Guinea, another in Brazil, and he used his speed to chase a train, rushing by in Algiers. In this Algerian train he had glimpsed a face, caught lit and rectangular as if on a celluloid strip, that might have been a fleeting vision of our long-lost father. It was an image from a dream. The bluish gleam of a film, the face blurring into shadows. The train headed straight off a suspension bridge and hurled in a curve with terrific sparks into the chasm below. Montefiore watched it glide to its fiery end. Observing from a cliff, he could not say if there were any survivors of the crash.

'It seems pathetic, I suppose, to claim that these stories helped us all. But they did, they truly did. My sisters were always more ingenious than I, and they too imagined sightings, fictive and inconclusive. We entertained each other with our endlessly disappearing father.

'Letters arrived from Australia – we saved the kangaroo stamps – and for some time we suspected that our father had emigrated and would one day admit it and send word for us to follow. But the letters turned out to be from my father's brothers. One brother, Mauro, wrote regularly, once every few weeks, and the other, Luigi, wrote only occasionally, but in vividly excited prose. Our mother would regale us with tales of Down Under. It was like a Zembla to us, every description serving as the footnote to this extravagant distant land. In our stories we sometimes sent our characters to Australia, where there were many madcap adventures, all fuelled by childish conjecture and comically inadequate hints from the letters. Luigi wrote that in a pub somewhere in Queensland he had seen a snake twirling like a dancer on an overhead fan: this was the kind of exotic detail we loved. With this slim image we concocted an entire chorusline of dancing snakes, swaying on a stage.

'There is another set of stories that compelled and formed me. My mother is Jewish. Before the war her family lived in Via Amerigo Vespucci, on the other side of the Tiber, where the old Ghetto had once been. She was a little girl of just four when the Italian Jews were rounded up. She was hidden away and then adopted, by a Catholic family. I don't know many details, but her family was lost. I am named for the old man who was her adoptive father. He was a watch-maker and she was apprenticed for a few years before she was married; so she practised arcane and mechanical skills. With a set of watchmaking forceps her second father had left to her, metal instruments with slim bodies and fine grasping hands, she liked to open up watches and then put them back together again.

'It is a combination that imparts to me an unfathomable sensation: a lost family, and the disassembling and reassem-bling of watches. I thought the minute cogs and levers, the clever fit of the parts, the gold circle into which everything perfectly slotted: I thought these all very beautiful. For a while I imagined I would grow up to be a watchmaker, without knowing that it was a craft – centuries old – about to disappear. This virtuous grandfather died before I was born; his wife, who had no children of her own, died when I was an infant. I would have liked to have met them, since my mother's parents never returned, nor any member of her extended family. I know their names, that's all; and there are one or two photographs. But their fates in Germany and Poland are entirely obscure.

'At some stage my mother's hands began to stiffen and cripple and now she no longer tinkers with old watches or disassembles and reassembles them. These days she rubs her own watch on her wrist with an air of nostalgia; it is a habit she has; I see her turn and turn it again. Perhaps she's remembering the substitute father, or her own disap-peared parents and her two older brothers. I see her drift into memory, and I see death moving towards her.

'The deportations were of course all over Europe, the camps . . .'

Here Marco acknowledged Victor with a soft, humane glance.

'And our story, I know, is not an unusual one. Disappearances. Adoptions. Conversions. Secrets. But she is still alive, my mother, and she still wants to know what happened. I tell her that I will one day write the history of our family, and that there will be a recompense in words for those who come after.

'The uncles in Australia paid for my education. I don't know why. I guessed Mauro had been in love with my mother – there was something about the oblique way he expressed private sentiments in his letters. Or perhaps both simply felt responsible for their brother's abandoned family. When I wrote to them as an adult, neither could tell me his whereabouts. They seemed unable even to confirm if he was alive or dead . . .'

It was speaking of the father that wounded Marco's speech. It pained him to explain that there was no resolution. They waited patiently for the return of his voice.

'At La Sapienza, at university, I discovered silent propinquity. A pompous term, perhaps, but this is how I think of it. Reading. Imagining. I discovered the vast population of others also trying to make sense. Books of poetry and fiction extended what it was possible to think, not just in fact, but in feeling; not just in the primitive accumulation of stores of knowledge, but in the questions we are faced with every day. I felt these questions unwind like a spiral inside me. I felt myself becoming at last an adult.

'And as I grew older my epilepsy gradually receded – the medication is so much better these days – so I was able to become more social and more confident.'

Cass heard the echo.

'But my thinking and reading nevertheless set me apart. There is an isolation to reading, just as there is a community. There is a philosophical learning, impossible to unlearn, and we have all, each of us here, discovered this form of enchantment. Forgive me, I'm sounding like a preacher, like a fanatic.'

'Too many mysteries,' said Gino.

'Yes, you are right. Mankind cannot bear too many mysteries.'

Victor laughed at the exchange. Some inexplicit tension had been released.

Cass thought again, not for the first time, that Gino and Marco seemed sometimes like brothers.

'For some reason, some reason I cannot quite understand, telling you of these things makes me recall the end of Nabokov's story about his governess. The narrator is walking late at night beside a misty lake and sees a white swan floundering as it tries to hoist itself into a moored boat. The poor bird flaps ineffectually, stumbles in air, struggles with ungainly wings to rise and to nest itself. The narrator is repulsed, but also fascinated. He describes the swell of the water, and the slippery sounds, and the sensations in the dark that are impossible and dreamlike. You all remember this, I'm sure. He reflects that his governess, now dead, exists somehow in the agony of the struggling swan . . . and that unhappiness impedes the development of a soul. This was a scandalous idea, a shocking idea.

'I had of course read of Romantic swans ascending. I knew how writing and imagining works with these typical symbols. But the misery of Nabokov's ending was a true surprise. This childhood is told in a mode of tedious irritation; yet love for the governess becomes apparent, so that when, at the end, the swan is a kind of monster, the creature is also more truly "art" than Tchaikovsky's lovely dancers in *Swan Lake*, with their fluffy low curtseys and slow drooping arms.'

Marco paused, and it was clear he had stopped. It seemed both a capricious and confusing point at which to leave his story.

'That's all. That's all I have to say.'

'*Bravo, Montefiore!*' Gino sounded drunk.

'*Bravo,*' chimed Yukio.

'And here ends Therapy Session Number Five,' announced Victor.

Silence followed in a shockwave. The others looked at Victor in quiet alarm. He was instantly contrite; his expression of triumph fell away. He realised he had casually offended Marco and the others, and that he had denounced and ridiculed the commonsense trust of their speak-memories.

'A joke!' he objected, raising his hand like a traffic warden.

Marco tried to placate. 'No problem,' he said.

But the exchange had dispelled the calm the story inspired.

'So you think that's what we're here for?' asked Gino. His tone was unmistakably aggressive. 'You think we're here for cheapskate psychotherapy, to hear each other confess and sob?'

'Of course not . . . Jeez.'

'You want to know our foolish inner selves, our clowns?'

'Now you're not making sense,' Victor said feebly, his face dark with hurt.

'You want sense? Explanations? You want your damaged life explained to you?'

'*Basta!* Enough!' Marco spoke something in brisk Italian. He had looked exhausted at the end of his story; now he looked angry and dismayed. Discord had arrived so rapidly. Cass saw that Mitsuko appeared upset and Yukio had disengaged, perhaps unable to follow the entire exchange. Gino seemed to sulk: he muttered as adolescents do, making audible, but not entirely, his undercurrent protest, his body pulled tight into an indignant slouch.

It was like delirium, Cass thought. In this over-decorated room, reeking of tasteless excess and bookless ignorance, images from Marco's story had saturated and disordered them all. It had startled her, the swan. Why had he mentioned the flailing swan? And she had seen too how he felt he had to account for his epilepsy, how he had made it historical and the side-effect of a fatherless child-hood. She had never been to Rome, but saw it in her head as a sequence of pre-empting monuments, the Coliseum, St Peter's, the Trevi Fountain; instead there was nothing at all definite in Marco's Rome, but names without images: Trastevere, Via della Luce, Via Amerigo Vespucci. As if each must invent for themselves the world of the others, from barely comprehended scraps and faint associations. What mattered, she told herself, was the human element: his mother, her old hands, gracefully disembowelling a watch. The boy painfully atremble, his brain alight in zaps and flickers. Montefiore. The sisters, the protective sisters.

Marco was by her side. She felt the shudder of a reawakening and jolted back to the present world.

'When can I see you again?'

There was an intensity to the question, slightly fevered, slightly anxious.

'I'm meeting Victor tomorrow. Perhaps tomorrow night? Or the next?'

'Tomorrow night then. May I return to your place? Gino is staying with me. It's been a little tense.'

Cass looked over to Gino and saw that he was watchful and still unsettled after Victor's tasteless joke. She must defend Victor, she thought. There had been no malice in his remark, and no snide intention. Dear Victor, playing the comic, mistaking the genre. So much depends, Cass reflected, on correctly determining the genre.

Gino was scratching at his neck. He was drinking too fast. There was psychoactive fizz and a countermanding note of exhaustion. And at that moment Cass saw him look at her and register that Marco had revealed something. Faux priestly, with a sneer, Gino raised a hand to acknowledge them.

'Come for dinner,' she said to Marco. 'Come about seven.'

14

There is a short story by Vladimir Nabokov called 'A Guide to Berlin', written originally in Russian and first published in 1925. In this story, a man sits in a pub and describes to his friend, his 'pot companion', five topics that compose his personal guide to the city. The first is *Pipes*. He simply describes the pipes of the city, its black iron entrails, which he saw that morning laid out and exposed on the pavement in front of his apartment. He is charmed by white snow recently fallen on the black pipes, and by the fact that someone has written 'OTTO' with his fingertip in the virgin snow.

The second topic described is *The Streetcar*. This is a lyrical sequence on the specific loveliness of a tram, and the particular beauty of the tram conductor's hands and uniform, noted because trifles are meaningful, and must be cherished in the future. The tram will vanish, the conductor will die. The future will devour them, so they are both sad and remarkable.

The third is *Work*, in which the man, recalling his journey on the tram, also recalls the forms of work he witnessed looking out of the window: two men pounding an iron stake with a mallet, a baker on a tricycle, a postman emptying a postbox, and a butcher who carries a heavy carcass on his back. It is the butcher who most impresses him, because the meat (chrome-yellow with bright-pink arabesques and splotches) is carried on a colourless winter's day into a red-coloured shop.

The fourth is called *Eden*. In this segment, the guide recommends a visit to the aquarium section of Berlin Zoo. In winter the tropical animals have been hidden away, but one may see the fish tanks of sea creatures and a gigantic tortoise. This is a pure counter-world of imported wonders. One may see a starfish, five-pointed, crimson and possibly Bolshevik, resting alive at the bottom of a murky pool.

The last is *The Pub*. The friend responds to his 'guide' with a mournful yawn: what do trams and tortoises matter? he asks. How boring. How dull. The guide then notices the pub's mirrors and the billiard table and the publican's wife. He sees a little boy eating soup at the far end of a long hallway. All these he notes with the most languorous and tender regard. Imagining that the boy has caught his gaze, he thinks of his companion. 'How can I demonstrate to him that I have glimpsed somebody's future recollections?'

This was the story Cass had discussed with Victor the first evening she met him. His face had beamed at her. He was delighted that she knew 'A Guide to Berlin' and also considered it wonderful. Regarded by critics as slight, almost an affectation, or a trivial and somewhat formless exercise, both Cass and Victor were its champions, fond

127

of its exceptional humanity and modesty, and the fact that Nabokov thought a city guide might include items as mundane as pipes and billiard tables. No monuments, no Brandenburg Gate or linden-lined boulevard, only what is noticed in a single day.

When Victor had leant close and whispered, as though it was a secret, that he wanted to visit the aquarium, Cass had immediately agreed to join him. It was the only named location in the story, the aquarium at the zoo, the only remnant of the fleeting world of the 'Guide'. Victor wanted to see if the Bolshevik star was still visible and thought it possible that the tortoise Nabokov had seen might still be there, since they live for ages, he said. For ages and ages. Cass had charmed him by relating the story of Harriet, a tortoise taken by Darwin from the Galápagos to Australia in 1835. Harriet was estimated to be 176 years old at her death, in Queensland, in 2006.

So she waited now, hugging herself, for Victor to arrive at the aquarium. He was late. Her feet were damp and burning with cold. New boots. She really must buy a new pair of boots. The sub-zero weather and black slush had emptied the streets. Only a few people were entering and leaving the zoo, adorned, inexplicably, with pagoda-like towers and an oriental archway held aloft by two majestic stone elephants, condemned to ceaseless burden. Cass watched the elephant archway, in case Victor mistook it as the aquarium entrance, but then could endure her frozen feet no longer. She hobbled into the foyer of the aquarium building to wait for Victor there.

In the toilet Cass hid in a cubicle and removed her boots. She unpeeled her damp socks and rubbed her marbled blue feet to try to return them to the rest of her body. They were hard foreign appendages and stung appallingly. When she had revived them a little, she wrapped her feet in toilet paper, Egyptian-mummy-style, and wedged them carefully back into the sticky cavities of her inefficient boots. She was foolish to be so unprepared.

The toilet was drab, with smeared windows and a coppery mirror, apparently unreconstructed since the 1920s. She rested, dressed, on the toilet seat, and contemplated sneaking away, inventing an excuse for later, should Victor eventually arrive. But as she opened the door back to the foyer, she saw him there, depositing his coat in exchange for a small plastic token. He gave an exaggerated wave across the room, already in high spirits. His greeting was so fulsome and warmhearted that she was again drawn to him immediately.

Arm in arm, like father and daughter, Victor and Cass walked into the dimly lit corridors in which the aquaria were held. On each side of the walkway, underwater lights shone within round and oval worlds, separate, artificial and entire unto themselves. Soft bluish radiance shimmered around them. Cass loved the windows into underwater, the chambers of slow, languid fishes with sullen faces, the fake grottoes, the undulating weeds, the simulated beams of sunlight shot from some electrical heaven above. Simple maps showed in red the region from which the sea-life came, but it was all tropical to Cass, all appeared warm and sequestered. She was reminded of diving in the ocean with goggles as a child, blinking and astonished by what she then saw. She remembered her own arms pushing away the water, how mottled they were, how thin and how pale. The bubble-trails of her own breath, wavering upwards. The hot rays of sun, shining on her back.

Victor was one of those embarrassing companions who read every sign aloud.

'Get this! *"Gefleckte Qualle*: Spotted Jelly, *Phyllorhiza punctata"*.'

Cass stood with him before a high blue tube of jellyfish. They pulsed up and down, aimlessly beautiful. They were indigo with gathered water, and waving threads of pale tentacle.

'Umbrellas,' Victor said, in a low, bemused voice.

He had cultivated, Cass thought, a personal aesthetics, derived from childhood enchantment and the authority of ideal forms. Perhaps he saw these shapes everywhere, in cloud formations and in ice-creams, in architecture and topographies. Perhaps umbrellas were evoked by certain feelings, or melodies, or a retrieved infant scent.

'What?' Victor asked, turning towards her. He might have read her thoughts. He gazed quizzically in her direction, then looked again into the water.

'Isn't that something?' Victor exclaimed. His face was so close to the glass that she saw his image there in the aquarium, huge and distended. It had the distortion of a ghost, stretched like a balloon. Cass pulled him back. A young couple nearby were taking photographs with their smartphones. They each had their arms stiffly upraised, as if in a fascist salute. Victor noticed too. But they could not draw away. The domes of the spotted jellyfish, their glistening propulsion, their silver luminosity and simple lives: there was a kind of exemplary peace, just here and now, in merely standing and observing them.

At last Victor said, 'The starfish! Where is it?'

What they found, in the end, was un-Nabokovian, not a notorious emblem signifying hoped-for-utopia pitched into murky depths, but a blotchy and rather sad-looking specimen, more brown-coloured than crimson, more superfluous than emblematic. It was small and singular, a disappointment. They stood together patiently, waiting for others to appear.

'The Berlin Aquarium is deficient in starfish!' Victor announced, a little too loudly. He sounded like a complaining American, brash and entitled, when he wanted simply to enthuse and entertain.

Cass could not look into his face without remembering his speak-memory. This was the man whose father had worked in an umbrella factory, who as a boy plunged his face into piles of washing, who saw his grey-haired Polish mother rage and disintegrate. This was a man who had whispered 'umbrella, umbrella' because the word and the thing were his especial inheritance and it had entered his dozy intention as the verbal pathway to sleep. She knew more about him than his colleagues – this for sure – or possibly even his oldest friends. He had spoken so bravely to strangers of all that was lost. Cass remembered the names: Solomon, Hanka, Leah Rabinowitz. New Jersey. Ferry Street. Keer Street.

She imagined Victor with a younger face. He had sunken cheeks, pimples on his chin and a Mets baseball cap on his head. He wore unflattering geek-glasses then, as he did now. He bore a baffled and slightly defeated expression, and possibly possessed a minor, self-revealing habit of some kind, a flickering of the eyelids when he spoke of his parents, a sagging mouth when he attempted Yiddish, an unselfconscious tic or repetition that his students later noticed, and wondered about. She wanted to ask questions, questions, in particular, about his saviour, Leah Rabinowitz, but this was not the right context.

On the second floor, in the impossibly steamy 'Reptile and Amphibian' section, Victor and Cass saw a tortoise. It may have been, said Victor, *the* 1925 tortoise. It was utterly still, certainly ancient, and the only sign of life was its glaucous, slow-moving eyes. Cass noticed the array of the tawny scute plates that made up its shell and thought of stumble stones, tessellation, the interconnection of parts. Patterns continued to complicate. Victor gazed at the creature too long, wanting some historical nod from its wrinkly head, a Galápagosian confirmation of the proximity of the past. It refused to comply. It was inert and indifferent. In the counterfeited swamp, pumped with warm water sprays and planted with limp foreign grasses, it had lost all momentum and would look exactly like this – inanimate – when one day it was discovered conclusively dead.

In the coffee shop Victor recovered his good humour. The sight of so many non-human creatures had engaged and invigorated him.

'Give me a zoo over a museum any day,' he said.

'An aquarium over a library?'

'Hell, yeah, why not?'

He was in a jokey mood.

'That tortoise sure was something,' he added.

'Yes, it was.'

'Hey, I remembered a word: "ocellated".'

He waited for Cass to ask, but she did not, so he rambled on.

'The eye markings on animals, some of the fish were ocellated: they had eyes on their cheeks.'

Cass knew the word from butterfly descriptions: there were butterflies, too, that carried ocellated spots; they swept high on wind drafts, gliding with opaque eyes on their diaphanous wings. The Apollo. The Apollo was one butterfly that had ocellated wings. She sipped her milky coffee, only half-listening to Victor. To her left sat a young couple who spoke in English with New Zealand accents: it took all Cass's willpower not to turn around and greet them, and try to forge a global connection. She glanced sideways. The man, bearded and New Zealand-ish, clad in superior hiking gear, was swiping images on his computer pad, flicking from one polychromatic fish to the next. He might have been batting flies. The woman, Mansfield-ish, was unimpressed. She sat back in her chair, twirling a toggle, bearing an expression of haughty boredom. There are couples everywhere on the globe that look uncannily familiar, replicants of others, sly double-takes. This was such a couple. Cass observed them longer than was polite, but neither saw her. Three tiny female Germans, possibly three-year-old triplets, dressed alike in tight parkas of strawberry pink, rushed in a fan formation towards the door. An encumbered mother plodded behind them, hopelessly calling.

Victor had moved from ocellated markings to smudges.

'Smudges,' he said. 'There's a section somewhere in Nabokov – it must be at the end of the autobiography – where he stands with his son and looks down at a flowerbed of pansies. The dark smudges on the pansies' faces remind him of Hitler's moustache, so he says to Dmitri, "Hey, a bed full of Hitlers!"'

Cass was not sure what purpose this anecdote served. Victor chattered on. She knew she should ask him about his research, but she liked his manic mood, his lighthearted banter. Scholars asked about their research become dourly existential and feel obliged to account for their being-in-the-world. Victor talked as children do, sure that he was interesting. And in this manner he released her, as Karl sensibly had, from the burden of her part in the conversation.

It was unclear at what point a certain gloom descended. She was thinking ahead, to new boots; then she was thinking again of ocellated wings; then she was recalling a section in W. G. Sebald's novel *Austerlitz*, in which he writes about moths. Not butterflies, but moths, the dismal cousin. Struck by their immobility, clinging to walls at night, Austerlitz decides that moths on indoor walls know they have lost their way, so simply stay still, completely still, until they stiffen and die. The anti-butterfly. Ragged-winged, plain, taupe and grey-coloured. Staying completely still until they die.

Victor pushed the remains of his cheesecake in Cass's direction.

'Try it!' he insisted.

They parted on excellent terms, each agreeing they had joined in the spirit of 'A Guide to Berlin'. Cass walked unevenly in her paper socks, determined to shed them as soon as possible. The damp wool socks in her shoulder-bag, furtively stowed, were already giving off a sour whiff of must. She needed fresh socks and waterproof boots.

The sky was white overhead, but no snow fell. There was ice aplenty, even rows of small icicles, hanging like sea-animal teeth from eaves and above the mouths of windows. Dainty, serrated, sharp with caught shine. But again she wanted snow. Cass wanted that powdery light, that world-filling softness. She wanted total immersion.

15

In the hours before Marco arrived, Cass was restless; her thoughts had a reeling, unstable quality. He was no longer arbitrary in her life, nor was he yet essential, but she felt the need to fortify herself against too soon a surrender. A surrender then of what? A surrender *to* what? What is it that a woman gives to a man, apart from the curve around him in darkness, apart from a moment of freefall from one body into the deep space of another? What do any lovers, of any arrangement, most truly exchange? She had enough experience not to fret, but was still uncertain of her feelings. He reminded her of areas of dissatisfaction in her own life: not enough sexual elation, not enough untrammelled joy.

From her laptop drifted No. 3 in G Major of the Brandenburg Concertos. Third movement, the less popular one. She listened for the curlicue refrains and baroque swings and roundabouts, then decided on something more fitting to her mood and more tonally restrained: Mischa Maisky on cello. Music was one fundamentally reliable pleasure. She would be an old woman one day, alone in a dark room, with only Bach's cello to keep her company.

Cass prepared a minestrone, which she hoped would impress, but then realised it was too early to cook anything further. With only two gas rings on her poor excuse for a stove, with a small number of pots and a single frying pan, it was impossible to prepare a full meal ahead. She had bought too much food and had nowhere to store it. A large loaf of rye bread – huge for two people – sat like an outback boulder on the sink. This 'studio' was meant for the lonely and indigent, not for entertaining. It had a punitive aspect. At least there were two of everything, two plates and two glasses, two cracked soup bowls; and the reassuring touch of her pink tulips, still unfolding and other-worldly, that stood elegantly detached in the cheap vase she had bought the day before.

'I met your friend Karl,' Marco said as he unwrapped his scarf. 'He intercepted me at the front door. It was a shock to see him here, the man from the Pergamon Museum. I didn't know of your connection. You didn't tell me.'

'Did he mention his son?'

'Yes. And when he discovered my knowledge of German he launched into a rapid-fire explanation of his history, his family, his experience with epilepsy. His son is a gangster, apparently.'

'Karl's from the East.'

'Yes.'

They smiled at each other, amused by what might have been a crass cultural joke. Marco stood still, appraising her.

'New boots?' he said.

137

They kissed with slow confidence, taking their time. When they drew apart he produced a bottle of wine from somewhere.

'Let's start again. No talk of epilepsy. No Nabokov's girlfriends.'

Now an easy atmosphere settled between them. Marco was relaxed and contemplative; Cass was patient and circumspect. This is how it is, Cass thought, between men and women. There are endless tentative beginnings, some in words, some in touch, and these stand in for intermittently true connections.

'I'm glad it's over, the speak-memory. The anticipation filled me with dread. It's a relief to have spoken – you'll feel the same, I promise. It's a relief to have selected what to say and not say.'

'Will you tell me, later on, what you did *not* say?'

'Perhaps after your own speak-memory. Perhaps we can talk of it then.'

Marco paused. 'There's been a disturbing emergence of memories since,' he continued. 'I'm just beginning to realise that the speaking, even with all these constraints, even in our strange little drinking ceremonies, and with our eccentric group, is like a door slowly opening.'

So they entered a neutral territory in which Marco's talk was left unexamined. The missing father, Montefiore, the sisters, the epilepsy. For her part, Cass felt guarded and careful, as if his dreadful anticipation had in the last minutes transferred to her. She must now consider what she might say to the group, and how to fit, unlucky last, with their trusting disclosures.

'I've become rather obsessed with the weather,' she said, opening an unoriginal topic.

Marco smiled. 'So let's talk of the weather, in detail, after the English fashion.'

It was not superciliousness but humour. Relaxation had made his tone easier to read.

She told him that she found winter terrible, but for the sublimity of the snow. That darkness fell too early. That there was a kind of sorrow to everything. That she felt a lethargy, a fatigue, when her spirit was normally lively.

'What nobody tells you is that Berlin is haunted in winter, truly haunted. You need to see the city in the spring, when all the ghosts move on, when they've all gone on vacation, somewhere else. In spring the city's full of blossoms and bright light, and people eating ice creams on the pavement. In June there's the scent of strawberries in the air and whole booths of them, piled high, great pyramids of strawberries. Berliners swim in the lakes, and take over the streets with bicycles. It's another city entirely.'

'So everyone says.'

Cass was thinking: why does everyone say this? Why does everyone defer the 'real' Berlin until spring?

'And trains,' she said, 'I seem to have my imagination stuffed full of trains.'

'Ah, this makes you a Berliner. U-Bahns, S-Bahns, they are the skeleton of this city. No citizen is unaware.'

'Skeleton,' she repeated. 'Of which particular body?'

'And now you're waxing metaphysical. Tell me about your outing with Victor.'

Cass saw the change of subject. She had the impression that Marco too was interested in this business of trains, as others in their group were, historically or indirectly. The U and S Bahn routes continued to cast a net in her head, as the sticky pads of neurotransmitters, sprouting and interpretive, are placed outside the skull of some unfortunate woman in an experiment. This is how she imagined herself, within a web of buzzing connections and charged cognisance. And when would she tell Marco of the body beneath the train? She recalled Mitsuko sobbing as they rode, creating a mournful soundtrack. She recalled night-time Berlin, traversed from above, sliding below them in streaks of light and blurred, glossy images.

'Do you know "A Guide to Berlin"?' she asked.

'The short story? Of course.'

'Victor and I went to the aquarium today. We walked arm in arm through corridors of semi-dark, we peered into fishes' faces and shallow-water wonderlands. The jellyfish were especially exciting. Victor was just like a kid, exclaiming, chattering away.'

She was thinking: there was nothing adult about our visit; it was regressive and naïve and not at all Nabokovian. Aquaria and zoos do that, cancel the adult mind. She saw again the reflection of Victor's avid features, opening like an umbrella. It had swum there, the slick film of his searching face.

'The tortoise? Did you see the tortoise?'

'Yes, we saw a tortoise. I couldn't say if it was *the* tortoise, the one in the story. But it was old and venerable, as such creatures are. Victor waited for it to whisper a secret to him. I think he believes he has looked into an eye that in 1925 looked into Vladimir Nabokov's eye. As if a creature, not a place, is the custodian of his phantom. There was a delight to Victor's attachment, a real wish for material connection.'

'Nabokov would have been, what: twenty-six?'

'Yes, the same age as me,' Cass said shyly.

'I love that section on the tram. The tram conductor's unusual hands, the way they dabble and rummage. They are thick and proletarian, but also busy and agile . . .'

The wine was uncorked with a friendly squeak. Cass reheated the soup and fried portions of salmon. The boulder of bread was sawn, a lemon was sliced. It was a simple meal, which they ate unromantically. In the studio there was a gentle enfolding of dull light, and a limpid calming down as each became silent. Two lovers, newly met. A promise, implicit or imagined. Time had adjusted, somehow. There was an expanding sense of the present moment, full of his complex other-existence, and an invitation to imagine a coupled future, however short-lived. Cass suppressed an instinct of ironic recoil. And she remembered Marco's elegant phrase, 'silent propinquity', and wondered if it might describe forms of intimacy, as well as reading. She wanted to ask, but vacillated between expression and reticence.

There was no hesitation in their physical meeting. Later, as they lay tipped towards each other in Cass's cramped little bed, they spoke in hushed tones about the others in their group. Though a contrived association, it had unusual affections and affinities: they agreed on this. Marco said there was a dignity and convergence he'd not expected, and an unspoken trust. Cass had been surprised, too, she said. She'd joined half-expecting a polite social club, flimsily premised, dilettantish, a few dislocated bookish expats with time on their hands, but had been overcome by a vast tenderness in hearing the speak-memories. From the moment Victor

141

had begun, on her first day, she had realised how unusual they were, how fortuitously well met. His words had moved her, she said. There was a soft continuation of this feeling. Would it be old-fashioned to say that they would be friends forever?

It was too early for Marco to say more about himself, and he refrained from asking Cass about her life before her chance to speak of it on her own terms. Instead they shared more sleepy reflections and observations on the weather. Marco recommended the third chapter of Pliny the Elder's *Natural History*, which he said was full of oddball speculations and historical musings on things like lightning, sunshine, tornadoes and shadows. Pliny died near Pompeii, said Marco, covered in ash and pumice, having set sail to observe the eruption of Vesuvius. He said the Elder's nephew, Pliny the Younger, closer than any son, waited on the far shore for the boat to return, but was met only with the spectre of the old man's death. A cargo of stones. A beloved uncle, fallen. The year was 79 AD.

'I'm a pedant,' he concluded. 'You must have guessed this by now.'

Cass did not know how to respond to Marco's tale of ancient disaster. She thought of no witty comment, laced with seductive wit. Instead she explained in imprecise terms why snow was exotic to her. Her own account was deeply banal. There was no convincing language, these days, for epiphanic surprise, no verbal nuance or refinement that might explain etherealised seeing or the quality of novelty usually reserved for describing children's pleasures. She was tempted to tell Marco of the discovery of the frost, superincumbent on glass in Yukio and Mitsuko's apartment, but it seemed too obscure a moment to describe. Not yet, she thought, not yet. And how, without sounding provincial, would she say it had seemed an apparition?

At some point their conversation returned to Nabokov's story.

'Gino's own "Guide to Berlin",' Marco said, 'will be something remarkable. He writes beautifully and audaciously; it will be an extraordinary book. He's now calling his Guide "The Book of Conclusions".'

'Conclusions?'

'Who knows?' Marco paused. 'Conclusions are everything. In the Nabokov story, what matters is that the guide is one-armed and scarred.'

Cass had forgotten. How could she have forgotten?

'It's in the last couple of sentences. The guide imagines that the little boy eating soup in the pub will remember him in the future, with his empty right sleeve and his old scarred face. He's a war victim, I guess.'

In her discussions with Victor, they had never spoken of the ending. They had both forgotten that the guide is historically damaged, and that the future recollection includes his disfigurement.

'It's the whole point of the story,' Marco insisted. 'Not an angel looking backwards, seeing ruins and history blown away, but an old man, gentle and kind, looking at ordinary things, and seeing mystically into the future memory of a small child.'

Cass was annoyed and embarrassed. She did not wish to be told that she was a poor reader, or that she had missed a vital detail. She would not tell Victor. She would keep to herself Marco's revelation and preserve their ignorant delight.

They were happier, she reflected, not talking of Vladimir Nabokov, his life or works. In the mental life of couples there are these reticent areas, of which, both know, it is better not to speak. She suspected Marco would have been academically stringent, and a tough perfectionist. When they knew each other better she would ask more about his ideas; and she might discover the real nature of his relationship to Gino.

Marco prepared to leave around midnight.

'Forgive me,' he said. 'There's no way two can sleep here. And I should check on Gino. He's been disappearing again in the last couple of days, scoring from the dealers at Görlitzer Park, or hanging out with the homeless who camp under tarpaulins in that wild strip behind the zoo. Then he returns, haunted-looking and edgy, and he wants to talk all night. It's exhausting. Sometimes he sobs. Sometimes he punches the wall.'

Marco waited for Cass to ask for details. When she didn't he added, 'Be careful, Cass.'

He was sitting on the bed, leaning forward, tying the laces of his shoes. Cass leant over him and kissed the nape of his neck. His springy hair curled there, she felt it graze her moist lips. She encircled him with her arms and rested her face on his back. Fully dressed now, he was no less desirable, and she was reluctant to part with his warmth and the skill of his embrace.

What had been remote and impersonal was now becoming individualised. Each tale of childhood was a gateway, each observation he made, or new word he taught her, was a personal effect he left in his wake. Holding herself above him, looking directly into his eyes, she had seen the sallow child swooning and the Madonna sisters nearby. She had seen the exemplary pathos of a small convulsed boy.

When Marco left, Cass returned to the warmth of her bed. In the darkness her room had a violet sheen. Her insomniac mind wandered. She thought of Vesuvius and the deadly wallop of ash and stone from the sky. Catastrophe: the wracked scope of every history. She thought of Victor, alert, watching the unalert tortoise. She thought more generally, and yet again, of their visit to the aquarium. Almost asleep she saw anew the subdued world of sea creatures, alight in the dark and liquid corridors, drifting, on display, gleaming meekly and seeming – this was the trick, surely, of aquaria and zoos – to be prolonged, or even imperishable, in their own dwarf kingdoms. The paradoxical attraction was in their remove from the world, their apparent self-sufficiency. How safe they all were. Needing no true ocean and no true sunlight; needing no actual freedom.

16

In the underground station at Innsbrucker Platz, an old man was playing 'Nessun Dorma' on a saw. It sounded Martian, thought Cass, like a Theremin whine, like the tune of titanium spaceships approaching in a dream. The bent-over musician looked Central Asian and poor. He wore an ill-fitting jacket that might have belonged to someone else, borrowed perhaps, or raided as a cast-off. His face was scabby and squashed and spoke of many hard winters. The saw was caught between his legs and he played it gently with a bow, lifting, lowering, lifting and again lowering. A saw, she thought. That a saw could sound so extraterrestrial. The musician did not look up; he was intent on his recital and in a world of his own. Some sort of quivering, ineluctable spirit contained him. In this drear and lurid tunnel, with its rushing commuters, he was seancing Puccini.

Cass and one or two others stopped in their tracks to listen. The passage between the U-Bahn and S-Bahn was a perfect chamber for music: the saw sounds reverberated loudly, rang in the concrete shadows, travelled paranormal in thin waves through the dingy tubes. A concert audience of three. They each offered a few euros.

Gino was there to meet her, as they had planned. He stood at the exit, smoking. When he saw her approach, he dropped his smoke and cowboy-style, without looking, ground the butt with his heel.

'What would Pavarotti think?' he said, as he leant to kiss her in greeting.

'Or Joey Ramone?'

'Both dead. Touché.'

It was a fatuous exchange, completely contemporary.

Gino's face was ice cold. Cass wondered how long he'd stood there, waiting for her to appear. He looked tired, she thought. His handsome features were drawn, his eyes were inflamed and baggy. Around him hung the fusty reek of too many fervid cigarettes. She wondered when last he had used.

'Come,' she said. 'I promised you good coffee.' Together they walked up Hauptstrasse and into the backstreets of Schöneberg; Cass led Gino into the pokey place she considered her local. They sat on uncomfortable chairs that indicated hip Berlin, and gazed in the direction of Apostle Paulus church. A light snow fell. Cass stared calmly out of the window as Gino fidgeted and stirred, touching at his clothes like a man who discovers he has lost something and immediately feels a wild need to locate it.

'I've lost my wallet,' he confirmed.

'I can pay, don't worry.'

'No, I mean *really* lost. My credit cards, everything.'

He was ruffled by his misfortune. He stood abruptly, pulled upwards, and the wallet appeared as in a trick, fallen in a plop from somewhere inside his jacket. There were tears in his eyes.

'Jesus, I'm such a mess.'

Cass remained silent. She would let him recover his dignity, she would watch the snow. The windows were slightly fogged with damp, but there it was, still apparent, a pure-white scrim descending. Already the streets were halfway transformed, becoming crème-smooth and beautiful.

'Don't you think,' she ventured, 'that one of the effects of snow is to make everything, even people, appear almost motionless?'

Gino looked vacantly at her face as if not comprehending the question. Then he reconnected, and calmed.

'Yes,' he said quietly. 'Yes, almost motionless.'

After that, they could speak. Gino leant close so that Cass caught the scent of his masculinity intermixed with the tart cigarette smoke. He spoke, as Marco had, of their tight little group. Victor was inauthentic, he declared, but he was unable to explain why he knew this to be so. It was a feeling he had, a definite feeling. Victor was inauthentic. Yukio and Mitsuko were the real thing: they were true lovers who had found each other, they were a paradigm case, a rare modern example. Marco, well, he was Marco; he was the exceptional Marco.

'Has he told you yet about Pliny the Elder?' Gino asked. 'He has these points of obsession: the uncle who was really the father, the death of excessive poignancy as Vesuvius gushes fire, the encyclopedic, and scholarly, and finally futile life.'

Cass lied. 'No.'

'He knows a huge amount, really, but it's all self-referential.

History is full of allegories that he considers marvellously personal. Don't trust him, Cass. He has crazy theories about everything.'

Gino's face was close, insistent; he had the tone of a fanatic. For all the details Cass knew of them, Gino and Marco were still unknown to her. She ought to defend Victor, she ought to speak of her own judgements.

Instead she said, 'And you? Is there some historical story you like to tell that is the marvel that tells you?'

They both sipped their coffee. Gino was moving a forkful of chocolate cake across his plate, without eating.

'Later,' he said cautiously.

The café was full of mothers with hefty babies and hipster-cool men. Everyone was young, relaxed, leaning back in their chairs, talking in polite and respectful murmurs, charming each other, kindly amusing. Here they were, by contrast, mere faltering strangers. Cass wondered why Gino had felt it necessary to warn her off Marco. There was a secret somewhere between them, and a vague animosity. The snowfall outside was growing faster and more dense. Both paused and stared into its fluctuating and dimension-less depths. The church before them was disappearing, fading into white.

'Me too,' said Gino, intuiting her thoughts. 'I also love the snow.'

Conversation turned to politics. It was a relief to consider social meanings, to acknowledge real urgencies and those not their own. Gino was still upset, he said, by the mass drowning of African refugees, a few months back, off the island of Lampedusa. Cass knew the figure: 366 lives lost and not one child under twelve who'd survived.

She knew that the survivors were heading to Sweden. She knew some had burnt off their fingerprints with melted plastic bags so as not to be registered as refugees in Italy. Gino looked shocked at the details.

'In Australia,' she added, 'we have a government policy of hard hearts. In Australia we are meant to accept such calamities as inevitable. To enjoy our own good luck.'

She restrained herself. How national shame diminishes us all, she thought. How brutally the lucky country guards its unearnt luck.

Gino looked away.

'Don't you hate luck?' she asked, in what must have seemed a somewhat perverse and irrelevant question. She was thinking of the German word: *glück*, luck; *glücklich*, happy. Such a sticky word.

Gino did not answer. Instead he seemed to drift off into private thoughts.

'I had a holiday in Lampedusa only a year ago,' he said. 'I swam in the sunshine at the beach where all the bodies were retrieved. When I watched the TV reports it was all so familiar – that bay, those rocks. I thought of this again when Yukio told us of seeing his subway on television as a child, how somewhere is stained with tragedy and becomes an intolerable memory. Those people, wanting escape. All those poor people, Jesus Christ . . .'

Gino pulled out his cigarettes. 'Do you mind if I smoke?'

They left the warmth of the café. The heavy door did not smother or close away their feelings. Gino lit up immediately.

'We can go to the Ramones Museum, or to Oranienplatz,' he said.

Ramones Museum? 'What's at Oranienplatz?'

Now they moved together from single to communal stories. As they continued moving towards Oranienplatz, Gino explained that it was an occupied space. Refugees from Africa seeking asylum, seeking a warm, safe haven, had built there a shantytown of tents and shelters. There were ramshackle huts, stretched canvas beneath bare trees, there were signs that read: *'Kein Mensch ist illegal'*; 'Refugees are welcome here; Deportation is murder'. It was a community, said Gino, an ephemeral community.

When they arrived the Platz looked almost deserted: few people were out and about in the cold. Snowfall lay heavy and threatening in the deep folds of the large tents, the sag and strain of the load looked fundamentally precarious. Snow was piled high on park seats and clung to a few stranded bicycles, and Cass could hear it being scraped away, somewhere nearby, the raw shivery grind of metal on a concrete path. It was an impediment now, and an inhuman threat. Some of the tents, Cass thought, would surely sink. She looked around her. On the corner stood a boarded-up building, so firmly closed, so untended and dead that it was hard to believe living people had ever been inside. Posters for yoga, cinema and punk bands were stuck haphazard across its walls, and everywhere lay strata of garish graffiti with impossible-to-read messages. High up, almost beyond sight, there was a sign in English: 'Reclaim your city'.

A man wrapped in a purple sleeping bag emerged from behind the flap of a tent. He strode towards Gino and held out his hand. They shook, then they embraced, and then they stood patting each other's back, like old drinking buddies or revolutionary comrades. Cass was still, observing. She was in her new waterproof boots, she was warm and she was lucky.

Gino introduced Ahmed from Eritrea. He had come here via Libya and Italy. He had come, Gino added softly, via the island of Lampedusa.

Ahmed reached out from his sleeping bag cocoon and shook Cass's hand. Cold stung at her eyes. Her chest felt tight and congested. She took the hand of the man who greeted her and wondered if she might be crying or if the nip of the cold had simply generated tears. There was such confusion in her response, such sensory and extra-sensory overload; and Ahmed did not seem to concede his sorry state, so that it was she who seemed pathetic, it was she who was floundering, and caught up in twisted emotions. Ahmed smiled broadly in welcome. His face reminded her of a kid she had known fondly when she was a child, a kid with a dazzling white smile in his open black face. If she had come earlier, Ahmed said casually, she could have met his wife.

'Come again. You can meet her.'

Gino opened his wallet and emptied it into Ahmed's hand.

'Thank you, my brother.'

Behind him a man with matted blond hair was donating a crate of potatoes. Cass saw his breath in the air; she saw the slowed and deliberate motion of his half-frozen movements. In a few seconds he was gone, as if never having existed. Now, no other person was visible. The pall of snow fell between them all, damp and obscuring. Flakes settled in a delicate skull cap over Ahmed's dark hair. Gino leant towards him, curled his bare hand to his ear and said something confidential. Ahmed replied in a whisper, 'Yes, my brother, yes.' They spoke briefly in Italian.

The others were all sheltered from the cold at some sort of meeting, Gino said. Wisely sheltered. The three stood still, in a moment of silence and social inertia. Then Ahmed stamped on the ground and pulled his sleeping bag closer. He announced, 'Things to do!' and turned back towards the tents.

Gino took Cass's arm and led her away. He seemed almost happy now; his gaze was lit and he smiled with satisfied ease as he left behind the encampment of Oranienplatz. It had been such a small encounter, so modest and swift. But Cass felt that her chest was still tight and her feelings were still snarled.

Gino's face was close. He hugged her arm as they walked. He said: 'Now. Let me tell you now the historical marvel that tells of myself.

'I'm very interested in Descartes. Everyone knows "*I think therefore I am*," everyone knows of the *Discours* and the wax example, but he was much more interesting than that, and more philosophically strange. He was a mathematical genius, he wrote on psychosomatics, on passion, on meteors, on the weather. He wrote a treatise on snow and drew images of rare, twelve-sided snowflakes. And in 1633, at the age of thirty-seven, Descartes visited Rome. While in Rome he observed the phenomenon of parhelia, which is an odd optical effect in which there appear to be several suns in the sky. Descartes saw three. He did not panic, he did not lose his religion, he did not resort to lunatic theories or apocalyptic speculations.

Instead he stood looking up at the sky, with its three bright suns, and knew how good it was to be a man, with his senses fully alive, his brain figuring out all the equations of angles and reflections. He was jubilant, he was curious. He was self-possessed.

'Marco told me this story, but it has become my story. It has become the weather story that I most adore.'

They parted at Kottbusser Tor station, just as the snow at last began to ease. Gino borrowed his fare. He said, 'When you tire of Marco, I will be waiting.'

Cass felt herself blush. It was a sensation of disorder, of unexpected feeling. She was both irritated and pleased at Gino's presumption. He squeezed her hand, holding on a few seconds longer than he should. They stood awkwardly, awaiting separate trains. Before them, a young man collected beer bottles from rubbish bins and stowed them in his backpack. They watched his focused searching and his quiet desperation. Something stiff in his manner implied old age, but he couldn't have been more than thirty, Cass thought, not much older than she. When her U1 train arrived she bid Gino a hasty farewell and sprang into the carriage without looking back.

She might have been swimming, or drowning, in a twilit aquarium. Stopped faces blinked by. The air seemed watery and blue. Her carriage contained her behind glass, less as a person than a notion; the particulars of her own life had fallen away. Prinzenstrasse, Hallesches Tor, the golden tiles of Möckernbrüke. Heading towards the west. In motion she felt bizarrely neutral, and disembodied.

Parhelia, a new word.

The sky was a white ceiling. Not even one sun, not one, was visible in the sky.

17

On the day of her own speak-memory, Cass busied herself with chores and casual distractions. She washed her clothes in the bathroom sink, rolled them in a towel and hung them along the iron heater to dry, placing her socks just so, and spreading evenly her underwear. Across the back of a chair she draped her wrung jeans. Festooned in this way, the studio apartment looked even smaller and more cramped than usual. It was like being a student again, imagining the intermediate time before adult tidiness is obligatory, not having space enough for simple tasks, feeling temporary and derided and unimportant in the world. 'Nessun Dorma' played a maddening riff in her head. Cass was surprised at how tenacious remembered musical interludes were, how they play and replay, how like madness or dementia the repetitions begin to seem. It was a fickle irritation, its jingle replay tormented her. She had a residual memory from somewhere, probably from television, of Luciano Pavarotti belting out the final 'Vincero!', his mouth hugely open, hugely appetitive, as if he might gobble the entire world. She was more a Bach person, she reflected, less operatic, more baroque. She would listen to the cello suites again, later on. She enjoyed a dilettante comfort, knowing little of music and unable, if pressed, to speak intelligently on the subject. There were many areas of knowledge in which she felt entirely a fraud. But the pleasure was definitive, it was incontrovertible. Against 'Nessun Dorma' she pitched Brandenburg phrases and passing seconds of melody.

There was a knock at the door and Cass was startled. She saw the mess of her room, she was half-dressed and unfocused. She threw on her coat, hanging near the door, and drew it open to discover Karl.

'I thought you might like to talk,' he said hopefully. 'Coffee?'

He was unkempt, he looked bored, and his appeal, painfully tentative, was that of a lonely old man. Dimly, he seemed in the hall light to twitch and shuffle.

But Cass sent him away. She pretended she was dressing to go out, and knew now that she would have to dress and leave the apartment, because he would be watching and she must make her evasion seem true. How often she performed a quality of seeming, not being. The anticipation of her speak-memory was undermining her good sense; she was disproportionately tense and in a state of seizure and dread.

'Come up for coffee tomorrow afternoon,' she said. '5.30 okay?'

Karl looked concerned.

'17.30,' she corrected.

He beamed in return. 'Kein problem!' He mopped his forehead with a handkerchief, as if he were ill or unseasonably hot, then turned away and headed slowly down the poorly lit stairs. Cass felt a twinge of guilt and the need for female company, to be exempt from male demands and conversation. She needed to dissipate her nervousness with a walk in the cold air of the city.

When she stepped out into the street, she decided to ride the ring line. She passed the apartment that had been burnt on New Year's Eve, boarded up now, but not yet repaired, the paisley shape of smoke, immemorially delinquent, still defacing its surface. The streets were mostly dismal, abandoned and awash with black slush. On Martin-Luther-Strasse many shops were deserted, the large mattress shop on the corner was entirely empty, even the bakery, brightly enticing, had just a single customer. A few shoppers well-rugged in scarves came and went from the Turkish supermarket; this was where life was. Cass peered at the bulging plastic bags of non-European delicacies and found herself hungry for pita and something loaded with garlic.

From Innsbrucker Platz Station she headed east on the S42, sliding past the border where the Wall had once stood, then sliding back to the same side later on, finding in the train a calming rhythm and the slumberous satisfactions of automation, of being carried somewhere, of doors opening and closing, of the regular announcements and toneless instructions to depart on the left. It was a soothing circle, moving her in the legless fluency of a dream. She felt almost airborne. As she rode her thoughts drifted to celestial speculations – dust clouds from volcanoes, the multiplication of suns, the curious possibility of twelve-pointed snowflakes – and already she was considering how her new friends had changed her, what knowledge, explicit or implicit, they had imparted. This was the kind of association she had often longed for: an avowable community and the trust of shared biographies, small stories offered as symbolic tokens.

Passengers stepped on and off the train in silence. Winter brought with it this dissolve of conversation. A man with a tattooed face and a German shepherd plumped down beside her, the dog stinking of rough nights and what might have been spilt beer. Both had glazed, hungry eyes and a fatalist passivity. She was relieved when they rose and disappeared at Wedding.

Cass rode almost the whole circle before she alighted one stop from where she had begun. At Bundesplatz, under a darkening sky, she left the station and headed to a coffee shop to daydream and read. She would spend a few hours hidden away, waiting to speak and rematerialising after her wraith-like journey. She felt somehow tenuous and unbelonging; her riding was the symptom of absent centre and inexplicit purpose.

There was no snowfall now, but sharp frosty air and ice on the pavement in wafers, which cracked beneath her boots as she stepped. The afternoon was fading fast; the little daylight that thinly penetrated was already flowing away, disappearing into *the dark backward and abysm of time*. I must not quote Shakespeare, she thought to herself. I must be clear, and true.

In the former home of Kępiński, Cass faced the group, determined. Yukio and Mitsuko wore matching denim outfits, long and sculptural, and for the first time it occurred to Cass that they were probably rich. This was high-end fashion, not mere costume; this was the casual exhibitionism of wealthy artists. They greeted her with embraces. Marco and Gino were both more formal; and Gino appeared unshaven and tired, as if he had not made it home after their excursion together and displayed the stale and bruised look of a sleepless night. Victor, playing the fool, was wearing his shapka inside. He alone seemed to be in high and robust spirits.

'To be honest, I wasn't sure I could participate in your speak-memory. I have been surprised by the candour, and by how much trust has been established. I've not known anything quite like this before. And I guess I still feel like the newcomer, a little outside your circle. The kibitzer, you might say.'

The beginning, she told herself, would be the hardest part. Once she launched her voice into the group, it would take energy from their listening. It would be enabled.

'I grew up in a remote part of Australia, in the northwest. So, like Mitsuko, I come from beyond a city, and am marked, I suppose, by a distinctive place. As I travel I begin to learn how cities govern our imaginations, how difficult it becomes to recover the humble place that has no special renown, or world-historical importance, but exists as a little constellation of lives, somewhere largely forgotten by the rest of the world. When Victor began with his magnificent list of cities, I thought, even then, as he spoke, of an alternative list, of places whose reality to others is more like Zembla – possibly fictitious, not wholly substantiated, too small or unremarkable to warrant outsiders' attention. In Europe, Australia is regarded as a fiction of beautiful lies.

It pleases me that this is so, and I can't really say why. But it is also a scattering of settlements, modest places that no one knows or cares about, where real lives happen, where there is a density to knowing and a quiet certainty to existence.

My parents, now retired, were both schoolteachers dedicated to working in small communities. I had three older brothers, two of whom are also now schoolteachers. So, I am the black sheep in the family, I am the one who left. I am the one who was captured and taken away by words.'

Had the others found it this difficult?

Cass realised that she moved habitually in the zone of her own allegiances, those things that were sensitive for her, and private, and without need of expression or exaggeration. When she spoke it was with an awareness of a kind of betrayal and a tendency to generalisation. There was no way she could speak in detail of her parents, modestly hardworking, serious and sane, living together in a tiny country town with a single store and a petrol bowser and a weatherboard town hall. Or indeed of her brothers, and their quiet integrity, and their meaningful, hidden lives.

'The house I grew up in was once the hospital of a former quarantine station. It stood on a peninsula, beyond the north-west town of Broome, and had been a place where soldiers returning from the battles of the Second World War were sent to recover or die. These were men with fevers – typhus mostly, and dengue, and malaria. In our house they had seethed, or so I imagined, afraid and alone in the thrall of their tropical illnesses. They had called out in the night, they had suffered, seen ghosts, had themselves become ghosts. I knew in my heart that our house was haunted. How can one live in a former hospital without imagining the deaths that might have occurred there? How is it possible to ignore remnant presences and the traces of suffering lives? I believed that I heard their voices. I believed that they called out to me. My brothers teased me and said I was crazy. But still I persisted in my childish belief.

'I had a room to myself. Ours was a long house, raised on stilts, in which the rooms had once been wards, opening to a common verandah running along both sides. The rooms were not joined: one stepped out onto the verandah to enter another room. So I thought of this house as a flute, or a harmonica, or some yet unknown musical instrument, because the wind blew straight through it, making high, eerie sounds. At night, with doors at each end of the rooms left open in the heat, there was a pitch that could only have been human wailing, or someone lost in the dark calling to find their way home. Beyond this lay the sound of the waves and the Indian Ocean, pulsing and beating. So the air was full of ocean noise, and quasi-human voices. At least this is how I thought of it then, waves and voices. I was an imaginative child, burdened by vivid speculations.

'Just as Gino described the resonant atmosphere in a cathedral, there was a peculiarity to the dark night air of my childhood, there was an amplification, and an immanent mystery. For most children, I suppose, the night is large in this way, framed and intensified by their own imagining. The night fills up with all they sense, but do not comprehend.

'There was a lighthouse too, nearby, set high on a sand-hill. It flashed its stripe of white light directly over our house; it created an intermittent dark that I have never really known since. This other-world of night-time was my surest reality; I cannot tell you how profoundly it has left its mark. Nabokov describes a child's night-train ride in this way: the world oddly rocking and swinging, images enlarging and speeding into vision, omnipresent shadows, presences half-seen, the silver coating to objects and the creepy moon-glaze that hangs over everything. As he falls asleep the boy fancies he sees a glass marble rolling beneath a grand piano. Somehow that mattered to me, that unconnected detail. And the train ride sounded so like my own childhood experience of night – of animation, and of ill-defined presences. And then waking mid-night from the current of sleep to find things slower and more visionary, the lighthouse blankly continuing, the walls sliding away, ordinary furniture, the little there was, made spooky and fantastical, discarded clothes on the floor looking like writhing monsters.'

Cass checked herself. She was babbling, babbling aimlessly about the night. And she was sounding literary when she wanted to sound more straightforward. She'd not anticipated how easily one might become carried away, how the descriptive task dragged her narrative along an unexpected track. Opposite, Yukio, Marco and Gino were all staring at her. Mitsuko, sitting beside, lightly touched her hand. They might have been schoolgirls in the playground, sharing a confidence.

'In daytime my brothers and I lived in a rough kind of utopia. We fished and swam, we rode through the bush on the back of a truck into the town to attend school. We were a gang, living apart, mostly running wild. Cricket, we loved cricket. I took my turn at the batting and my brothers indulged me with slow, easy bowls. I remember their bare legs streaked with red dirt beneath filthy shorts and their arms turning like windmills. Dust puffed from their heels as they skidded for the ball. They liked to leap up and shout "How's that!" as if we composed a real team, with real opponents and serious scores, not just sibling mischief and fake competition. I wanted desperately to be a boy and tried hard to act as my brothers did, and to be tough and masculine. I was a very good fighter – even they conceded it – driven by the foolish need to prove myself equal. I loved to wrestle but never had the weight or the strength to win, so I developed a ruthless repertoire of dirty tricks. I was an arrogant child, clever and self-assured. And of course I was spoilt as the youngest and the only girl.

'My defeat – at least this is how I thought of it then – came when at eleven I developed a bad case of ringworm. My skin flowered in repulsive circular lesions. My mother dabbed me all over with gentian violet and my head was shaven. I was forbidden to touch my family, and bound, like one guilty, to constant hand-washing. I was purple-speckled and bald, unrecognisable even to myself. Not a serious illness, of course, not disability or catastrophe, but simple humiliation, and a kind of disfiguring.

'By that time my two older brothers had been sent south to boarding school, and Alexander, one year older than me, remained. He did not contract ringworm. I remember he looked at me with a faint expression of disgust, his face averted. I remember a kind of flustered pity.

'A feral cat had deposited a litter of kittens beneath our house and my mother said I had ringworm because I'd fondled them. It was true. I'd crouched in the shadows and lifted the kittens to my face, kissing and playing and wishing them fat and adorable. I'd pushed them into my shirt, felt their silky small throb, and held them against my chest. Something in their fragility moved and compelled me. Their puckered faces. The squint of their newborn eyes. That squirming being, not yet fully extended into the world.

'I watched as my mother drowned the kittens in the laundry, in a hessian bag. I remember how the bag stretched and twitched with their thrashing panic, how she had to hold it down, how I wept and pleaded. It was a loss of power, I think, a loss of that sense of having one's own dominion. The kittens were killed and I looked hideous. I was confined, my parents were strict, Alexander was distant. As a child it is hard to believe the transformations of illness or injury will reverse. But somehow I knew then that things had irrevocably changed.

'At twelve I was sent to a boarding school in the south, in the city of Perth. It was a kind of exile. I had been vain and self-centred, now I was ignored and punished. Possessing no girlish social skills and eccentric in my tastes, I was isolated and had difficulty making friends. I developed an interest in butterflies, which other girls ridiculed, preferring pop music and magazines. I thought myself a specialist in spotting the Amaryllis Azure, but more than anything I wanted to see the Ulysses butterfly, *papilo ulysses,* known to Vladimir Nabokov as the Australian swallowtail. It is startling in its beauty – iridescent blue, outlined in black. The drab underside is a furry brown. I copied images from books and went on spotting expeditions, climbing alone through the sodden, murky undergrowth along the banks of the Swan River. You will know of course that Nabokov was a specialist of American 'Blues' and spent almost two years classifying them on the basis of their microscopic genitalia. He also created butterflies. There is a fine drawing he did, as a present for Vera, which is derived from his knowledge of the Australian swallowtail.'

'I have a photocopy of this image,' said Victor. 'I can bring it next time.'

'Mostly I saw Common Browns, those with marbled wings and eye-spots, or Monarchs, orange-brown, with distinctive white dots on the black band of their outline, and now and then a Painted Lady, a *Vanessa kershawi*, blown down from Indonesia – tangerine with black and white markings, white spots at the wingtips . . .'

'Ocellated,' said Victor.

'Thank you, yes – ocellated. It is hard to explain to you how completely absorbing this can be, how fastidious one becomes looking out for a passing fritillary, or the flit of a bluish wing, or eyespots flying, or the glimpse of some shape, yellow or cinnabar, suspended in mid-air, beating at the sky, jerking just beyond the reach of one's hands.'

'I have also seen the Painted Lady, the *Vanessa kershawi*,' Mitsuko interrupted.

Cass halted, aware suddenly of how she had revisited her adolescent enthusiasms. What was it that made this artificial tale-telling, once begun, veer into flowery declarations and indulgences?

'Most butterflies live only about two weeks. As a child this knowledge moved me as the scrawny kittens did . . . I wondered at the value of something so barely enduring. Or rather I wondered at a new idea of value itself.'

166

Cass halted again.

'I'm not sure how to explain this. The scrawny kittens.'

The others remained silent, and waited.

'Shadows of the chessmen,' said Yukio in a distant voice.

Her story was stumbling. She changed the subject.

'I studied painting at first, then I studied literature. I wanted to be an artist. All that I saw and knew needed an analogy of some sort; I wanted the world fixed and intelligible, not flowing away behind me, not disappearing into *"the dark backward and abysm of time"*. I wanted images to stop, for my quiet inspection. I needed for some reason or justification to look more closely. I understand why serious collectors pin butterflies in trays and write tiny labels, why they range specimens carefully, one after another, in diminishing size. But I never did this, truly; I was never a collector.

'At art school my eccentricities were valued for a time, but then I became tiresome to others, and to myself. I was a failed painter, bold but not remarkably talented. Self-portrait in purple speckles, that kind of thing. It embarrasses me now to think of it. I fled art school to London for six months, then returned, moved to Sydney and turned my attention to literature. I took a series of part-time unskilled jobs, and finally settled in a bookshop, a small independent bookshop, where I felt most at home. Then I left, I simply uprooted. Travelling revives the intensity of images. It recovers curiosity.

'And now here I am.'

'*How long is now?*' Gino asked.

She could not go on. Cass was aware that her story was thin beside the others'. It was secretive, almost sham.

The night was true: it had been just like that, the Australian Gothic house on stilts, exposed to winds from the ocean, wailing, hysterical. There had been relentless flashing light and the echoing of dead voices and oceans. It sounded invented, she knew, but it released her from speaking of more difficult things. What had happened to Alexander. It released her from speaking of the unspeakable Alexander.

'Well done,' said Victor, determined to be supportive. The others murmured approval. Gino excused himself absentmindedly and rose for a cigarette. Marco was smiling warmly. Expecting them all to reassemble, Yukio and Mitsuko began laying a small collection of oriental snacks on Kępiński's table. Cass could not help it: she was disappointed in herself. She knew she had somehow not fulfilled the narrative contract; the others were all less reserved, more confiding and more open. She was provincial, she was a failure. She perceived a radical lack of clarity. In not producing a coherent story, she was not possessed of those properties of necessity and fullness that make a plausible self. And why had she mentioned the kittens? And gone on about the house? Why, though Nabokovian, had she described the butterfly spotting?

'All good,' whispered Marco.

This time they stayed. This time all of them sat together around Kępiński's impressive oak table and continued to drink and to talk and eat tidbits with chopsticks, and gradually to recover a dimension of unselfconscious ease in their conversation. Victor did not remove the shapka, and in the vapid opulence of the apartment looked somewhat droll and comically displaced. He was telling everyone in cheerful terms of the visit to the aquarium, how the ancient tortoise was very likely the one Nabokov himself had seen, how it had made eye contact with him, as if some glimmer of the distant past moved like electricity between them. A living creature, he said, still persisting, and *in situ*. Mitsuko and Yukio agreed that animals possibly apprehended time in ways unknown to humans. Gino scoffed, and raised his glass.

'Here's to the superiority of non-human creatures! Who outlive us, and judge us, and know vastly more!'

Victor looked confused.

'It was wonderful,' he continued. 'It was really something, that tortoise.'

Talk ranged across animals and books and the harsh winter in Berlin. No one questioned Cass on the details of her speak-memory, or thereafter alluded to it. She was relieved by the return to relative impersonality.

Now that they had all performed their speak-memories, Marco suggested, they might next time talk of the city, and the ways in which they personally knew it. There was vague, muttered assent. It would be informal, he added, it would be much more informal.

Alcohol began muddling and tangling their conversation. Gino was retelling a short story by Italo Calvino. A man heads an agency that attempts to archive all the knowledge in the world. It is a mammoth, absurd task, and he inflects the data with banal and unregarded things, the dull things that make up the true texture of everyday being: yawns, pimples, obscene ideas, whistled tunes . . . These he folds into public knowledge in an act of subjective subversion. What seems most untransmissable, said Gino, is what is most human. The story is finally about jealousy, he said; it is finally about evil and the wish to control.

Cass sat at the head of the table, as though the guest of honour at a ceremony. As she drank more, now both careless and relieved, she saw how strategic Gino's story had been. Here, in Kępiński's, he needed to remind them of the self-serving selection of remembrance. He needed to claim and to advertise his own right to record. They looked at each other. Gino paused in a sip of wine and offered a flabby drunken smile.

'My version,' he said, waving a leather-bound notebook. 'My own "Guide to Berlin".'

18

She had wanted a day staying in, seeing no one, finding her independent shape. But as soon as she woke Cass remembered that Karl would arrive in the afternoon. She lay in her bed and was tempted to remain. The air in her small room was mean and chill; she would have to find her socks to go to the bathroom; she would need to rug up just to move the few steps to make coffee. It was a long time since she had felt so seriously hungover, and now she recalled Yukio and Mitsuko guiding her into a taxi, and Karl – could it have been Karl? – helping with huffs and puffs as she dragged and pulled herself up the stairs. That fuse-effect of drunkenness was something she'd rarely known, being a careful drinker, and judgmental of others, but now the night returned to her in the viscous form of bodies merging and imprecise recollection. She had sent both Marco and Gino away, this much she remembered. Victor, dear Victor, had passed out, at some stage. And yes, Marco and Gino had together carried Victor from Kępiński's. This morning they would all be feeling seedy and nauseous. They would all be trying to unfuse the united moments in which their bodies and minds swum together, and they touched each other suggestively, and were given to rash declarations and smudgy kisses. She had slumped between Yukio and Mitsuko in the back of a taxi. Their faces had looked oily and gleaming.

Behind the window, snow was lightly falling. How pure it looked, and how unsullied. Cass put her head beneath the pillow and tried to return to sleep, but wondered now what she had said, and how she had acted, and if she had managed to disgrace herself by an irretrievable word or action. Unaccountably, she recalled some words of Nabokov: when he dreamt of the dead, he wrote, they always appeared silent and bothered and inexplicably depressed, quite unlike the bright selves they had expressed alive. Her sense of the night before was like this – that her friends had shed their bright selves and were in the shadows of another state, bare and intangible, as in a dream existence. There was a slightly sinister bend to her post-drunken recall.

At last she rose. She saw her bag on the floor and her scarf and coat discarded. She must have flung herself into bed; she must have been out of it.

Cass spent the morning reading, battling a headache. She read a detective novel, trashy and ham-fisted, then flicked in a casual way though a guidebook to Berlin. Recommendations for clubs and decadent nightlife seemed to predominate. One club offered 'post-human pleasuring', another had erotic booths and blue movies as sidelines to the dance floor. The young music scene was impressively huge. Techno, house, remix, rasta. Rap, electronica, funk, hip-hop, soul, punk, gangsta, electro-pop . . . Her tastes were antique, she knew; she was outside her own generation. She vaguely noted the names and location of a few famous clubs, but was essentially uninterested. There were the expected photographs: the Reichstag, the Brandenburg Gate, the silver spear of the Fernsehturm. And there were any number of outings – a world of non-conformist restaurants, minimalist or maximalist concerts and gleefully perverted art galleries. Museums of every kind offered sober histories, of the wars, or the Wall, or Germanic triumphs and failures. So much theatre, high culture, so many memorials. Dutifully, Cass noted a few 'attractions'. She had been merely a woman riding on the U and S-Bahn, observing ordinary Berliners. She was both democratically curious and committed to her own inclinations; she was clearly a failure as a tourist.

When Cass stood she felt ill; when she sat or lay, her head throbbed. It was a wasted day. At some point the buzzer rang and she heard Yukio's voice echo in the resonating space of the lobby: it surprised her that they had visited without prearrangement, and she felt sacrificially unprepared and murderously antisocial. Hastily, she tidied. When she opened the door Yukio and Mitsuko looked flushed with good health, and were again dressed in garments of distinctive and showy uniformity. Beneath their coats they wore matching suits of navy vinyl. Yukio handed Cass a plastic bottle of Pocari Sweat.

'Hangover cure,' he said.

'We travel with our own pharmacopoeia.' Mitsuko explained. 'Pocari Sweat is for *veisalgia*. Ion supply.'

Cass invited them in. Each had snowflake traces clinging to their hair. They disappeared as she looked at them.

'Snowing again, yes? All those hexagons.'

She was trying hard to be social and entertaining, though she wished them gone. They would see her facile indifference and her lack of engagement.

But Yukio was immediately and enthusiastically responsive.

'I know that English word: *hexagon*. It was a Japanese man, Ukichiro Nakaya, who wrote the first real scientific study of snowflakes – in the 1930s. I read it in my *hikikomori* days. Nakaya knew how crystals form and why no two snowflakes are the same.'

Cass couldn't be bothered responding. She politely drank the sour Pocari Sweat and made a pot of tea, setting her two teacups in the centre of her table. The lovers showed no signs of wanting to leave. Just as she was running out of conversation, when she thought that her headache was finally abating and she might have some peace at last, there was a knock on the door.

Oh no, she thought, Karl. He stood in the doorway, smirking. He was unfazed by her visitors and shook their hands with vigour. Almost instantly he commenced his loud chat in German.

'*Japanisch!*' he exclaimed, genuinely impressed. He pointed at their suits.

'Yes, also *Japanisch*,' said Mitsuko. She translated for Yukio and soon the three, apparently, were talking about snow. Cass couldn't entirely follow: Mitsuko's German was excellent and far beyond her own level of competence. But she heard the name Ukichiro Nakaya once again and knew then that Yukio must be explaining the science of snowflakes to Karl. She made another pot of tea. Since she had only two chairs, Karl and Mitsuko sat on her bed, and Yukio and she drew up the chairs and pulled the small table beside them. Karl was enjoying himself hugely. His large hands clutched his knees. He looked ten years younger, altered by youthful company and *Japanisch* novelty. At some point in their conversation he excused himself, went back to his room and returned with an old book on natural science, full of tatty bits and pieces of bookmark. He proudly opened it to a few pages of snowflake sketches – exquisite prints in fine-point etching, dated 1905. He was saying something like 'nature does not age', he was expressing a naturalist's delight. Cass was compelled to revise her knowledge of Karl: he was, after all, an educated man, and one with assiduous – bookmarked – intellectual passions. With Yukio he inclined his head over the images. Mitsuko leant forward, her vinyl suit creaking.

'It is one of Yukio's special interests,' she explained in English. 'When we first met it was in winter, and he liked to tease and call me the *yuki-onna*, the snow woman. She is a beautiful lady of mythology, but exceptionally dangerous. She kills men with her cold breath. She floats through the snow and leaves no footprints.'

How enmeshed they all were. It was startling, Cass reflected, how they overlapped and repeated in their private fixations. They were a group of random foreigners, passing at this moment in history, through this specific city, and they were continually discovering symbolic convergences. Interpenetrating knowledge made their association unique. In their para-literary life of drinking and ritualised talking, outside usual social forms, a leisure class all of their own, they had discovered the *gestalt* of apparently shared perceptions. No footprints necessary to lead their way.

'Let me show you something,' Mitsuko said.

She extracted a pile of stiff papers from her bag, pushed the teacups aside, and set about fussily manipulating a single square page. She said she was constructing an origami snowflake. Her fingers fiddled at the sheet, pressing and folding, following crease lines, flattening corners with her fingertips, deriving a pointed star from an entirely ordinary plane of paper. With a slight bow of her head, she offered the shape to Karl. He received it with two hands, in a delicate gesture. Then Mitsuko bent again, and folded again. This time she folded into existence an origami butterfly. Her fingers pinched at the corners and pulled lengthwise at the paper body. She displayed the completed shape on her open palm.

'It's a female,' she added, handing it to Cass with the same quiet formality. 'The male is slightly different.'

With the gentlest of pressures, Mitsuko urged Cass to open her hand and accept the butterfly. Cass had always thought it ingenuous, this playing with paper, and above all despised the decorative motif of butterflies that infested women's scarves and bags and summer clothes, ubiquitous as the skull. But now she held the little object with new regard. Its combination of exactness and austerity moved her. Such a rational thing. Such a marvel of reconstruction. 'Implicated', that was the word, the mystery of folds. From a humble planar void, this 3D surprise. She glanced at Karl and was moved to see that he had tears in his eyes. He nodded politely. With endearing charm he held up his paper snowflake, swinging it from two fingers.

When at last they all left, Cass realised that she felt both lucid and well. Her headache had gone, her laconic mood had disintegrated. Her body was no longer clogged with excess alcohol and toxins. Darkness had fallen very early, so she had no sense of the time, but when she looked at the clock she discovered it was nearly seven. She set about rinsing the teacups to make way for preparing her dinner. She felt a vast, dreamy ease, a sense of moving in a state of peace and equanimity in her room. Minutes passed unnoticed: she seemed to drift through absent time on shallow associations, the Japanese origami, the bookmarks in Karl's book, the slow lamination of memories of the last few weeks, and of what she had said, and of what others had said, and of how there had been a hundred small intersections and correspondences; and how these had given her such subtle and unexpected pleasure.

She was aware of a distant sound in the hallway as a door slammed below, and of footfall somewhere, and of the spooked quality of indistinct sounds in the stale air of the apartment block. She was aware of the warmth she now felt, and the enveloping comfort. Beyond the windowpane the darkness of Berlin was thickening. She pressed her face to the window. She held her breath, to see. Outside, streams of snow were swirling in nautilus curves. She watched them turn, the whorled shapes of a beneficent sky. It seemed too that she heard a faraway sound. Something like a phone disconnected, or the blurred hum in a seashell.

19

Now she returned to where the associations had begun, to Nestorstrasse, Wilmersdorf, 10711 Berlin. Vladimir Nabokov's Nestorstrasse. Marco Gianelli's Nestorstrasse.

The message from Marco told her that Gino was staying for a few nights somewhere near Oranienplatz; would she join him for dinner? Cass all at once felt a kind of trepidation. It was serious now, now that she had spoken of herself, now she had exposed her eccentricities and her odd selection of tales. She must prepare for questions and curiosity and the seductive power of mutual confession. She thought of the curve of his bare back, and her own arms encircling. She thought of how sex both generalises and stipulates, how it was this all-purpose lust, vital and urgent, and this glimpse of an individual, singular spine.

Cass buzzed 'Gianelli' and was admitted to the building. She found the light switch inside the doorway and illuminated the stairs. It was a shabby-looking lobby, stinky and dim, with paint flaking from the walls and a grimy stairwell. Four leaning bicycles crammed the hallway. She climbed nervously to meet him. Waiting in the doorway, Marco hovered above her. Cass looked up and saw his solicitous gaze, and the way he held the door open, bending slightly, and the calm contentment with which he awaited her. He kissed both cheeks, slowly uncoiled her scarf, lifted her coat from her shoulders and ushered her in.

It was a relief to discover that the apartment was stylish and clean. The lobby had suggested depredation and miserable tenants, but Marco's place was orderly, even expensive-looking, in its furnishings and arrangements. In the sitting room there was a wall of bookshelves, stacked full, to which Cass was immediately drawn, and beneath it a beautiful tan sofa and a beechwood coffee table. She stood scanning the titles of the books – a habit she always succumbed to – lost in hasty calculation of his intellectual tastes and predispositions.

'Make yourself comfy,' Marco said.

'Comfy': it was unlike him to sound so casual. On the wall she noticed a Rembrandt print of a small shell she had collected as a child: a cone, or was it perhaps a *volute*?

'Not an original!' Marco sounded happy. He ducked into the small kitchen and returned with wine and two glasses.

'I was worried about you, after the speak-memory. We were all a bit drunk, I think.'

'I was well looked after.'

So they began. There were olives with the wine, a good Bordeaux, and the affable ping of lightly touched glasses. Each sensed a harmony descending, and a recovery of expanded time. Marco said he had returned late from work and apologised in advance, and unnecessarily, for the hasty simplicity of the meal. Cass stood beside him as he stirred a mushroom risotto, and spoke of how as a child he had liked to watch his mother cook.

Their conversation settled, with relaxed irrelevance, around childhood matters. In response to a question about school, Cass told how often in her primary years they were given the plastic template shape of Australia to colour in, and how the fashion among kids was to outline the island in a fringe of blue. 'The Island Continent'. Meticulously schoolchildren indicated feathery ocean, following the irregular coastline, making the island float. It gave her a sense, she said, of the Australian shape as a squat body, set adrift, lost, aimlessly floating. A country all alone. A body all alone. Marco was amused and encouraged her reminiscing.

'I love these details,' he said. 'These past intensities.'

In his primary school – and in Gino's – they were given the shape of the Coliseum to colour. The Ring, they called it. Every Italian child was required to colour the Ring. Marco said he remembered the fearful pleasure of gladiatorial stories, their atrocity and splendour. He remembered the musky smell of pencil shavings and the dank interior of his oak desk.

'Children love stationery,' Marco went on. 'Coloured pencils, with tiny golden writing at one end, the oblong eraser, the little zipped pouch for odds and ends. The metal pencil sharpener, what a brilliant invention . . .'

Cass imagined his curly head bent very close to the paper, colouring with special care within the lines, then pausing only to change pencils, or earnestly to sharpen. The avid hand of a small Roman boy, filling the *Colosseo* with colour.

Soon they were laughing together. Trivial childhood

details blazed carelessly between them. It was all so much easier now, buoyed by their unimportant stories, those that needed to fit no community or explanation.

Only later, much later, did they speak of difficult matters. Marco asked why in her speak-memory Cass had not named her brothers, but for Alexander, and why too she had described herself in such negative terms. She paused before she answered, partly returned to inhibition. Marco did not press or hurry her. Yet when she responded it was easy, and without the anxiety of performance. It occurred to her that she had waited for just this opportunity, to speak at last of her secret, to find relief in the tender satisfaction of telling a single person.

'My brother Alexander was killed,' she said clearly and in a steady tone. 'He was killed in an accident just before I left the north.

'I was twelve, he was thirteen, we were both about to leave at the end of summer for boarding school. There was a cyclone, a fierce one, which swung in from the ocean.'

'I see,' said Marco.

'We were inside with my parents, crouching under the kitchen table, which was bordered with mattresses. We could hear our dog, Nip, barking frantically outside. Nip was running in circles, going completely crazy, and would not be commanded or whistled in. Alexander lunged from our shelter and rushed out into the storm to retrieve him. That's all. That was it. He just ran out into the storm. A falling tree struck him on the side of his head. My father struggled through dangerous winds to locate him, then returned within minutes carrying his wet, bloody body. Together we pulled him beneath the table. We sheltered against the roar of the wind and the shaking of the house.'

Here Cass halted, her voice thinning.

'Blood was draining from Alexander's head. He rested in my mother's lap and I watched her skirt soak red. He was dying then, I know that now. But I felt nothing, really. Not grief, not understanding. I had no sense of consequence, then.

'It took hours for the cyclone finally to pass. When it did, it was dark. We crept from our shelter to find the house half-blasted away. I remember there was a full bright moon, fantastically shiny, and the lighthouse still shone, entirely unharmed, so that in its intervals we could see that everything was wet and shattered, everything was strewn about, everything was destroyed. And everything was beautifully glistening, like polished silver.'

It had been a vision, an anomalously charming vision. Cass knew that this too was part of her shame, that she had found the wreckage alluring.

'My older brothers, Michael and Robert, came back for the funeral, but somehow we didn't dare speak of the cyclone. We didn't speak of Alexander, or of what we had all lost. My parents implicitly prohibited it.

'I chose not to mention the death in my speak-memory, because I was afraid I would cry. And because, during the storm, I had felt such shameful excitement. And because I have never told anyone before, anyone at all.'

She might have been humiliated telling him, or simply relieved, but it was some other kind of feeling – a listlessness, an exhaustion. Soon after she must have fallen asleep, because when she was next conscious, she was in darkness and Marco was snoring beside her. His body seemed to emit an extraordinary heat. His arm was flung heavily across her chest and she experienced a sense of suffocation. She lifted the arm and slid from the bed, making her way to the kitchen, where she switched on the light and filled a glass with water from the tap. Marco's apartment was warmer than hers, and much more comfortable. She stood naked, thin and hard as a candle, wondering how long it would be before she began to shiver.

It was almost frightening to have spoken of the family secret. Perhaps her parents had felt responsible; perhaps this was why they wanted never to acknowledge or speak of it. Perhaps they had loved Alexander best of all their children – she had often thought this, intuited it, even as a child. Standing at the sink, lonesome in the night, Cass was confronted by the question of what is at stake in staying silent or in speaking; by what intimacy with Marco she had created or supposed. She recalled, vividly now, that Alexander's face was unblemished. He had lain in her mother's lap with his eyes placidly closed. They were so still together, mother and son, so apparently eternal. Now, simply remembering, she felt what she had never remembered feeling before. Now she felt ill.

From the kitchen window there was a clear view of Nestorstrasse. Across the road Nabokov's building looked undistinguished. It was a blank façade, stern, with a metallic lunar glow. Like many buildings in Berlin it was possibly a reconstruction, an address, rather than the walls that had actually held him. There was no snow in the sky to entertain or to distract. No cars passed by on wet pillars of light, and there were no clip-clopping pedestrians, abroad so late. Cass saw only the bareness of the night and its ghastly stillness.

In her half-awake reverie, caught by the flowing past, she began to think of Vladimir Nabokov's brother, Sergei. Eleven months younger – as Cass was to Alexander – he had been the doomed, the unsuccessful son. Afflicted with social awkwardness, physical frailty and an incurable stutter, which worsened as he grew, Sergei was also homosexual and an embarrassment to his brother. Vladimir considered him indolent and hedonistic. He despised his bowties and his make-up and his handsome boyfriends, but loved him too, with an inadmissible, furtive affection. Vladimir was safe in America, on a butterfly-hunting expedition, when Sergei died in the Neuengamme concentration camp, just outside Hamburg, in 1945. By all accounts the younger brother, the awkward, the frail, the incurably stuttering brother, the brother who was always slighter and much less successful, exhibited extraordinary bravery during the time of his imprisonment.

Standing at the kitchen window, staring into the night-chasm of Nestorstrasse, Cass in her nakedness began quietly to weep. It may have been self-pity. She was not really sure for whom she wept. Alexander and Sergei conflated into one abstract cause. It was an affectation, or something like it, to mourn a historical figure, brother of a writer, a man famous for his family connection. But looking at the blind windows opposite, and imagining the Nabokovs living there, this amorphous double grief was a convenient displacement. She had sat with Alexander's body, beneath the table, in the roaring wind, and felt an indecent sense of adventure.

She had refused with a lazy soul – an indolent and hedonistic soul, perhaps – to imagine him truly and permanently gone. Now it was easier to attach to a remote historical example. Poor Sergei Nabokov, poor gay war hero. Dramatically taken by the Nazis and killed in 1945.

20

The plan was to meet again at Kępiński's.

After the drunken conclusion to Cass's speak-memory, the group had met in twos or threes to recalibrate their links to each other. Apart from the meeting with the lovers and Karl, and her night spent with Marco, Cass met Victor at an English language bookshop in Prenzlauer Berg. He was still talking of the aquarium: for some reason it had become the ever-ready answer to his directionless search for meaning. He said yet again that he loved the jellyfish as well as the tortoise; that he had sensed the presence of the master; that he had seen in the fluid bluish light some kind of mesmerising confirmation. Did she know that Nabokov had proposed marriage to his seventeen-year-old girlfriend, Svetlana, at the aquarium, in 1923? It was a place of ardour. Ardour, he repeated, tapping the side of his nose like a comedian. For Victor, idiosyncratically fixated, all Berlin turned in a gyre around the liquid centre of the aquarium.

They sat together on a freezing bench not far from the Watertower. Cass had complained to Victor of the macabre element in Nabokov's work, and he responded simply by declaring that it was the joy he read for. Look at the stories, he said, there are murders and deceptions, there are grotesques and mistakes, but there is also humour, a theme of happiness, and the great adventure of being. Victor had quoted one or two of his favourite passages, then Nabokov's aphorism: 'We are the caterpillars of angels.'

'Corny,' said Cass.

'You bet,' said Victor.

'I don't believe in angels.'

'No one does. Kids maybe. Only kids. But in this weary flux of sensations, why not love the enchantment of a symbol? My temperament allows me to pretend. Call me old-fashioned!'

They spoke of imaginative knowledge and the impossible drive to precision. They spoke of the enchantment of symbols, and how the defects of language required a more figurative gesture. At length, Victor asked Cass about her childhood. He liked the detail of the lighthouse, he said; it must have been so *romantic*. No lighthouses in the third ward! There was a lighthouse in New Jersey on the Hudson, a red-and-white-striped candy bar, but it was a tourist site, he said, and good for stoners and skaters. Nothing like a working lighthouse, dominating the night. Cass verified, as best she could, the adequate romance of lighthouses, not lying exactly, but protecting his lustrous vision. He was satisfied with her answers. Pity about the kittens. Poor little kittens. He had a black cat called Sirin that his daughter was looking after back in her apartment in New Jersey. Sirin liked to tear at the furniture, a psycho cat, and attack rival felines and strangers to the house.

Cass had not seen Gino, nor had he contacted her. No one had seen Gino. Marco had met Yukio and Mitsuko at a bar after his work; Mitsuko had texted her saying she guessed of their affair. 'Have you slept together yet?' Cass wondered what had been said to prompt such a direct question. She did not answer, and now felt the offense of exposure and the need for distance.

So they were all orbiting each other. They were a human orrery. The six eccentrics were swinging through deep space in close or faraway circles.

This Kępiński meeting would be easy and carefree; it was the meeting at which they each felt more secure and connected. The completion of the speak-memories had given them access to each other, and paradoxically its formality had strengthened their interconnection. There were inevitably misunderstandings and strange attractions, inevitably misconstruals and hypersensitive reactions, but they could greet each other warmly, and with a kind of love. For all the cynicism their age had bred in them, there were these discoveries of affinity, made simply in speaking and listening.

It was Cass's turn to contribute the alcohol. Since they had all recently suffered the drastic power of spirits, she bought wine, excellent wine, more expensive than she could afford. Marco came by to help her carry it and together they walked to meet the others, escorted through the darkness by the soft chink-chink of the bottles.

She had waited to meet him again, to recommence their conversation. At her disclosure of Alexander's death, Marco had said little other than to offer more or less conventional condolences. But now, on their walk, he said how much the story of her brother's death had shocked and affected him. He had dreamt that night that it was he who was under the table, with the wind spinning around them. It had been his father – looking young, looking a lot like himself – lying dead in the blood-soaked lap of his mother. At some point in the dream they moved to the centre of the Coliseum, with the mad Roman traffic surrounding them in its cacophonous roar. He'd woken with a start, he said, his heart massively pounding.

'I don't usually remember my dreams, except for a rare image or two. And this one, though dramatic, seems somewhat transparent in its meaning . . .'

Cass heard the effort in his voice.

'Almost a cliché,' he went on, as if feeling responsible for the lack of originality in his dream.

This was a closeness, now, that he had spoken of a difficult dream. She understood that they might discuss it later, and that in the bold presumption of dream-logic, symbolically assertive, he had confused his own uncompleted mourning for hers.

The lamplights they passed under cast little radiance, but it was a companionable walk, less dark than either expected. Cass was aware of the rhythm of Marco's limbs and his rapid, light step. The swing of his coat, the steady bulk of his body. She liked walking beside him. Other pedestrians would have thought them a long-term couple; they walked easily together, they were comfortably close.

For her part, something crucial had lifted and shifted. Having spoken finally of Alexander, Cass still felt only relief.

And after the night standing naked at the Nestorstrasse window, stricken by what she had said, desolated by memory, she was now recomposed. Almost sane, she thought wryly. She was now almost sane. Alexander could rest in peace and she could fall in love with Marco. It felt as if she had scooped at a pond of icy water, dashed her face clean, felt a shock intake of breath, and then come suddenly alive.

For once, they all arrived at the apartment at exactly the same time. In threes they rode upwards in Kępiński's small metal lift; Cass with Yukio and Mitsuko, the others following. Gino was looking rumpled and worn, but was making an effort to be sociable, especially with Victor. With exaggerated politeness he was asking Victor about the tortoise, knowing this was the topic that would most engage and delight him. Gino looked across at Cass, who smiled her approval. Accord; there was a sweet if tentative accord. Victor was saying, once again, 'It was really something, that tortoise.' For a literary scholar his expressive powers seemed sometimes rather limited; or perhaps, thought Cass, he had reverted to adolescent wonder, when encounters have their own form of 'something' that exceeds description.

Cass sat next to Marco, who was explaining the German expression '*toi, toi, toi*'. 'It's like saying "touch wood",' he explained, 'but it represents the sound of spitting. And since we are all superstitious, perhaps we can bless this meeting with a traditional German spit: *toi, toi, toi*. Lucky. It will make us all lucky.'

They laughed. Jointly they felt both happy and non-German. There had been times all were aware of their exclusion and foreignness, but now asked to speak of Berlin they set about summoning a connection. Marco said, 'Let's have a free-for-all.'

'Fountains!' said Mitsuko.

'The Stattbad,' said Yukio.

Victor paused. 'You all know mine: the Berlin Aquarium.'

'Gino?'

'Too many sites to choose one. Perhaps the Anhalter station. Or the Cemetery of the Nameless.'

There was an uneasy silence. To fill it Cass said, 'The trains, U-Bahn and S-Bahn, and all those stations along the way.'

'I'm a bit like Gino,' Marco said. 'Hard to choose. But I shall start with Bebelplatz.'

Each was enjoined to say a little more.

'So me first,' said Mitsuko. She was dressed in jeans and a jumper, as was Yukio. Cass was surprised to see them appear so unexceptional.

'There are so many fountains in Berlin. I noticed them straight away when we arrived in the summer, because people clustered there, and there were children bathing and frolicking, and because so many seemed frivolous, and even comical, in this very serious city. They have no water now, of course, because it would freeze in the pipes. Everybody knows the golden deer on the pedestal in Schöneberg, but there is a four-penguin fountain in Boxhagener Platz; a yawning rhino in Friedrichshain; and a frog fountain in Mitte: so many creatures! In Leon-Jessel-Platz, not far from here, there's a huge toadstool; and in Barbarossaplatz there's a fountain that features eight babies, all sitting in a circle staring at a spray of water. Cute! My favourite is the Medusa head in Henriettenplatz. It's a great monstrous thing, extremely ugly, and I can imagine it would give any child nightmares. It's a severed head, just stuck there on the pavement with the usual Gorgon snakes for hair and bulging sad eyes. When I first saw it I wasn't really sure what it was. And each time I look at it now, it's still something of a riddle.'

Mitsuko was pleased with herself. She had shared her fervour. Yukio followed.

'I make a blog in Japanese. It is called "Japan in Berlin". And I tweet, and have Facebook with many, many friends. So, I have many stories for Berlin and they are all sent to Japan. The Stattbad in Wedding was a swimming pool; now it's a club. Now you can dance in the pool to super-cool DJs. There's a basement room, with tunnels and taps and old water pipes; but Mitsuko and I love to dance in the swimming pool. The sunken dance floor means that the low sound . . .'

Yukio played air-guitar. 'Bass,' Mitsuko said.

'The bass is very boom-boom; there is a feeling of being in another world.'

'Truly,' said Mitsuko.

Victor was entirely affable, with his tortoise affirmed. What more to say? He sat back in his chair, holding his thin belly like a sage enlightened.

'The other world is those living beings who carry their own lives inscrutably. We gawp at animals in the zoo, and fish in the aquarium, with little thought they gawp back, and see in our looks another strangeness. Do you know I'd never been to an aquarium before? And this one – perhaps it's not special at all, because I have no comparisons – this one was such a joy.'

This was Victor's word, thought Cass, *joy.* This was a man who had retained some early skill, the ineffable pleasure a child feels – lavish and quick – when a butterfly alights on the back of her hand. He was unafraid of expressive emotion, its metaphors and its forms of knowing.

Gino hesitated in the face of Victor's delight in his own location, but when he spoke his voice was languid and thoughtful.

'Anhalter Bahnhoff. It used to be the largest railway station in Europe and Hitler wanted it to be one of the centres of "Germania". The architecture was grand, all arches and round windows, and the building massive, with a magnificent façade. More cathedral than station. An underground tunnel connected it to a fancy hotel, "The Excelsior", and the whole construction was entirely luxurious. Of course, it was bombed in the war and today there's only one fragment of wall, standing alone. There are three circular windows, up high, and three empty arches. It's in the middle of open ground and looks pitifully abandoned.'

'Theresienstadt,' Victor said. 'It was the point of departure for Jews being sent to Theresienstadt.'

'Yes,' said Gino. 'So many stations in Berlin, even the glamorous ones, have these awful dark histories. And it's hard to feel sentimental with the Topography of Terror just around the corner. But this ruin interests me because it is so meagre and nihilistic: it speaks of emptiness and demolition. The ruin above, the tunnel below. It represents something fundamental to what we meet here, in this city.'

Mitsuko and Yukio did not know this ruin, they said. Cass was recalling when she had first seen it, and her sense of bewilderment. She had expected more, somehow – more ruin, more remains.

Cass considered Gino's contribution corrupted by romanticism. She would say so, afterwards. But she was chastened by the knowledge that she was also attracted to sites of destruction, and to empty spaces, to havoc, and to things broken persisting.

'My sense of Berlin is entirely dominated by the trains. I carry the route map in my head and think often of the shape of the city, and how essentially it is netted and webbed by the rails. There's a sense of a circulatory system, a sense of the conveyance of energies and the very pulse of life. I like the shadowy, tiled U-stations, with their varying fonts and colours, the familiar smell in there, so thickly human, and the loud sounds of the trains coming and going. The iron arcades of the S-stations are beautiful too, and I have a special fondness for the green struts and arches of Eberswalder and Schönhauser Allee. There is something both old-worldly and futuristic in the vision of overground rail – and the rise of the tracks across the city, the curve past buildings and highways, and the way they make an extra, and another, architectural level . . .'

'Dahlem-Dorf,' said Victor, 'with its fairytale station building. And the Gothic script names on the S25.'

'Or that little station in Schöneberg, with the lake outside.' Mitsuko's favourite, clearly.

It may have been that each of them was mentally entering their station. City portal and place mark, and the satisfaction of a punctual train. Cass knew she had summoned communal imagining, had invited them to salute their especial station.

'I'm interested,' Marco was sounding more serious, 'in memorials. Berlin has many, of course. One of the least conspicuous is the rows of empty bookshelves underground in Bebelplatz. They commemorate the book burning there by the Nazis in 1933. It's such a simple thing, the empty bookshelves. Have you seen it?'

Only Victor knew of the Bebelplatz bookshelves. 'Best seen at night because of the supernatural glow.'

'Yes, you peer into a lit square, as down a deep well, and you see only empty shelves. I like the simplicity of this installation, and the accuracy of the idea.'

Marco fell silent. He rose and stood staring at the window, as if he expected a book to materialise there. The window was black and opaque. No text would emerge. They watched him, their leader, wondering what would come next.

'To books!' toasted Victor. His voice flew up to the ceiling.

Dear Victor, funny Victor. They all toasted books.

Then, sounding like Groucho, and holding up an invisible cigar, he asked in a briskly slapstick tone, 'So who was this guy Kępiński, anyway?'

21

It would seem like handwriting in snow, or in the breath adhering to a windowpane. There would be no visible trace. The obliterations of winter had use-value, after all. Later she would remember how still the day had been, how all motion but snowfall had seemed abruptly to stop.

They had all agreed to two weeks without any meetings, to recover their lives apart. Cass missed Marco much more than she expected, but enjoyed the white radiance of the winter and the return to her own preoccupations. Gradually the city was unfolding for her; she saw that she might know herself more subtly here, that the pressure of history, imposed like a spy mission, required her to develop a kind of inner sincerity. Small in the face of a terrible history, foreign, young, uncool, antipodean, she might find here an expression of her accumulated questioning. It was a challenge, she decided; there was a logic she must achieve, there were encryptions, there were passwords, there were possible solutions. Not only the train system, but littered everywhere: signs and symbols, implications.

When Cass arrived for their next meeting at Kępiński's

building, Marco and Gino were outside, standing beneath a lamp in the cold dark, smoking on the pavement. Both greeted her warmly. In the aqueous brown lamplight Gino looked wild-eyed and hyper. Cass saw how altered he seemed in so short a time. He looked thinner, pale; his body and mind on the errant edge of crystal meth impulses and tics. But he was also friendly and somewhat crazily verbose; as if wanting to entertain, he greeted her with a racy description of their train ride.

Marco touched Cass's cheek as he gave the formal greeting, a sign of all that still remained unspoken and hidden. It was a claim, she understood, and a promissory gentleness. Gino noticed the gesture. When he leant into the hello kiss he seized Cass's forearm and gripped. She decided simply to ignore him.

They could not use Kępiński's, Marco said: another agent from his company would be showing someone around. They needed an alternative. He suggested they meet in Cass's apartment, since it was the closest option, only a ten-minute walk away. Marco and Gino would wait and tell the others. Cass would go ahead, and return to her studio.

It was foolish, she knew, but she felt anxiety at the idea of them all gathered in her single room. The ignominy of it. Her poor, undecorated existence. Practical trivia was rushing through her brain: she had only two wine glasses. Four could be seated, two on the bed, two on chairs; the others, she and Yukio perhaps, could sit with pillows on the floor. She must duck into a shop on the way to buy more glasses. She must buy snacks and more alcohol, just in case. It alarmed her to have been given this role so casually, and with no time for preparation. Indignantly she thought

Marco should have suggested a café; and why did she not have the presence of mind to recommend and insist on it? She felt her privacy was to be invaded, just as she had, rather meanly, when Yukio and Mitsuko arrived.

How then would she describe it all, if she was compelled?

It had begun well enough. They had arrived in one group, clomping up the stairwell, their voices echoing upbeat in the narrow and dreary space. They all shrugged off their coats, sprinkled with snow: it must have begun to fall again soon after she'd arrived home. There was the damp smell they brought with them, and slightly loud exclamations at the novelty of a fast walk all together to the new location. Cass offered them tea to warm up and the lovers both said yes. Gino was picking up her books, scanning them without permission, moving restlessly, back and forth, as he flicked through random pages. He scratched at the back of his hands and was evidently agitated. Victor stood alone looking out of the window, peering with a frown into the dark, sunken square of the cemetery, and Marco was busy opening wine bottles at the sink. They were crowded, she felt it; they all felt the pressure of confinement. Mitsuko sat on the bed sipping her tea; Marco soon joined her. As anticipated, she and Yukio were seated on the floor. She will remember that Yukio lolled a little, as if half-asleep; he may have been stoned. She will remember the shine of hot water in his teacup, a perfect circle of shine, one of those entirely incidental images that in retrospect returns as a small, certain thing.

So, what did they speak of? There were Nabokov stories:

Victor was pleased to tell them that Nabokov shared his rooms in Cambridge with someone called Kalashnikov. Like the Hitler-pansy story there seemed to be no point, other than Victor's literary delight at the unusual association. Gino visibly sneered. Marco thought perhaps they should all nominate 'transparent things': those according to Nabokov through which history mysteriously shines; those objects that carry time past or the ghosts of our childhoods. Bright things, he said, metaphysically admitting light. There were no takers, this time. No one wanted prescribed conversation or Marco's intellectual guidance. He accepted quietly and poured more wine.

Mitsuko spoke of how Nabokov had loved to go to movies in the cinema palaces around the Gedächtniskirche; how sad it was that they'd left the bombed ruins of the old church standing. Better gone, she insisted. Better to start again. Ruins are too sad. Sometimes forgetting is better than remembering.

Yukio, awoken by tea, said that he liked the sporty Nabokov – the man who broke his ribs and was knocked unconscious playing goalie for a football team at Fehrbelliner Platz. When he came to, Yukio added, they'd had to prise the ball from his frozen grip. They were all quiet then for a moment, contemplating this image of their writer, parting the air with his body, sideways flung; the writer with his two arms outstretched, seizing the ball from its fleet arc, just as his extra-clever head struck the waiting goalpost.

Such disconnected conversation; such irresponsible idleness.

And what had she spoken of? Cass could not remember. But she remembered the tone and the content of Gino's speech. In the studio together they became very warm. Cass saw that Gino was edgy, sweating and ill at ease. He scratched at his chest and had trouble sitting still. He was drinking quickly. There was a sense they all shared of the dissolution of narrative order; there was a decline to arid blather and unacknowledged tensions. Conversation at some point turned unexpectedly taut. Sentences seemed to twang in the air; there was the strain of pulled wire and the threat of something retracting with a vicious whip of release. A prolix energy emerged, a warp factor that may have been a consequence of their lack of structure and ceremony.

Then Gino made his speech. Biochemical mixture fuelled an articulate hostility. Unprovoked, he stood and spoke in a hissing, loud voice. No one dared interrupt.

'We are all shits, my friends. We are all literary snobs in this vicarious little room of our own, dilettantish, smug, hidden from the fucked-up world. We are enslaved to the folly and the whirlpool of our own obsessions. Where is *now* rather than our own deeply intoxicating pasts? Where is Lampedusa, where is the tragedy of others? What do we think of a man playing "Nessun Dorma" on a saw in the shadows of a U-station? The lost homeless in Kreuzberg, the drug pushers in Gorlitzer Park, the illegally immigrant prostitutes, freezing their arses at Hackescher Markt? And all the other foreigners, wretched foreigners, who don't have wine and company? Why do we meet for this writer who laments his lost Russia, when losses are everywhere, and always inestimable? We adore him because we find some cracked mirror there, we think that words will save us, that a fine description will drag us away from our own disap-pointments, and offer consolation, or explanation, or the return of a disappeared father. We want to cancel our nothingness with his vigour of incarnation, we want to believe, truly believe, in literary salvation. Who else tells us that a twig reflected in a puddle in the middle of a black pavement is worthy of our notice? That it looks like an undeveloped photograph, that it symptomises something inside us, that it reminds us of the entanglements of words and things and reflections; that we must all notice the withering as well as the blossoming; and that the immortal gesture is always present and exists inside the word . . .'

There was a stunned silence. Cass was struck less by the anger than by the eloquence of the speech. It was Victor who rose and gently took Gino by the elbow. Gino pulled instinctively away, but then submitted when Victor insisted and tried again, leaning in close and whispering something that none of them could hear. If it was a reconciliation of some kind, it was quiet and easy; they saw Victor summon verbal authority against Gino's unfocused fury. There was kindness in Victor's manner, and a gentle fatherly command. They saw Gino's shoulders sag, then he moved into Victor's embrace. The two men stood there, silently communing. They made a strange sight: Gino was so much taller than Victor, yet he was the one supported.

After a few seconds they turned, pulled open the glass door and stepped out together onto Cass's small balcony. Gino lit up and Victor remained with him, talking. They appeared to float together outside in the semi-darkness. The tiny star of Gino's cigarette appeared only when he inhaled. The flare, then the shadow of his arm, falling to his side, faint light from the studio only partially revealing them.

The others watched, transfixed, then slowly and surely, and in a tone of concern, they began talking quietly among themselves. It reminded Cass of the decorum of a funeral, where there is one exceptionally grieved person, comforted singularly and especially, and others hover at a distance, knowing for certain that their own pain cannot possibly be so great.

Without warning, Gino raised his voice, and then he was shouting in Italian. They were not sure what he said, but his tone was angry. A black ferocity possessed him. In profile they saw him push forcefully at Victor's chest, then push again. They saw him lift Victor up and onto the iron edge of the balcony, balance him for a second or two on the railing, and then let him fall. Simply that. Gino lifted Victor, rested him, and then let him fall. It must have been a surge of incredible strength and perverted will. Victor seemed to offer no word or physical resistance – he was there balancing, seeming inanimate, teetering over nothingness, and then he was gone.

There was a moment of delayed response, in which nothing was felt, or could be felt, at such an incomprehensible act.

Gino was at first motionless, outside, looking over the edge down to the street, then the glass doors burst open, and he stood before them, guilty. Nothing could be said. Gino's mouth was slightly open at his own shock and derangement. His face was unearthly white and his expression distracted. Marco pushed past him in a great rush to witness the fallen body. They all knew it without seeing: Victor had crashed and was shattered.

'Oh Jesus,' Gino was saying. 'Oh Jesus, oh Jesus.'

Mitsuko was already sobbing and Yukio had his arm around her. He appeared to screen her eyes with his hand, as though the sight of Gino was too awful. Cass saw Gino's desperation and stepped forward to touch him. But there was ice in him now; he was stiff and remote, glittering with his own act and its terrible enormity.

In a tight voice Marco said, 'We must call an ambulance, the police.' But instantly Gino wailed, 'No, no!' And again they were stopped in time, two men halted and confused, robbed of the strength of sensible volition and rational decision. The room filled with the sound of Mitsuko's hollow sobs.

How much time passed? In truth none was sure, none would be able to say. There was a magnified quality to their responses, and a stylisation, yet all was hopelessly fixed, somehow, in inactivity and indecision. Marco argued with Gino, but nothing moved forward. There was a knock at the door, then the alarming pound of a fist, and they all returned to the present.

'Jesus, oh Jesus.'

Cass opened the door and saw not the faces of *polizei* or strangers, but Karl, sturdy Karl. In the hallway light he looked unusually solid, monumental. He was heaving from a hasty climb up the stairs.

'We must get the body inside, into my room,' he said.

The body. He had said it – he had called Victor a body. The directness and lucidity of his statement was scandalous.

And already Marco was trying to rewrite history.

'It was an accident,' Marco pleaded. 'I was talking to him on the balcony and he leant backwards onto the slippery railing.'

But Karl was not listening. 'Come,' he commanded.

Why had Karl arrived? Why would he involve himself in their affairs? Cass wondered if she was the only one feeling such puzzlement. Yet having been shocked, and stuck, they were now overcome with the momentum of authority.

They followed mute and miserable. The six of them, the new six, filed down the stairwell, saying nothing. Karl had asked no questions and seemed simply activated by his chore and the pressing need to tidy up. He was focused and deliberative. The others were united in blank disbelief and the altered speed of the world, together with their own rising fear, which came in sickening surges.

In Karl's room Mitsuko refused to sit, so Yukio waited with her, held in his arms. Karl led Cass, Marco and Gino out into the night. Gino held back, but was also compelled. He was riven by the need to see and not to see, and so too Cass and Marco needed to confirm what they dreaded, if only to meet a settled image when so many were uprising as possibilities.

Such a beautiful night. New snow was everywhere, lightly fallen, and it collapsed in soft crunchy pits beneath their feet. None had taken a coat as they left, so they stood unprotected in the cold. Yet it seemed appropriate somehow, that they should feel the sting and the risk of it, that their bodies at this moment should feel frail and assaulted. They all looked around anxiously. No one. No one visible. There was not a soul on the street. It was possible that no one at all had seen. On so cold a night, and so late, everyone was indoors. A body might hurl from above, darkly and undetected.

Victor was lying face up, a brazen corpse. This was the first surprise. Cass had somehow not expected to see his face. 'Unblemished' was the word that sprang to mind, and she hated herself for the instant comparison. Victor's head was ringed with blood, in a slick, bright halo, and his eyes were fixed open, snowflakes falling shallow inside them. Tiny crystals glittered there, giving a semblance of live alertness. Cass bent to her knees. She moved very near to his face. She closed the eyes with her hand as she had seen done in the movies. A gentle push at the eyelids was all it took, then a little more pressure, a calm resting of the fingers. The bushy moustache was also covering with snow; she wiped it away. Gino gave a little groan and rushed back inside. Karl and Marco lifted the body, Karl at the feet and Marco with his arms hooked under Victor's, while Cass continued to brush snow from his still-warm face, delicately, carefully, with her open palm. She was still brushing, as if it would make any difference, when Victor was lowered onto a blanket Karl had hastily spread on the floor of his room. Marco reached for Cass's hand and held it firmly, in silent command, to stop her brushing movement, then pulled one corner of the rug over Victor's face. Now that he was a shape, not Victor, it should have been easier. But Cass felt a rising, queasy, ungovernable panic. This was the second surprise. That it was the hidden face that truly panicked her.

In whatever madness they were enduring, Karl had taken over. He telephoned his son, Franz, speaking far too loud. There was a garbled conversation.

'Truck . . . Now.'

'No, now.'

'Yes, yes.'

No one stopped Karl and called the police. No one wanted to be blamed, but all felt implicated and guilty. Later it would seem impossible, entirely inexplicable, that they had become so passive and indecisive, that the repercussion of Victor's fall had made them all crumple like children, that without discussion or decision they had let Marco and Karl take control.

Gino was by now curled alone in a corner. Cass saw that he held Victor's spectacles; he must have found them in the snow. Mitsuko and Yukio remained together, facing away. Karl offered them all a shot of vodka, but only Marco accepted. They clinked glasses – a habit, surely, but a vile gesture in the circumstances – and drank. Cass saw the blood on Marco's hands and shirt and held up her own hands in a mute sign, like a Muslim blessing. Wash, she was signing. *Wash your hands*. She too had a tidying instinct, and wanted death cleared away, wanted it all put right, wanted the night to stop spinning.

It was Cass who offered to return upstairs and retrieve their coats and scarves. She found her own coat and put it on, drawing it close, then with the bulky bundle stood for a minute outside her door thinking what a comfort it would be, to have their warm clothes with them. The blast of freezing night air had seemed extreme, but it might have been shock, or the sensitivity of her nervous condition. She remembered how death changed everything, time and space, the significance of small objects and creature comforts. Death had its own weather. Death was uncontrollable as cyclones. She reeled a little, unsteady, as she descended the stairs. In those few moments alone carrying the coats, cautious and silent, relieved to have her own chore to perform, relieved to be active, not still, she experienced a sudden sense of her own life congealing. Alexander had also been wrapped in a cloth – not a blanket, but a curtain, pulled from beneath a fallen window frame. Her father had lifted the heavy frame to extract it. She saw him now, pulling at the fabric carefully to keep it intact. Was he crying? He may have been crying. Her usually reserved father may have been crying. The curtain bore a decoration of autumn leaves of a kind she had never actually seen – European leaves of an unbelievable orange, regularly shed in unbelievable seasons. They matched her sense then of things misaligned and incredible. The shape of her beloved brother, wrapped in a decorative cliché that meant nothing; the expedient offence of it, the simplification.

When the truck arrived – old and rusty and rattling down the street – the man who climbed from the driver's seat looked a lot like Karl. He shook hands with Marco, only Marco, selecting him as the leader, or the one inherently blameworthy. Perhaps too, she thought later, Franz had been told about Marco, or perhaps he had come to help out of a brotherly instinct for the medical condition they shared. Perhaps Karl had bribed him in some way, or offered to pay for his assistance. Cass would never know. The handshake was like the clink of vodka glasses, unseemly and incongruous. Franz acknowledged the others only with a brief nod of his head. His manner was businesslike, gruff and dourly preoccupied. They all noticed he had the gait of an injured man, leaning to the right and slightly lurching.

For now, they piled in, Marco up-front next to Gino and Franz, she with Mitsuko, Yukio and Victor in the back. Seated with her back against the cold metal, her legs outstretched, it was Cass who held Victor. There, in the trembling tray, surrounded by ropes and tackle and an indistinct smell of raw meat, she held the precious shape of his head in her lap. They pulled away into the night. They did not know where they were going. They did not know why they were in the truck, or what unspoken obligation bound them to this reckless response. Cass's last glimpse, before Franz lowered the metal roller door, was of Karl shovelling red snow into a plastic bucket, still busily tidying up the scene of the death.

22

The third surprising thing was that they had all accompanied Franz.

It would have made sense if they had dispersed, all gone their own way; it would have made sense, of course, if they had rung the police, and told a credible and exculpating story. But instead they consented without discussion to go together with a stranger, to who-knows-where, in the darkness, in a noisy old truck. Having no burden of consistency in their experimental community, they now slipped into a genre, into driven action, not reflection. They cancelled disquiet for deed; they wanted a procedure, a decisiveness that would take Victor away. In the future there would be no consoling explanation – in the disgrace of the event they were simply cowardly and passive. There will be fleeting moments in which they will consider otherwise, what might have happened if they had acted in a manner more responsible; but for now an irrevocable plot had taken over, now they were compromised, and submissive, and must pretend they knew what they were doing.

The cold metal floor of the truck was almost painful to sit on. The air was foetid, freezing and horribly closed and Cass felt woozy with dread and the weight of the death that she held. Mitsuko was quiet. Yukio was wide awake, but lost in the world of his own thoughts. Now and then light from outside entered the crack beneath the back door, but for most of the journey they were riding in almost total darkness. They did not say a word. They were still a group then; they were still hypothetically together. For all that it was a nonsensical circumstance and fate, they had without question and in unanimity joined forces with Gino.

The truck drove for too long. They felt it slow, start again, enter traffic, swerve away. They felt confined, like prisoners. There was no way of knowing where in Berlin they were heading. Blind journeying carried its own kind of fear and Cass was overcome by grim misgivings. When at last the truck stopped, she felt enormous relief. Now she would know what they were doing, what plan Franz and Marco had hatched. She heard the front doors creak open, then she heard them bang shut. The truck shuddered. Footfall, and then the unlocking of the metal door: Franz flung the door up into its roller with the emphatic gesture of a conductor at the end of a huge symphony. Marco and Gino were standing close, and each by prior arrangement took charge of the blanketed body. Neither spoke. They lifted Victor down between them, and only then did Cass and the lovers descend.

'Where are we?' She needed to know.

'It's the Havel,' said Marco, 'the river. Near the canal.'

It was snowing densely but she made out the city lights in the distance. They were near the bank of the river in what seemed to be a wild space of rubbish and dead wood, surrounded by sentinel, leafless trees. Franz switched on a torch so that she saw the swing of a yellow beam and stripes of snow flurry briefly aflame. But it was a mystifying dark they inhabited, away from street lamps, semi-erased, and full of slow-moving snow. There was the sense of texture around them, of drifting presences, as if the air was remade with another substance, as if the air itself was altered and atomically changed. And cold. Bitter cold.

In the distance the water shone with plates of ice, jagged near the shore. Further out lay a stretch of profound deep black. Something inside Cass crumbled, subsided and gave way.

'Not here,' she said to Marco.

'Further up. A clean space, I promise.'

Franz offered no help with the body, but seemed to be lugging over his shoulder a lump of iron – an anvil, was it? – attached to a soft-clinking chain.

'This isn't right,' said Cass in a small voice. But Marco and Gino continued to walk ahead, disappearing into the dark, carrying Victor's body. As she watched them ignore her, she experienced a flash of outrage.

'Stop!' she called out.

Their faint shapes turned. They all stopped. The anvil glinted on Franz's back.

'This isn't right. We haven't discussed this. You're going to throw Victor in the river? Just like that, like garbage?'

A gash had opened in the night, an intimation of atrocity. Around them were the stiff shapes of bare branches and the night shadows of unfamiliar woods. There was something underfoot Cass couldn't name, something compressed and uneven. She heard the chain metallically rattle as Franz moved his burden.

'You don't understand,' Gino shouted. His voice was shattering in the cold night air. And they had already begun moving on, they were turning away from her.

'Stop!' It was Mitsuko this time. It was Mitsuko who yelled her anxiety into the night, who wanted to halt whatever morbid plot was unfolding.

They saw the shadows of Gino and Marco halt. Franz swung the torch again; his yellow light faltered, as he did. They saw its dispersed beam concentrate and turn downwards, the cone focused brightly at his feet.

'What are we doing here?'

'What?' It was Gino again, sounding angry.

'What are we doing here?'

Ahead, Marco and Gino lowered the body. Franz remonstrated. Cass heard the German word 'hurry'. Gino stood his ground, but Marco was slowly approaching them.

'Gino can't return to prison,' said Marco. 'We must do this for him. We can't leave him alone to deal with this. We've come this far.'

There was no explanation of 'prison'. He was speaking urgently and fast. But in the effort to sound reasonable his voice was almost tearful. It was overwrought with too much yet unexplained. What story was this they had entered, or failed to enter? What might both men be attempting to conceal?

Yukio called out, 'Fuck you, Gino! Fuck you!'

His face was caught by the disc of the torch: Franz had returned without them noticing.

And then Gino, propelled with furious distress, sped

from the darkness and threw himself onto spotlit Yukio. It was a sudden rough tackle, a frightened will to hurt, so that Yukio fell backwards into the snow and the two men were rolling together. Gino was attempting ineffectually to pummel Yukio's face, lifting his fist, pushing wildly, heavily flailing. There were grunts and hard thwacks, but it was more a wrestle of two boys, with nothing much occurring but impotent rage. Within seconds, Gino had stopped. He was suddenly still, lying on top of his opponent, heaving, sobbing.

'I'm sorry, Yukio,' he blubbered. 'Sorry. So sorry.'

In a single move Franz had seized Gino's jacket and lifted him upwards, forcing him into a headlock and pulling down on his own wrist to tighten the pressure. Yukio clambered sideways to upright himself. Under his breath, he let out a curse in Japanese. Beside him, Mitsuko was brushing rapidly at his coat and flicking wet flakes of snow from his hair. As Franz loosened his grip, Gino sank groggy to his knees. Cass could not bring herself to comfort Gino; and now he wept without restraint, apart and undone. There was a slow settling down and a slower reunification.

They all stayed there looking downwards, seized in tense indecision.

'We have to do this,' whispered Marco. 'But it can just be Gino and me. You can all go now. You can wait for us in the truck.'

He spoke like one rebuked. They heard his uncertainty. Again, Gino sobbed. They saw that Marco was shivering. He paused to blow air into the shell of his cold cupped hands.

Mitsuko and Yukio were conferring in Japanese. Cass stood alone, stupefied. In the end a peculiar solidarity

213

overtook them. In the end they trudged together into the darkness with the body of their friend. Gino was hopelessly distraught so Yukio took over, carrying Victor with Marco. Victor made a neat bundle. Mitsuko and Cass flanked Gino; now they were holding his hands, almost pulling, in a half-dragging grip. Ahead, Franz walked lopsided, leading the way to a narrow path, and down to the water. His torchlight was pallid and skewed and let nothing in the world remain stable.

What she would remember was the unusual clarity of the words and actions that followed. The snowfall had eased to an uneven sprinkle. In its place was scintillating night and a smothered calm. Now they heard the sound of their own footsteps, crunching the new snow, and the rasp and effort of their own frozen breathing. Somewhere a stream of traffic issued a blurry, murmurous hum, somewhere meaningful life was still going on, warm and oblivious. Cass thought of Victor's flecked face, *unblemished*, his eyes wide open; she thought of Karl shovelling snow, of the drive closed inside the truck, and of the form, Victor's form, resting in her lap. She thought only in questions of how the night had accelerated to this, this trudge into a death zone, this despicable trudge. Snowdrift was piled at an angle against what looked like the remains of a wall. What was it doing here, what purpose might it serve? Symbols resolved round her, the contraction of time felt like a noose.

Yet there was no more protestation. They acted as one group. At the bank of what might have been the river or the canal, they looked over ice that lay unnaturally flat and shining on the water. Franz swung the anvil around his head and lobbed it onto the black ice. There was a sharp cracking sound as the ice plate broke apart. It broke as if a mirror, spiked and dangerous. Franz pulled back his missile, hauling it hand over hand as one would an anchor, then flung it again. It rose higher this time, a mean dangerous missile, and came down in the darkness with another loud crack. Then he instructed, 'Now. Now the body can go under.'

They all paused. Gino had fallen silent. It was the moment in which they might all have come to their senses, but there was a drive now to completion, and a sense of inevitable mission. With bent, sorrowful heads Yukio and Marco weighted the body with Franz's anvil. They wound the chain around the feet and rested the block of iron in the centre, on what was still his belly. Victor's belly. Taking one end each they heavily swung, then swung again, and then let go. The body arced only a little and landed hard on the ice; and they all looked with alarm at what fell there but did not immediately disappear. Franz prodded a plate of ice with his foot, and they saw the form list slightly as the shelf tilted, then tilted a little more. Across the shine of angled ice, Victor slid into the water. There was less a splash than a sound like a mouth opening and closing. Then bubbles breaking at the surface, like evidence of posthumous words. Then nothing at all.

A little wind had risen, so the light snow began to turn. They were heading back to the truck, quiet, each enclosed in their own deep misery, when Marco asked them to stop. Franz kept on walking, his torch wobbling, insecure, and they watched as his swooping angles of light took him separately and further away. The friends stood in a circle, finding their night vision, so that they might look directly into each other's funereal faces. They oddly resembled each other:

Gino and Marco, Yukio and Mitsuko. In snowlight Cass saw that they were radically alike. Each had dark eyes that twinkled like aluminium foil; each the same pinched guilty face, tight and withdrawn.

Marco gave a little speech, absurdly formal in the circumstances. He said that the death of any human was without metaphor or likeness. The death of any human was incomparable. It was not a writerly event. It was not contained within sentences. It was not to be described in the same way as the beauty of an icicle, or three wrinkles parallel on the forehead of a remembered governess, or the play of shadow and light on a swimming body, or the random harmony of trifles that was a parking meter, a fluffy cloud and a tiny pair of boots with felt spats.

He said Victor's name. Beloved Victor. He said, 'Rest in Peace, Victor.' They remained silent. No one else could speak. They were as specks in the dark of a shocking event. Then, in a tiny voice, Mitsuko said, 'Umbrella, umbrella.'

Ferrule, Cass thought. The release of something deadly.

The headlamps of the truck flicked on and off, on and off, their sickly glow both faint and far-reaching. It was Franz, annoyed, signalling them to return. They stood a little longer, ignoring him, stuck in a star of five. Cass heard a low susurration that might have been a phantom whisper, but then realised, coming to her senses, that it was traffic, Berlin traffic, distant and mechanical and streaming away.

23

When she walked into her studio, hardly vertical, completely exhausted, Cass saw that the glass doors to the balcony had been left open. No one had thought to close them. In the hectic aftermath of Gino's crime, they had all fled her room as though it was contaminated. Now weather had entered; the outside had swept in. Snow from the balcony had been blown in streaks across the floor and the edges of her little world had been made indistinct. She stood for a few seconds in rapt attention to this evidence of a new state: no geometry of flakes but a chaos of elements, no poetic impulse, but disgust and ruination. The tense shimmer, the snowy sky, was an unbearable thing.

The room was sub-zero. Her spirit was lost. Cass pushed the balcony doors closed and leant for a moment against them, as if holding back a still clotting darkness. Keeping her coat and scarf on, ignoring the mess of their meeting, and the puddles on the floor, she collapsed into her bed, made herself as warm as she could, and lay defeated, in a tired pile. She drew her body into as tight a shape as possible, abbreviating herself, becoming smaller and smaller. And almost immediately, perfectly still, she fell into a deep, dreamless sleep.

Cass had kept Marco away, and insisted she could return alone to her studio apartment. But in the morning it was he whom she thought of first. Not Victor. Not Gino. Not the dark ceremony by the river. She wanted an explanation of the events of the night. Outside, the sky was white, but no snow fell. It was a dead-looking day. When she turned on her phone there were several messages waiting, flicked open in a radiant, expectant rectangle. 'Come.' 'Come now. Please.' These had been sent an hour ago. Cass wasn't ready for conversation, or the sound of his voice, so she messaged Marco simply, 'I'm on my way.' She stayed in yesterday's clothes, not even bothering with fresh underwear, and drank a glass of water. She was not hungry. She was numb and feeling empty. She brushed her teeth and washed in haste, withdrawing from the mirror and the glimpse of her pale foreign face.

There was no sign outside the building. Karl had indeed cleaned away death. Cass looked discreetly as she left, seeking bloodstains or a dropped article, and wondered if he now watched her, half-concealed behind his window. She would not turn around to acknowledge him. At this moment he was someone whom it would pain her to acknowledge. Guided by Marco's message, driven in his direction, she felt again relieved to have a chore when all around her felt tumultuous.

Last night's snow was banked high along the streets. The roads were churning into black slush, and cars were becoming smeared, but there was still a purity and cleanliness to the fallen drifts and mounds. A few children with sleds were playing in the park near the cemetery. There was just enough of a rise to give them the velocity of a slide. They shouted in high squeals and ran with the energy of small dogs. She saw them veer and twist and fall laughing from their sleds. They fell, and rose again. They chased each other up the inclines and then flew excited and atremble into the waiting arms of their parents. It was archetypal in its appeal, this liberated play, this return again and again to a loving embrace. Pock shapes of small footprints threaded up the slope, lovely in their regular spacing.

A snowman had been built. The simple white form, corpulent and skewed, stood in the centre of the park, commanding his own mini-kingdom. There were sticks for the fingers and a halo of stick rays springing from its head. It had a crucified shape, Cass thought, and then she reproached herself for so vulgar an exaggeration. It would be like this for a while; signs would correlate and extend, there would be a deathliness to ordinary bodies and a kind of pathology to associations.

Cass was walking north, in the direction of Marco's apartment, when she saw the U-Bahn sign of Viktoria-Luise-Platz. She was fond of the U4, a short, old-fashioned line, the station a slightly antiquarian monument in green and white tiles. Victor had loved it too. It occurred to her that she might ride the U4, change at Nollendorfplatz to the U2, then pay a quick visit to the aquarium before she saw Marco. It was already late enough, the aquarium would be open, and it was a way of thinking about Victor not within the confines of the group, but exclusively, as only she had seen and known him. Victor was demanding attention, like Hamlet's father; he was ghosting her thoughts.

Cass entered the underground and was carried away. The ride was a blur. As she emerged at the busy Zoo station she was overcome with a clear sensation of retrieved affection, and the memory of waiting by the aquarium entrance with cold feet for Victor's arrival. She climbed the steps, bought her ticket and walked as if back in time through the glassy corridors.

She saw again how enticing were the windows of swimming creatures, how the chambers were shrewdly lit to suggest timelessness and drift, how the comedic element prevailed – the antics of miniature creatures, their circus-toned colours, the far-fetching and bemused look of some of the larger marine animals – how overall the blue light led to dreaminess and contemplation, and a wish to slow down and childishly dawdle. What was consoling here, she realised, was this eradication of history, this facile escape.

She was heading with a certain dread towards the tubes of jellyfish, wondering if she might lose control of her feelings, when a crowd of schoolchildren appeared and swept from behind her. She had been alone, in a kind of memorialising spell; now she was among chatty thirteen-year-olds guided by their ponytailed teacher. They were an anarchic group, uncontained by space or authority. None wore uniforms and all seemed to have multicoloured sneakers and scarves. They filed here and there, gathered for photographs, mucked about in rowdy and jovial groups. Three boys were pressing their lips against the glass, making human fish lips and obscene sucking sounds. The place was at once lively and over-run. Victor would have loved this, Cass thought, all these kids, going mad. The world of selfies, bad jokes and impudent observations.

Cass saw ahead the tube of jellyfish and decided to wait until she was alone, until the crowd had moved on. It took a while – she began to worry Marco would think she was not coming – but then the children moved to other novelties and other misbehaviours. She walked up to the display of jellyfish and peered again into their world: the light-filled bodies, drifting and pulsating. Victor's lovely face was no longer there. It amazed her how quickly the faces of the newly dead faded, how within hours they were watery and cast away.

She stood watching what Victor had so recently seen, with his own alive eyes. She saw the loops of trailing tentacles and the perfection of jellyfish domes; as every being, after all, was entire and perfect. She noticed now how there were barely perceptible currents in the water, motes floating down as the gelatinous shapes pulsed up, the blooms of perpetual motion, the opening and closing of loose cavities. Vivacity, too; she noticed their bright vivacity.

Cass had not yet felt what she needed to feel. She stood vacant and quiet, afraid to feel anything. Practised at control and the suppression of disturbances, she remained fixed in a pointless stasis before the glass. But she must also move away and return to Marco. She must keep on moving. She would not look at Victor's tortoise, she suddenly decided. She would not remember last night, and would leave before what she suppressed could no longer be held down. *Now*. She would leave now. There was a precise anxiety that kept returning and flooding her thoughts: how could they possibly tell Victor's daughter? Might she come to Berlin to seek her father?

On the U-Bahn, returning, Cass saw with new clarity the mortal faces of Berliners travelling alongside her, passengers all together, all moving in the same direction. Sweeping around the city without effort, skimming on silver lines. She listened to the voice over the loudspeaker, saying, 'Exit left.' She watched people rise and leave, and others enter and take their places. A woman sat beside her who displayed the blue complexion of chemo. Around her head was a tight scarf, she wore an inaccessible look, she had the telltale sunken cheeks of one etiolated, slowly becoming skeleton. The woman stared directly ahead, not acknowledging anyone around her.

Two boys, about ten, flung themselves into the facing seats. The slighter of the two had Alexander's chin, angular, distinctive, and a tiny scab at his mouth. They had always been close, but after their brothers had left for boarding school, Alexander paid Cass more particular attention. He was determined, he said, to make her an A-grade cricketer. She remembered how he arranged her hands on the handle of the bat, his own knuckles shining, how he moved her legs into position and set her body at the correct angle. He liked to spit into his palms and rub them together; he liked to bowl with a kind of lazy, loping stride, as if spilling the ball rather than throwing it, as if it came whizzing with its own red life, extended from his arm. He loved the language of cricket: wickets, stumps, bails, fields, the innings, creases, overs and runs, and managed to use these terms to comment wittily on everyday moments and situations. His ambition in life, his sole ambition, was to become a legendary wicket-keeper for the Australian team.

Cass watched the two boys sprawling in their seats. They were heedless of adults. They had their own business to attend to, their own busy lives. All at once she was overtaken by a powerful urge to tell someone, not of Victor's death and her own dreadful complicity, but the delightfulness of children, and the astonishing beauty of jellyfish.

When Marco opened the door Cass saw immediately that he had been crying.

Victor. Her first thought was that Marco had revisited Victor in his own way, lost his sense of impunity, acknowledged in a quiet moment the horror of what they had done. His face was distorted and his eyes were red. He had taken on that childlike look adults acquire in the business of serious weeping. At least, unlike her, he had changed his clothes: there was no blood, no evidence. He clasped at her tightly, and held her very close and still. His mouth was warm against her hair.

'It's Gino,' he whispered. 'Gino has gone.'

'Gone?'

'Dead. Gino is dead.'

Cass drew back and stared at his face, which quivered with emotional saturation and strain.

'I got rid of the ice,' he said quickly, matter-of-factly, blurting out what he had waited all morning to tell her. 'But I've left the heroin gear. So they can see it's a suicide.'

He must have registered only then her startled incredulity. He must have realised the shock to Cass, and how severe his announcement had been. This sudden news had sprung from Marco entirely unmediated and incautious. He was a man distrait.

'Oh Jesus,' he said, echoing Gino. 'Oh Jesus, forgive me. I shouldn't have called you.' He took her hand and squeezed.

'But here I am,' she responded simply.

The sky was falling in. Victor, and the night by the icy Havel, and now this. Now Gino. Cass must withstand this news or be annihilated. She willed herself to stay collected and composed.

'No Franz.'

'God, no. No Franz. I've called the police.'

He went on to say that there had been no warning or indication. When they arrived home Gino had refused a glass of brandy and said that he just wanted to sleep. That they would talk in the morning. That he needed to lie down. It had been a relief, Marco said, that Gino didn't wish to talk it through, that they didn't say Victor's name, not even once. Marco had taken a long shower, washed himself clean, then fallen into bed. Since Gino was silent, he assumed he was already asleep.

'I didn't check,' he added, his lip and chin quivering. 'I should have checked.'

Marco's face was now becoming rigid, like plaster. It was the cumbersome mask that grief had given him. She had seen this stiff mortification on the faces of her parents and her brothers. She had seen their features harden and intensify. Marco slowly removed Cass's coat and hung it on a hook by the door. She was a comfort to him, being here, not falling apart. But now there was an agonising turbulence of thoughts to contend with.

She was thinking of the brutality of last night, the dishonorable stupidity. How could they? How? What bond existed that had made them act in this way? What corporate thinking? She had been in a daze of believing the crime was hidden, gone, but in Marco's words it had reappeared and cruelly increased. She looked away. She must fit her life into this collective drama again. She must tell Victor's daughter, she must somehow help Marco. It was not over, she thought, and it would never be over. Perhaps she would be questioned by the police. Yes, we both saw him late last night. Yes, he was a drug user. Methamphetamine, heroin. Yes, he had overdosed in the past. (Had he overdosed in the past?) She began to frame fictitious answers to imagined questions. The lovers would have to be told. Gino's sisters would have to be told. Marco would have to tell Gino's sisters. Two deaths now, and the blunt force of grief.

What followed was exempted from the new texture of time they had created the night before. Everyday principles, where one thing follows another, more or less with reason, where cause leads to effect, and where people behave, for the most part, sensibly and predictably – these had last night entirely disappeared. And yet now, in the quiet intermission in Marco's elegant apartment, there was a human scale once more, and a sudden slowing to real solemnity. Both saw again how one thing followed another. Order, consequence. Laws of motion. And because they were just two, a controlled response was possible. When she was ready, only then, Marco led Cass into his spare room to show her Gino's body.

He was just as Marco had found him, turned towards the wall, curled with his knees bent up near his chest and his hands tucked between his thighs. A syringe and a length of black rubber lay on the bed. The room was tidy and quiet. There was no desolating inclemency. There was no Nabokovian speech from Marco. Cass heard her own body as it moved, infinitesimally sounding, in small careful steps towards the bed. She heard the beat of her own breathing, regular and shallow. Timidly, she leant over to kiss Gino's forehead. His eyes were closed. His lips were pressed, like one petulant, or the way a child keeps a secret. He might have been fast asleep but for his bluish pallor. As snow shadows are blue, Cass half-thought. *Snow shadows are blue*. This principle she had learnt years ago in her painting class. She carried these stray associations, inappropriate, aesthetic, but no feeling response.

Marco stood nearby but seemed not entirely present. There was a code to his limited gestures, and to hers. He tugged at the end of the bed as though correcting something. She smoothed the surface of the doona, her hand slow and lingering. Both pretended they were calm. Their fingers touched once, but neither wanted touch now, neither could bear to take comfort with Gino so close, and dead. They stared at his face, which evoked shame and love in equal measure. They had done the wrong thing, hiding Victor. For ever and ever. It would always be the wrong decision. And now, now this.

Marco handed Cass a sheet of paper. On it was a handwritten message from Gino.

Sorry Victor.
Sorry Marco.
Sorry Cass.
Sorry Mitsuko.
Sorry Yukio.

Below, there was something scrawled in Italian, something just for Marco, or possibly written, and implicating, only for himself. There had been a moment last night, in the stillness of this room, when Gino had raised a pen, and written the simple word 'sorry'. Not goodbye. But sorry. He had been alone in this room and thought of each of them in turn. Cass scanned the text, uncomprehending, and picked out single words: *desolato*. Then *pietoso*.

She wept only then. The indirection of the Italian vocabulary had caught her entirely by surprise. Knowing no Italian, she saw only the English derivations there. And these words, Latinate, church-sounding, ringing with choral echoes and divine associations, seemed all at once to puncture and disable her. Marco stood apart. She felt tears stream down her cheeks for those she loved. And she loved them all: Victor, Gino, Marco, Mitsuko, Yukio.

Alexander. How she had loved her brother, Alexander.

She heard Marco clear his throat and shuffle out of the room, leaving her to the privacy of her grief, and carrying away his own.

Cass stayed for a long time at Gino's side. Not a body, but Gino. She stood looking down at him, caught in whatever turning vortex this loss truly was. She adjusted the doona once again, smoothing it once again, her fingers removing an imaginary piece of fluff. The feel of fabric beneath her fingertips was a comfort, and oddly precise. There was a ragged spot, tiny, but certainly there. She felt curiously both aware and unaware, like a child, or an animal, or a character in a book.

At last her weeping ceased. She stood silently, her face wet, her mind misty and unfocused. There was a lamp beside the bed; she leant forward to switch it off. On a table nearby lay Victor's spectacles. Cass took them and shoved them up the sleeve of her sweater. Then vaguely she considered whether it was proper, before the police arrived, to pull a cover over Gino's face.

24

In the opening to Wim Wenders' 1987 movie *Wings of Desire*, there are aerial views of Berlin in black and white that swing around in a slow, circular motion. From the point of view of angels, the city looks distant and dull, full of isolated individuals immured in their own unhappy thoughts. Some voice seems to say, *There are many immure-ments here, many walls and separations. See how walled we are. See how alone.* An early scene shows the broken-off spire of the Gedächtniskirche: a child looks up, mouth open, and sees an angel perched there. In another scene a man dies after a traffic accident. A Mercedes-Benz has hit a man on a motorcycle. He rests propped against the bridge that lies over the ring line in Schöneberg, guarded in his dying by a trench-coated angel. The man's face is undamaged but for a trickle of blood beneath his nose. He is thinking first of anxious things: 'Karin, I should have told you . . . I still have so much to do . . .' but as the angel stays with him and holds his head, the voice in his mind begins gradually to recall sites of joy. A murmuring voiceover speaks of distant places and loved locations – the Far East, Stromboli, the

Mississippi Delta; of loved names – Albert Camus; of loved visions – the morning light, a child's eyes, the old houses in Charlottenburg. The camera sways gently side to side as the actor looks upwards, seeing heaven. In cinematic terms it could have been a sentimental failure but for the restraint of the filmmaking, and the black and white of the scene, and the dignified, dreamy solitude shared and expressed by the angel.

Cass thought of this movie as she made her way to Oranienplatz. She was thinking of the beautiful, soft-featured face of Bruno Ganz, his sweet, boyish smile and wistful stare. She was remembering the glide of the camera, with his voice, along the winter track of the S-Bahn ring line, with the lacey basket of the gasometer just visible on the left, and the leafless trees, and the curved line, and the railway bridge passing above, in an ominous dark shadow. She was thinking how good it was to *glide*, and how the sweep under and over walls, through the trembling visions of stations, past faces glimpsed for a moment and then gone forever, was so like acts of consciousness, the mergings and separations of daily thought and perception. She had the sense of being on the periphery of things, she was not central to anyone's business, she was not of this city, or employed here, or with any particular purpose. She felt apart from things; she felt she was passing like a ghost.

After she had stayed beside Gino, and in those concentrated moments had begun, only begun, to feel what she needed to feel, Cass waited with Marco for the police. Two *polizei* arrived, checked the body, took the gear and called an ambulance. Apart from taking down their names, there was no interview, as such, and no questioning other than the most perfunctory. The police officers, both junior and regimentally punctilious, seemed bored. A suicide was principally uninteresting to them: it meant paperwork, official statements, arrangements for a coroner's report, but no crime to be solved and no criminal excitement. They took Gino's passport and said that the embassy would be contacted. They asked Marco to sign a form, and then another. They moved in an aura of function and workaday vacancy. Cass saw that Marco managed well to disguise his distress: he spoke fluent German with little trace of a foreigner's accent and sounded credible and trustworthy.

When Gino was at last taken away, his body sheathed in black plastic, Marco slumped in his armchair. He held his face in his hands, lost in distracted sorrow. Cass put her arm around his shoulders.

'I need to tell his sisters before they hear from the embassy,' Marco said. 'How will I tell them?' He looked at his wristwatch, irrelevantly. He was no longer obliged to hold things together and make sense.

And I need to tell Rachael, Cass thought.

She did not reply. She made coffee for both of them and not long afterwards she left. She felt suddenly the need for clean clothes and something to eat. The events of the past hours had not ceased her body needing, and it seemed that now she must return more fully to the world. Karl had reminded her of this attitude, this getting on with business, being competent, not waiting to be instructed to put things back into order.

*

With fresh clothes and new determination, Cass decided to revisit Oranienplatz, to see Gino's friend Ahmed. Outside their circle this was the only friend she knew of, and now there seemed to her an urgent responsibility to speak of the death and not cover it over. She'd met Ahmed only the once, obliquely and swiftly – he might not even remember her – but still she felt the pressure and compulsion of a duty. It would be easier, she knew, than telling Yukio and Mitsuko, but it was necessary, honourable. And just as she had wanted on impulse to revisit the aquarium, so Cass thought it proper and fitting to make a second act of return. Repetition, after all, was a kind of memorialisation. Devotion to modest tasks, carrying the news, speaking in a low voice: somehow these suited her. Again, she needed a simple task; and in this day given over to the weighing of disaster, she was reluctant to stay in her apartment and sit quietly alone.

At Oranienplatz, yesterday's snow was muddied with shallow footprints and the busyness of the community. As she approached she saw many more people this time. They were coming and going from the tents; these were their homes, after all. Cass saw a few women, as well as men, and understood only now the nature of her presumption – that she was entering a private space and might be unwelcome or in trespass.

She stood near the entrance to the encampment and patiently waited, not sure where exactly to locate Ahmed. She hoped she might spot him just walking by. A lanky girl of about twelve and wearing a hooded jacket far too large appeared before her and seemed to be sizing her up. She had a direct, penetrating stare and a confident manner. There was a tentative exchange of smiles. At length the

232

girl walked forward, took her by the hand, and simply led her into one of the nearby tents. There were five people there, four men and one woman, sitting on wooden planks arranged around a camp burner. Cass saw five black faces all turn in her direction, and sensed again how living in a tent left the refugees open to endless intrusion. The canvas walls told outsiders that they were essentially impermanent and did not have control over their own lives or space. Their hands were cupped around hot drinks, and their bodies hunched downwards, as if to find warmth that way. A tiny camp burner was heating a saucepan of water. Weather was in here, Cass thought. These people lived in perpetual cold, and with the snow banking close by and the callous invasion of wind.

The girl released Cass's hand and said something in a language she couldn't identify or understand. She pulled back the hood of her jacket to show intricate braids in her hair, displaying it for her, proud of her adornment. Cass resisted the impulse to run her hand slowly over the charming young head. She saw there plaits and ridges and complicated partings, painstaking hairdressing, neat and lovingly performed.

'Ahmed,' Cass announced. She felt foolish and out of place. 'I am looking for Ahmed.'

She heard the name repeated. The woman stepped forward and offered her a cup of hot water. Cass waved it away, but the woman gently lifted her hand and placed it around the cup. She felt moved by this spontaneous inclusion and hospitality. Everyone watched quietly as she took a sip. When a man stepped in behind her, she sensed him and turned.

'I am Ahmed,' he said. 'From Ethiopia.'

He was the wrong Ahmed. This man had an aquiline nose and slightly slanted eyes. He wore a mustard-coloured woollen cap pulled tight over his ears.

Cass said, 'Is there another man with your name? From Eritrea?'

'Today he is in Hamburg. The other Ahmed.'

This man was very tall, she noticed, and proud in his bearing. The girl with the braided hair was now holding his hand. Families, alliances, the linking of one body with another. This tall dark man and this silent child. Cass was unable to deliver her message. She looked into the pool of her drink and felt inept, redundant. Noble intentions and explanations were subsiding away, and in the brief time of her visit Cass saw that her motives were impure. It was for herself, not Ahmed, that she had returned to Oranienplatz. She had needed something to do; and she needed to pretend that she was doing good. It was then, when she looked up again, that she noticed the mattresses. There were two, propped upright in daytime, for protection against draughts of wind.

'Thank you,' she said, handing back the cup. The woman placed it on the ground near the burner, ready for the next drinker. Then Cass reached into her bag and drew out her purse. She stretched over and softly took the hand of the woman – as hers had been taken, with polite insistence – and emptied her purse of its contents. There was a look of surprise, but the woman did not refuse. She nodded a gracious thanks and turned away.

So money, the most crudely efficient of all signs, easily replaced the missing words. Cass was not given the opportunity to feel that she owned the news of Gino's death, that she had control, or that she might so easily gain absolution, or relief. Or just distraction, pure distraction, by passing on Gino's story.

By the time she arrived back at her studio, Cass was weak with fatigue. It was perhaps five in the afternoon and already dark, and there stood Marco, smoking alone, in the murky shadows outside her building. They embraced but had no need to explain their day to each other. Marco slowly followed Cass upstairs. He could not stay in his apartment tonight, he said. It would be difficult to return there, where Gino had died.

'Difficult here, too,' Cass replied.

Victor: why could they not yet speak of Victor?

When they entered her apartment neither had the spirit for conversation. Neither said they felt contagion, a sense of things tainted and base. Both were depleted, as true mourners are, hollowed by all that had been scooped away. A distance lay between them. Cass wondered what it was in Marco's past, and his past with Gino, that had enabled him, or compelled him, to wish to dispose of Victor. What might each or either have done? What crime had sent Gino to prison? She was almost afraid, but not quite, since Marco was smaller now; he was in some way less a presence and less a man. Still, she could not quite bring herself to ask. She was overcome with questions, but could not give them voice.

In darkness they lay close together, unsexual. Neither mentioned the loss of their friends or their unholy leaving. It was a temporary forgetting and another collusion. They talked in subdued voices of this or that. Marco began describing the trends in Berlin real estate and Cass understood that this was his form of abstraction and a way to avoid all feeling. She barely listened. Prices, places, what had these to do with her? Berlin as a marketplace, Berlin bought and sold. Prices were rising, apparently. Berlin would boom. Cass heard in Marco's voice the pitiless tone of real-estate evaluation.

When at last he fell silent, she told him of her visit to Oranienplatz, and of the missing Ahmed, and her confused reactions.

'There was a pretty girl, there,' she said, 'with braided hair. She took me inside. And mattresses, there were old mattresses leant against the wall of the tent.' Her telling was full of holes and incidental details. Now, in her conversation, there were more absences than presences.

'Lampedusa,' said Marco gloomily. 'Gino told me about Lampedusa.'

They had not yet managed a eulogy. Neither spoke in the conventional denuded forms: of what wonderful people the dead were, of what contributions Victor and Gino had made, of how much they were universally admired and loved. It would have seemed an obscenity to exchange these phrases, together or with strangers, when they knew so much more, and of what could never be spoken.

In the middle of the night, uncomfortable and overheated sharing her narrow bed, Cass woke with a start.

'What?' asked Marco, sounding bleary, unfamiliar. His head turned on the pillow.

'I dreamt,' she started slowly. 'I dreamt that the balcony door was stuck open, and there was no protection against the weather. But we were hot, not cold; we two, you and I. We were steamy hot.' She threw back her cover, exposing them both. Now they might shiver.

There was silence. The night grew huge and chilly around them. Cass thought that Marco had already slipped back into sleep. Alongside, she felt the regular rise and fall of his chest as he drifted away from her. Telling a dream, she reflected, beseeches a response. But then with the clarity and focus of one fully awake, Marco began to speak.

'I've just remembered.' He paused. 'A little thing appeared in my dream that I've seen in museums in Rome. It's a tear bottle. In ancient times mourners collected their tears in these beautiful vessels. Little pots, or glass vases, with stems that rested on the cheeks, beneath the eyes. I remember my mother pointing them out to me when I was a child. I remember thinking how ridiculous it was, in ancient Rome, to save one's tears.'

Then again they were silent. Eventually, they both slept.

25

The morning was frosty but clear. A grey sky hung above and the temperature remained low. Outside they heard cars moving with a sound like splashing ocean through the icy slush, and they opened the balcony doors to check on the day. Peering down, still remembering and not-remembering Victor's fall, they could see a few rugged-up people walking with care on the slippery pavements. In foreshortened perspective the walkers had the squat dimensions of fabled creatures: lumpish, with their faces obscured and their intentions unknown.

Further afield, four or five children were already running in the park, black shapes against the white, Breughel-like, and emblematic. The gasometer was hardly there, floating in the distance, but its insubstantial ring shape was what Cass most enjoyed of her balcony view. To Marco she pointed out the burnt apartment below, still unrepaired, the smoke-flare of darkness ever-rising above the boarded-up windows. Both saw but did not remark on the neat squares of the cemetery, picturesque compared to the melting, rough streets.

Had she been prepared to name it, Cass would have said

'rising panic'. This was the first time she had stood on the balcony since Victor's death and she felt in her stomach the shudder of that wicked act, one friend killed by another. It was lodged there in her gut. She retreated indoors. For a few moments longer Marco stood alone at the railing, scratching it with his fingernails.

Marco and Cass decided they would tell Yukio and Mitsuko together. Marco called, suggesting they meet at his place for a simple meal. For Victor, he told them. A memorial meal for Victor. He spoke as if their beloved friend had simply and gently passed away; and he said nothing about Gino, nor would they have guessed from his tone that there was a new devastation. They would come by at seven. It was a no-nonsense invitation like one in happy times, when what was anticipated was mutual pleasure and a few jokes, the clumsy telling of little tales over a meal and fine wine. Cass desperately hoped that Marco wouldn't make a second speech. She wasn't sure she could bear it – another set of pronouncements, another articulate statement invoking the inexpressible qualities of death, or of life. A Nabokovian cradle rocking above an abyss. A brief crack of light between two eternities of darkness. Now it sickened her, this degree of fluent abstraction, and the mendacity of words. Rhetorical flourish was Marco's way, but it wasn't hers.

When they left her studio, Marco to go home, then to work, she as an excuse simply to walk, or ride the trains, or look with time-wasting and anaesthetic distraction in shops, Marco swore that he saw Franz following at some distance behind them. Cass looked back and saw nothing but the bare freezing streets. There was a Turkish woman with a pram, who in her long coat and headscarf and confident stride appeared more persuasively solid and real than both of them. The Turkish mother turned into a side street and was gone.

But Marco was convinced and anxious. When they kissed goodbye at the steps of the U-Bahn, he looked around him with a darting glance, as one might look for a spy, and spoke to her in the agitated tone of a man who suffers delusions. Cass remembered 'everything is a cipher and of everything he is a theme'. Nabokov. Again. A useful writer on paranoia. Yet now they both saw nothing. Marco became apologetic. Cass began her descent into the underground, Marco resumed walking. There was a slight stagger to his walk, she thought, as if he was about to stumble.

In the syncopation of afterwards, after Victor, after Gino, after the defeat of all they had artificially and actually established, the day simply passed. Cass had offered to buy some food and come early to Marco's apartment. He would be home by six. She waited with her Kaiser's bags of shopping in front of his building and reflected that she should have returned that day to Oranienplatz, to seek again the first Ahmed. But the impulse had gone: she might not return at all. Ahmed would never know. He would be protected from grief – if indeed it had been that kind of intimate friendship – and would think simply that his handsome and generous Italian friend had inexplicably disappeared. No doubt white men do this all the time – express goodwill, then disappear. Ahmed would probably expect it. Besides, she bore no genuine responsibility, she thought. What had Ahmed to do with her? It was a matter easily dealt with by the decision not to act.

Marco arrived punctually, looking harried and tired. He took the shopping from Cass and admitted her into his dingy lobby, checked his mail – nothing there – then led her slowly up the stairs. The suave Roman Marco had entirely gone. He had loosened his scarf before he reached the front door; his face seemed to drag as he spoke, with the features of a prematurely older man. Cass felt such tenderness then, seeing him undone in this way, and almost not coping. Although she would not have admitted it, she liked the fact that he needed her, that her careful, poised presence was ballast to his rocking self. Her instinct was always the same, to place her open palm against his cheek, to claim privileged nearness and access to his face. In all the complications of what had occurred, there was at least this understanding: that each now had permission to touch.

Mitsuko and Yukio arrived typically early. Both wore white – whether by design or accident Cass could not know – as if formally dressed for an oriental funeral. Subdued, glazed, they stood close together, now and then reaching for each other's hands and the subliminal comfort of a glancing touch. Cass noticed that it was Yukio who seemed more competent in the aftermath of death. But there was no theatrical energy now, and a kind of empty politeness, distracted and depersonalised, had overtaken them. A few taut sentences were exchanged and Cass considered what effort it had taken to accept a dinner invitation.

Marco and Cass moved to the kitchen. The lovers stood watching them as they worked slowly, side by side, methodically preparing and chopping vegetables. Little was said; censorship and repression operated intuitively between them. Victor was not mentioned, and they had not yet asked about Gino, perhaps expecting him to be the last to arrive. They spoke of nothing in particular, but then Yukio announced that they had decided to leave Berlin early. They were flying back to Japan in two days' time.

'But we will keep in touch,' Mitsuko said. 'And you must come to visit us in Tokyo.' It sounded fake and insincere. She did not want to see them again. She was attempting the protocols of routine and idiomatic conversation.

'You can look at the images on my blog,' Yukio added. 'And on Facebook.'

So that was it: they had agreed to the meal so that they could take their leave, say goodbye and fly away from deadly Berlin. Cass ought not to have been surprised, but she saw that Marco was, too; that he had also imagined they might support each other through the next days and weeks.

'Gino has already returned to Rome,' he said suddenly. He did not look at Cass.

'Without saying goodbye?' Mitsuko looked vague. 'But, yes, I understand,' she added. 'We feel the need to get away, too. Did he seem okay?' she asked blandly.

'Yes,' said Marco, 'he seemed okay.'

Cass tried to catch Marco's gaze, but he was staunchly alone. He would not be questioned or contradicted. The fiction had sprung instantly to life, and now seemed firm and undisputable. There was no hint of doubt or fabrication

242

in his simple announcement: he spoke with easy conviction and assumed authority.

In the confusion that followed they reverted to insipid slogans: 'You must give us his email.'

'Of course, yes. Of course.'

'And keep in touch.'

'Of course. You too. We'll all keep in touch.'

So by inanities it was settled. By convention, they dispelled death. Cass felt ill, and stunned by the hasty pre-emption of Marco's lie. There was no excuse of drunkenness, or desire, or the wish to protect; it was a simple expedience, so neither would have to say aloud the word 'dead', or speak Gino's name in the past tense, or confront their crime against Victor, or contribute further to the brokenness of their group and of all they had shared. Mitsuko was rolling a tiny wheel of carrot beneath her fingertip, but Yukio looked directly at Cass, giving her the opportunity to contribute. None had yet spoken Victor's name. None had been brave, or true.

The buzzer then sounded, and Marco answered it without thinking. He pressed the admission.

'Right building, wrong apartment,' he said. He resumed chopping a line of carrot, and scraping it sideways into a pot. The impetus for irrelevant conversation had left; they stood like statues with fixed expressions, stranded in remote disquiet.

When there was a knock on the door, each looked at it with concern. The four stood there, arrested, all waiting together. The knock sounded a second time.

'Don't open it,' said Cass, already dismayed.

Marco hesitated, but then dashed forward and opened the door. It was Franz. Cass saw how large he now looked, taller than both Marco and Yukio, and how he loomed there before them, like a storybook tyrant exposed. In an atavistic act of courtesy he removed his cap and held it by his thigh, clenched in his fist. He looked fleshy and powerful, not the limping man in the shadows of two nights before, whose swinging torchlight seemed to hint at incapacity of some sort, alcoholic tremors or rotten, frayed nerves. Cass wanted to think *Nazi*, to make this man the guilty and responsible one. But instead, with a moral shock, she realised that his face reminded her of one she had seen in a photograph at the Topography of Terror museum. His was the face of a dissident, a Red, who had looked into the camera lens with an open, defiant stare. Cass had stood for some time before the portrait, taken from three angles, knowing that she saw something indefinable there, something that, ineluctably, refused to be cowered and captured. This was bravery, surely, to see death's glassy stare and to stare right back at it. To know violence, and more violence, and still not flinch or withdraw. She had written the name in her notebook, but could not now recall it. She recalled only that he had died there, at that very place, in 1943. From the wall of faces, each in three versions, this was this one that had singly addressed her. Now clear under fluorescent light, fully visible for the first time, Franz carried the certainty of a martyr's face.

They all expected physical violence to break the tension, but although Franz had entered the apartment, a few steps from the doorway, he was more interested in delivering a verbal threat. From what Cass could make out, he said he knew that Marco was a killer, and that he wanted €10,000 to stay quiet. He could tell the police at any time. At any time, he repeated. He could exchange information for immunity from prosecution, being an accessory to the fact.

Cass was struck by how smoothly Franz had rehearsed his crime-fiction scenario, how well the *krimi* genre worked, how it enabled him to find a role for himself and then to become the hero of his own story. To be the one, after all, who told the half-truths and one-and-a-half-truths. There was no caution in his voice: he knew his own terms exactly.

Marco invited Franz to sit down, but he adamantly refused. He was clever enough to know that kindly gestures would diminish his power. He remained standing, huge and strangely solidified, his cap still crushed in a purposeful, tight grip. In her revised imagining, Cass thought now of GDR monuments; she consigned Franz to some earlier era he seemed perfectly to represent. She saw too how closely he resembled Karl, and found herself disconcerted to see them so alike.

'So?' asked Franz.

Marco agreed to meet him the next day to discuss 'terms'.

Yes, he would discuss 'terms'. 'Money,' Franz said clearly.

Franz handed him an address on a scrap of paper. He spoke confidently:

'You come where *I* say. Tomorrow, 16.00.'

Then, almost as abruptly as it had begun, the confrontation ended, and Franz turned away and was gone. They heard his echoing footsteps clump heavily down the stairs. Cass was thinking: *this will never end; this will always follow us. Franz will always follow us.*

'What will you do?' asked Yukio.

Marco turned towards him.

'I don't know,' he replied hoarsely. 'I seldom know.'

All at once Cass saw Marco's anguish displayed in the entire room, in the faces of Yukio and Mitsuko, both staring in his direction, in the sallow lamplight that had earlier cast a modifying gentleness, in the disarray on the kitchen benchtop, the scattering of meal preparations, the chopping knife to one side, the soft dribble of tap water she'd not noticed before. Unassembled, partial, incomplete signs. From the stairwell came the sound of the front door banging closed. Franz was limping away, triumphant, into the night. There was yet another distortion of time in which none of them moved or spoke, the vindictive atmosphere and Franz's words still noiselessly hanging around.

There would be no meal and no fake memorial for Victor. Mitsuko and Yukio left soon after Franz. They made a poor excuse, but it was clear that they were afraid. As she embraced them both, in a melancholy goodbye, Cass considered that the lovers, of whom she knew such tender stories and modest reflections, might disappear completely, might with their Hagi histories and *hikikomori* pasts, with their Lolita affectations and affection for chess shadows, with whatever confessions or inventions they had sweetly offered to others, simply, snow-like, cease to be. The departure of friends carried an aspect of loss, but it was not simply that. In addition to Victor and Gino, it was the breaking down of their pattern, the rude crossing-out of what had held them all in a unique design. Carrying their stories, she was carrying their hazy traces; she thought them invisibly folded, somehow – voluted and convoluted into the texture of her own mind. Cass stood at the doorway and watched Yukio and Mitsuko move down the stairs, away into the darkness. Neither slowed, nor looked back. There was a dread finality to their leaving.

Cass moved shyly to Marco's side. She reached out, the

assertive one, and enclosed him in her arms. He was rigid for a time, then she saw his moistened eyes and lowered gaze and knew he could not bear her witness to his misery. As with the epilepsy, she reflected, this was the power of uncontrollable forces to take over a man, to cast him low, to require surrender to an archaic machinery once designated Fate. Of the body, of electrical flash, of the ignoble intentions of others, of the unfolding consequences of mistaken action. He shrugged, and touched her cheek.

'Tomorrow,' he said softly. 'Let's talk about it tomorrow. After I see Franz.'

A wave of muddled feeling flooded Cass's release. She stepped away from Marco, relinquished her claim to his attention and quietly gathered her coat and scarf. She saw a tremor ripple along his back and knew that he was crying. She felt she loved him most profoundly this moment, in which she was filled with a pity, much like a silent propinquity, that he wished her to leave unexpressed. She did not reproach him for his lie. She did not ask any questions. She left Marco to the solitude of his own burden, and his own justifications.

But the world continued to subside – with their joint indecency, perhaps, with their dishonesty and impassivity. There was a moment on the stairs when Cass misstepped and almost fell. In a vision she saw the lethal darkness surge and fly up at her; she saw the blunder that was a fall even further into loss. The fate of a coward: to plunge all the way to the basement in a chute of nothing. Then she caught the banister just in time, and just in time she saved herself.

26

As Cass returned to her studio in the dark, her thoughts were dismal and incoherent. In part her effort was to hold back images of Victor and Gino. Some process began in her mind that pulled Berlin sites into coalition, and expressed her sense that the world was altering, even as she considered it.

She was thinking of the roof of the Reichstag as the ribbed dome of an umbrella; that the Thälmann monument in Prenzlauer Berg looked remarkably like Franz; that the remnants of the Wall were an abomination. She was thinking that ghost stations in the U-Bahn still existed and were proliferating; she was thinking of a begging woman with a bruised face she had seen once at Kottbusser Tor; of the bleak museum called the Topography of Terror; of Nestorstrasse; and of Nabokov, writing under tulip lamplight at an old desk. She was thinking how strangers look at each other, without seeming to, riding opposite on a train; how randomly people gather, historical accidents merely, and how they are then broken, and pulled away, and possibly lost forever.

Now Cass wanted above all the company of a Berliner. Not Karl, but others, of her own age perhaps, and wiser, and authentically of this place, who would explain and make intelligible her scrambled feelings. Residents here knew more, she told herself. Daily they dealt with historical gravity. Residents of Berlin might be born, she thought insanely, with an inbuilt capacity both to memorialise and explain. She needed explanations. She needed a dream of reason without any monsters. She wanted to sit down with a Berliner and find a conclusion. Cass was worn out improvising a functional self against all that had made her feel so dysfunctional.

When she arrived at her building, Karl was waiting in the doorway. His bulky shape appeared before her, backlit and persuasive. She resisted moody and portentous *film noir* comparisons. Not again, she thought, oh no, not again. His knowledge of Victor made her cautious and a little afraid. Yet closer, in the half-light, Karl's face was again friendly and kind. She saw that he wore a crimson-checked dressing-gown over blue-striped pajamas.

'Coffee?' he asked.

And for some reason, she agreed. Again in his room, again surrounded by his knick-knacks, and his pride, and his native hospitality, Cass unwound her wound-up body into his capacious lounge chair and collapsed there, sad and floppy as an overtired child. She noticed Mitsuko's origami snowflake displayed with his other treasures, set prominently in the centre of the small table that held his souvenirs. It was an anomalously frail thing, propped among the glass ashtrays and plaster curios of another kind of life. In demented tiredness, in quasi-Nabokovian thinking, in which inconspicuous objects found a capacity to startle, and coincidence everywhere appeared, and accumulated, and found novel expression, Cass thought of the paper snowflake as an asterisk for which some important meaning was missing. Magical thinking, literary thinking. There was a scent of coffee and another she'd not recalled from her last visit, of old wood, of furniture polish, of a close-by forest. *'I found myself in a dark wood, for the straight way was lost.'*

Karl excused himself and returned with the coffee, which must have been brewing for some time. He added hot milk from a Turkish pan and handed Cass a mug she'd not seen before. It bore a miniature profile of Mozart and a pattern of musical notes. She sensed she was being honoured with his finest china.

'I have spoken to Franz,' he began, 'and I know what he has threatened. But he will not do this, I have warned him. He will not tell anyone of your man's crime.'

'Marco. And it was not his or anyone's crime. It was an accident. It was a terrible accident.'

'Of course it was,' said Karl. 'But I am telling you that Franz underneath is a good boy and will obey his father. I am still his father.'

The last sentence was spoken emphatically, as if it held the key to other certainties.

'Yes,' Cass said faintly.

What could she say? Karl looked sincere and nodded to encourage her to drink up her coffee and believe. She heard him begin to ramble. She must not worry, no one would ever know. Bodies can vanish. Bodies in Berlin vanish all the time. Many visitors, from all over. Russians. Poles. They vanish all the time. He would be quiet as the grave, he said, and mimed zipping his own lips. The cliché appalled her.

He looked at Cass with affection, perplexing after such a ghoulish and facile pronouncement. *Bodies can vanish.* She reminded him, he went on, of his own daughter, Katharina, who was long gone. He had again spoken his daughter's name with no hint of emotion, or indication of the nature of her disappearance. Then, as he continued, Cass heard the word *Japanisch* and knew, only half-listening, that he was speaking of Mitsuko and Yukio. He would like to invite her friends to coffee in his room, she heard, they were a beautiful couple. Such a beautiful young couple. They were the future, Karl said firmly. The future, he repeated.

By the end she had entered a state of inattentive passivity. It was too difficult to respond to what seemed almost jolly chit-chat. At last, Cass made an effort and stood up to depart. She felt so relieved to be going that she stepped forward and embraced Karl lightly. He was pleased, and grinned, his grey moustache flaring. He patted her back and let his hand rest for a second or two, as if in protection.

With no idea what time it was, Cass hauled herself up the stairs. Though fizzing with caffeine she knew she must try to sleep. She would not permit herself to think of what had actually occurred; nevertheless the sense of exhaustion and grief was unendurable. And just as she had recalled the leaf-decorated curtain that wrapped the body of her brother, now she recalled that her father had scrabbled in the intermittent darkness to find a lamp. In the beam of the lighthouse she had seen him appear and disappear, appear and disappear. Then, bent over to shield the flame, he struck a match and, cupping carefully, lit a kerosene lamp. They were all contained there, father and mother and dead Alexander and herself, all contained in a weak circle of brassy yellow, lit to wait out the night.

Cass was aware that this was the first time she had remembered the lamp; the sharp hydrocarbon tang of it, her father turning the tiny notched wheel at its side to increase the flame, the way he appeared before them all, enlarged and drenched in yellow light. How in the past she and Alexander had loved it when the generator failed, and they had taken turns filling the kerosene and tending the lamp. How the night changed, held back and seemed under control.

What else did she know? That her mother had not wept. That she had copied her mother. And that she had hated and admired her mother's strength in staying calm and holding Alexander. The cats. This was why she had told the story of drowning the cats. To make her mother seem cruel. To separate and remove her. There was an implacable juvenile logic here: withdrawing the evidence of her own improper feelings, the selective forgetting, the determined self-centredness.

The only exactitude was in her memory of her own physical sensations. There had been such a roar; the sky was one long terrific howl. Shifting wind pressure had caused a painful pounding in her eardrums, and her limbs were stiff with discomfort from so long beneath the table. What weird delight to hear tin sheets on the roof rip upwards and fly away, and the screech of wood cracking and nails pulling free, and the giant concussive whack as the side wall fell outwards.

252

Afterwards, she had seen her parents' faces, incandescent before her, fixed and stricken, but more clearly she'd seen the garland design on her cotton dress, a motif of green and purple flowers shaped like trumpets, running from her waist downwards in a regular print. The blink of the lighthouse that night had been a tormenting transmission, but her father's lamp let them see a continuous world.

This was the door opening that Marco had mentioned, the inexplicable return of memory that followed spoken words. She had always been deeply suspicious of these convenient theories, of instant recollection that made sudden sense, of puzzles at long-last given a vigorous explanation. But here was a girl she had forgotten, on the night of her brother's death.

At this stage of the night Cass no longer considered herself rational. She undressed in her chilly room shrinking away from her naked reflection. She showered, empty and detached, closing her eyes under the water. Unbidden, came the sensation of her open palm pressing on Victor's eyelids, the downward sweep, the efficient closing up of his face. How had she managed it, to touch his dead eyes in this way, to act as a functionary, as a competent stranger? How soft he had been, how humanly warm. And what had he seen in the last seconds as his death sped towards him? It was a distressing question which, having been thought, she would never eradicate. And his daughter: how to inform his daughter? They were guilty of the death, she told herself, and they were guilty of making Victor into an object. They were guilty of panicking in the face of a life suddenly taken, and responding with thoughtless, collective, idiot haste. They were guilty of disposing of him crudely and in a manner untimely and botched, as if he were a mishap, a mistake, and not a man. They had assisted Gino without knowing what past story he was covering, or why he needed their help but was unable to let each of them mourn. They had conspired so that Victor was a thing, unhallowed, a bundle heavy and impeding, to be thrown away into the night.

And Gino, what private disaster had he been expressing? They had been tricked into believing that the speak-memories had told them everything, but in all that mattered, finally, there was no trustworthy knowledge there. The most earnest and open story still meant nothing assured. This was the surprise of other people: their wealth of remorseless secrets. And this was what she had learnt: the failure of any tale.

Cass heard a rumble sound at the dark windowpane of the doors to her balcony. A truck passing, perhaps. But alone and addled, she thought this an uncanny omen. It seemed less glass-shudder than something outside and wind-borne; it was late shockwaves conveyed on the currents of the night. She felt inordinately heavy. She felt her own decrepitude. She yielded finally to all the violence that had occurred in the last two days, falling onto her bed in the arbitrary configuration of one suddenly surprised and shot dead.

27

How did it seem to her, the next, the final day? Cass will remember that when she woke, there was illumination again: daylight was snowlight. She had slept late, and overnight the snow had wondrously returned. It pleased her to see anew the draped quality in the air, the muslin white descending, the animation, the plenitude. The symbol suggested itself – that there might be a white-washing now, and a more complete covering over. Snow is consolation, she thought; snow is this padding and cladding, this lush erasure of signs. She was surprised at how rested and serene she felt. Watching from her window, with the room once again rising upwards, she resolved to speak candidly to Marco, to touch his face with her palm, to suggest that in the days to follow they might take things more slowly.

Cass opened her phone to discover messages from Mitsuko and Marco. Mitsuko had sent her an image of a gingko leaf, which resembled a butterfly. The message was simple and sweet: 'I shall think of you when I see a high brown fritillary.' Marco's first message was practical: '5 pm, outside Wittenburg Platz U-station, church end, right side.' A second message said: 'I've found Gino's "Guide to Berlin".'

She turned away from the snow view, carrying a word that had bubbled into her head: *convolvulus*. This was the name of the flower in the garland design she had seen printed on her dress. Cass dismissed the word. She willed it forgotten once again. She dressed without haste, then drank a glass of warm water.

The day dragged and became dull. Cass filled up her time reading newspapers online. She searched initially for some account of a discovered body, name unknown, surfacing with morbid resilience in the icy Havel. An anonymous body. Foul play. Clear criminal involvement.

There was nothing. Her nervous and wandering attention turned to impersonal stories. Berlin was experiencing its coldest winter in many years. North Korea had announced its possession of nuclear weapons. There was a civil war in Syria, suicide bombings in Afghanistan and landslides in China. Capitalism was facing a fiscal crisis, in which the poor and meek would be savagely crushed. There were fires in Tasmania and floods in Queensland. There were refugees everywhere, forming drifts of miserable humanity, moving in tired, desperate clusters all over the globe. Cass glanced at celebrity tales, full of the deplorable zest. She read a book review or two, and saw nothing that aroused her interest. The world of reading and writing appeared stupid and cynical, keyed to trends of the marketplace and the flat world of known stories. She resolved not to read any more newspapers in her currently vulnerable state. Too much *weltschmerz* and failure of humanity. Too much tyranny and comprehensive disappointment. She closed her laptop as one might close a coffin, repulsed, sealing the sight and the stench of decay.

*

When Cass left her studio it was with a heavy heart and a racing mind. Already she was considering if she would stay in Berlin until spring as she had planned. She had paid the rent in advance, and could not afford to lose her deposit. This worry had already lodged with immoral primacy in her jumbled thinking. She wondered too what extra doom or shock might await, what further convulsion beyond this ruined present. It had been only seven weeks since she'd first met Marco in Nestorstrasse. She could not have conceived then how layered their association might be, how their satellite lives would mimic and consolidate, would form their own peculiar entity of feeling and words. And it might not yet be over, this patterning, or this ruin. Though she could not imagine more waste, there was a kind of fear in her now, a new insecurity, and a loss of composure. Fundamentally – this was it – the future had been spoilt. All was aftermath now. Afterwards and aftermath.

Cass rose up from the stifling carriage, and rode the escalator at Wittenbergplatz. She moved through the reconstructed deco hall, over which a four-sided clock hung, then stepped out into fresh air and sparkly light. Here were tourists and Berliners with neon-lit faces; here the shine of stores, ornamental in the dark Saturday evening. There were streams of busy people flowing by in waves. The half-destroyed church was a block ahead of her. The gigantic department store, glamorous and transnational, devoured shoppers whole. Yet the night had a translucent, winking quality. She was pleased to be *en masse*, to feel so impersonal and indefinite.

From the edge of the platz Cass could see the U-station building from a distance. It was not clear whether Marco's 'right side' meant facing towards or away from the train station, so she triangulated her vision so as not to miss him. On one side was a memorial plaque: 'Places of terror we should never forget': a grim list of twelve concentration camps in yellow paint on a black surface. She glanced away. On the other side, conspicuously halted when all around him moved, stood a young man huddled against the cold, smoking a cigarette. He appeared to be Gino Scattini, returned from the dead. *Gino Scattini*. Cass stared, captivated, at the intimation of afterlife. The posture was the same. The slightly nervy carriage. The tilt of the head. In a gesture she saw as deeply cinematic, the man raised his arm slowly to inhale, then, just as slowly, lowered it to his side. He might have been an actor staging Gino. He might have been rehearsing a resurrected life. But then the man turned more fully towards her and she saw his irrefutable singularity. He would not be made into another fateful sign. He was autonomous and securely outside her knowing. With surprising liveliness, the young man suddenly flicked his butt into the snow, turned on his heel, tossed back his scarf and sped beneath the bright archway of the station.

As Cass stood still in the moving crowd, she felt the dark cold enter her chest. She stamped her feet on the icy pavement. Frosty air entered her lungs and she drew her coat more tightly. She adjusted her scarf, rubbed her stiff hands, squeezed in her shoulders, as dogs do when truly cold. The blink of the green man and the red man went on and on, the mazing heave of the crowd advanced and receded. For a while she thought of nothing but this daze of waiting. Then she noticed a triple arrangement of globed lamps that reminded her of Gino describing parhelia. She turned the word in her mind. How lovely it was: *parhelia*.

At that moment, Cass made two lucid decisions – that she would return to Oranienplatz and find the first Ahmed; and that she would locate Victor's daughter, Rachael, and fabricate an honourable tale about her father. It would be untruthful, necessarily, but she might construct a fiction that would serve as a refracted or substitute truth; just as there only exists one sun, but it may, in a natural deception, appear as three.

Marco had chosen this place because it had an absorbing anonymity. He also liked to move *en masse*, obscured by others. He liked big city bustle and the camouflage of populations. It was half an hour, then an hour, and Cass at first wondered if she had missed seeing him, or mistaken the time. She stood vacantly waiting. But at some point, sombre and sure, she realised that Marco was not coming. She looked through the night for his face and knew, without a doubt, that he would not arrive. Marco had left Berlin. She was all at once utterly certain. He had returned to Rome, or gone further – perhaps fleeing like a fugitive to North Africa. There was no phone message – she checked – no excuse, or explanation. There was only her waiting and her freeze-frame emptiness, full of unanswered questions.

Cass rode the S-Bahn ring line, just to ride. She needed the gentle thrumming, the clockwise or anti-clockwise lapse and elapse, the repetitions, the orderly movement, the comfort of going nowhere. A sequence of mobile images attended her travelling: umbrellas, teacups, chessmen, pietàs. The memories of others had infiltrated and become her own; they exerted their influence as planets might, pulling time and space, oscillating in and out of far visibility, changing how the world itself appeared, and all that was inside it. Snowfall glistened and the sky outside sped away. The snow appeared as a maze of minuscule stars.

The S-station names: Storkower Strasse and Frankfurter Allee. Ostkreuz, Treptower Park, Sonnenallee. So like a poem.

There was a boy once who whispered 'umbrella' into the night and sought in stories frail hints of his disappeared family. Another who saw in a cathedral the horror at an explosion, and found himself, ever afterwards, exploding inside. There was a girl who smelt history, and loved the pottery of her father. There was a boy who noticed the tiny shadows cast by chess pieces, and grew to know both isolation and the promise of release. A child in Rome lost his father and sent a fictional envoy to find him, then fell in fits that expressed what his mouth could not say. And there was she, meaninglessly riding on a train through the night. Her mournful self, second-hand, carrying other peoples' images. Her self lovelorn, and sorry, and now simply sliding away.

Acknowledgements

This novel was written during an 'Artist's Fellowship' year, hosted by DAAD in Berlin, for which I'm enormously grateful. For advice, support and stimulating company I wish to thank Katharina Narbutovic, Laura Munoz-Alonso, Susanne Fladt-Bruno, Susanne Kalbanter, Lars Eckstein, Anja Schwartz, Mattias Fredrich-Auf der Horst, Helga Ramsey-Kurtz, Frances Calvert, María del Rosario Acosta, Chris Eagle, Janne Teller, Sarah Burnside, Beatrice Fassbender, Eliot Weinberger, Jennifer Wawrzinek, Heidi Kuhles, Bettina Fishcher, Susanne Becker, Walter Kaufmann, Hannah Boettcher and Gerrit Haas. Fellow DAAD writers, including Anjtje Krog, John Burnside, Pierre Char-Naudé, Helon Habiba and Dorothea Rose Herliany, offered solidarity and fine conversation. Martin Chalmers generously imparted invaluable advice, and I mourn his passing. My very special gratitude extends to Esther Kinsky, Priya Basil and Doris and Christian D'Cruz-Grote, who each shared more than can ever be expressed here. Thanks too to my German publisher, Hanna Mittelstädt, and to her wonderful team, and to my translator, Conny Lösch; to Banff, and especially to Dionne Brand for walks and timely ideas; and to dear friends who corresponded. I particularly thank Mireille Juchau for her thoughtful reflections on Berlin. I'm indebted to Professor Ivor Indyk for offering support at an awkward time; and to colleagues at the Writing and Society Research Centre at the University of Western Sydney. Thanks to Meredith Curnow and Catherine Hill, ever patient and professional, at Random House Australia. Kyra Giorgi and Robert Podbereski were immensely inspiring companions, last but not least.

This book is in memory of Margaret West, Martin Chalmers and Philippa Maddern.

Gail Jones lives in Sydney and teaches at the University of Western Sydney. Her books have won numerous literary awards in Australia. She is the author of two collections of short stories and five novels including *Sixty Lights* which was longlisted for the Man Booker Prize, *Dreams of Speaking* which was shortlisted for the International IMPAC Dublin Literary Award and longlisted for the Orange Prize, and *Sorry* which was longlisted for the Orange Prize.